THE BLOOD OF ANGELS

DAVID BRADWELL

THE BLOOD OF ANGELS

Trust no-one. Especially those who promise to save you.

Former investigative journalist Clare Woodbrook has committed the perfect crime, but it's come at a terrible personal price. So, when she's offered a chance at redemption, she grabs it with both hands.

But it means joining an organisation rooted in the espionage of the old East Germany. It's a world of secrets and lies, in which old allegiances and rivalries count for nothing, and everyone has a sinister hidden agenda. Worse still, she's being hunted by a psychopath, intent on bloody revenge. As Clare embarks on her first mission in London, Paris and Frankfurt, the bullets begin to fly, and she has to face up to a stark yet terrifying truth.

The Blood Of Angels is a gripping conspiracy thriller with twists galore, pulsating action, and flashes of dark humour. It's book one in a new spin-off from the Anna Burgin mystery thriller series - and the alternative sequel to the huge bestseller *Cold Press*.

ABOUT THE AUTHOR

David Bradwell grew up in the north east of England but now lives in Hitchin in Hertfordshire. He has written for publications as diverse as Smash Hits and the Sunday Times and is a former winner of the PPA British Magazine Writer of the Year Award. Aside from writing, he runs a hosiery company with web sites at www.stockingshq.com and www.tightsandmore.com.

Get in touch at:
www.davidbradwell.com

THE BLOOD OF ANGELS

A Gripping Conspiracy Thriller: Clare Woodbrook Book 1

The Blood Of Angels was first published in 2020 by Pure Fiction
Copyright © David Bradwell, 2020
www.davidbradwell.com

ISBN: 978-1-9993394-8-7

All rights reserved. No part of this publication may be reproduced, stored or transmitted in any form by any means, electronic, mechanical, photocopying or otherwise, without prior written permission.

The right of David Bradwell to be identified as Author of this work has been asserted by him in accordance with the Copyright, Designs and Patents Act, 1988 This is a work of fiction. Names, places, events and incidents are either the products of the author's imagination or used fictitiously. Any resemblance to actual persons, living or dead, or actual events is purely coincidental.

For Helen and John.

Chapter 1

Tuesday, December 29th, 1992

SOMETIMES things happen for a reason. And sometimes that reason is that you've had far too much to drink.

Tobias Mertens opened his eyes, tried to close them again, and then experienced an immediate sense of urgency. He had to get out of there. Back to the hotel. What was her name? No idea. But if he could escape before she woke up, he'd avoid all of the usual post-coital recriminations.

He got out of bed, and dressed quickly in last night's suit.

And what a night it was. Boys will be boys. Men will be men. And hey, while you're on, it's Christmas.

She was what? A six at a push? Probably significantly less in daylight, when sober. So, certainly not the most attractive girl he'd come across in Paris, but definitely the most willing. And if nothing else, he'd done it for Germany. He smiled, despite the crushing pain shooting through his head. Result. As long as he escaped before the horror of having to pretend he wanted to see her again.

A few minutes later, he was staggering back down the alleyway. It looked vaguely familiar. Actually, scratch that. He had no idea where he was. Nor what had happened to Karsten. Presumably he'd be back at the hotel already, sleeping it off. There must be a Metro station somewhere near, though.

Tobias remembered the club. Remembered chatting to the girl. Asking her about her studies at the Sorbonne. Buying her a drink. Then another and another. But after that, it was every man for himself. Boys will be boys. Men will be men.

Although Pascal Duclos applied the brakes, the rubbish truck continued its journey. He watched on, powerless, as the ice beneath the wheels gradually afforded some kind of traction. He hated this time of the year. It was bad enough normally, but somehow it seemed inhuman to be at work so early, while everyone else was sleeping off the festive spirit. And the amount of extra rubbish ... *Mon dieu*. At this rate they'd have to do two runs, which was the last thing he needed when he still had to apologise to his wife, for all the things he'd said to her father.

He checked his mirrors. Watching for the thumbs up that would allow him to move on. He frowned in frustration. Why were they taking so long?

Tobias Mertens saw the rubbish truck slide to a halt. Poor bastards, out before dawn. And especially when it was so, so cold. The two men had stopped loading bags, though, and were instead standing motionless. He took a step to the left to get out of their way, but then saw what had grabbed their attention.

The arm protruding from beneath the pile of cardboard.

You wouldn't want to be homeless on a night like that.

But how many homeless people wore a gold watch? How many homeless people wore a suit like Karsten's?

Tobias stopped walking, his eyes fixated, as his hungover brain tried to process what he was seeing. And as it did, his voyeuristic curiosity was replaced by the vicelike grip of horror.

Chapter 2

Tuesday, February 23rd, 1993

WE all have enemies. I've made a few in recent times. Not all of them want to kill me. I expect some would prefer eternal suffering. But aside from one recent lapse of judgement, I've always tried to do the right thing.

Occasionally I've taken a decision to ensure my own survival, but who wouldn't? I really believe I'm fundamentally a good person, even if, these days, I'm the only one who thinks so. Because the handful of people who don't already hate me now believe I'm dead. Rest in peace Clare Woodbrook, albeit with minimal emphasis on "peace".

I sat back in my leather armchair, in the mahogany-panelled Piano Bar of Cologne's Excelsior Hotel Ernst. Most people came here for the luxurious ambience, the cocktails, or the selection of eighty whiskies. I just wanted a safe haven to reflect on recent developments, trying to understand why getting everything I'd risked my life for should have left me feeling quite so hollow.

I extinguished my cigarette, and signalled to the barman for a second drink. My Mercedes 190E hire car had been soothing company, but now I'd returned the key, it was time to switch off and contemplate the future. There were so many decisions. What was I going to do with my life, now I had the money to be free, but perversely had sacrificed true freedom in its acquisition? Where was I going to live now I could no longer go home? I was beginning to favour Canada. Would they even let me in? Was thirty too early for a midlife crisis? *What on earth had I been thinking?*

Two men were making small talk at the bar. One of them left, but I continued to watch the other, quite taken by his well-groomed appearance, his chiselled features, impressive physique, smart navy jacket and highly polished brogues. He noticed my gaze and smiled at me, but I quickly turned away, embarrassed to be caught. It was tempting to get to know him, but my need for privacy and anonymity was greater than any urge for physical contact, however tempting the illicit thrill of transient passion.

Instead, I returned to my English-language newspaper, idly toying with the new ring on the third finger of my right hand. I loved the blue and white, the diamonds framing a beautiful blue Ceylon sapphire. It was bigger than the one I'd had to leave behind, but I felt I deserved it. It was strangely comforting; a compensation for the sacrifices I'd made, not that I imagined anyone would feel sorry for me.

I read the same story again and again, desperate to analyse every word, in case I'd overlooked any nuance. There was the helicopter crash, the disgraced former journalist believed to have died on board, and the details of the art fraud she'd committed. At least they'd got my age right, even if some of the other aspects lacked a certain forensic certainty. Finally, I folded the newspaper and put it aside. I was an admirer of the British press. It had paid well and given me a career, but that part of my life was definitively over.

The barman placed my cocktail on the table. I nodded in thanks, then my attention returned to the suave-looking man at the bar. He was perhaps in his early forties. On second thoughts, maybe an hour or two of reckless abandon would help me clear the mental fog. New life, new vices.

He caught me again, then stood up, and indicated a spare chair at my table as he approached.

"Do you mind if I join you," he asked in German-accented English.

I nodded assent, and he pulled out the chair and sat down, facing me across the table. A tingle of butterflies shot through my stomach.

"I'm Steven, Steven Ponndorf," he said.

Behind my eyes, recent events played back like a film on fast-forward. I reached for my cigarettes and offered him one. Then decided on a name.

"I'm Charlotte Sadler," I replied. That should do for now.

"What brings you here?" he asked, taking a cigarette and then offering me a flame from his silver lighter.

Now there was a question that was difficult to answer honestly.

"I thought it would be refreshing to have a few days in Cologne, getting away from it all," I said. "And you?"

"Very much the same I think. Taking in the scenery."

I should have been appalled by the wink that accompanied the obvious innuendo, but I didn't have the energy. It was a D for effort, but at least it proved we shared an agenda.

"And has anything in particular caught your eye?"

"It has." He smiled, as if any further underlining was needed.

"What line of business are you in, Steven?" I asked.

He hesitated, and I knew that whatever he said next would be a lie. It was part of the game. The less we knew about each other, the better. Just two lonely people, sharing a moment in time, destined never to see each other again.

"I'm in the exhibitions industry," he said, at last. "Let me guess what you do."

He leaned back in his chair, taking the opportunity to look me up and down.

"Beautiful clothes and your jewellery is quite spectacular, so I assume you're successful. Clearly independent. You're in great shape and appearance is obviously important. I love your dark red hair. So ... " He pondered for a moment. "You run an international company, perhaps in fashion. But live in a prestigious apartment in London with a private gym. Am I close?"

"Close enough," I said, returning the smile. The apartment aspect was worryingly accurate, although I could never go back there now.

I took a sip of my cocktail. I was tempted to finish it there and then, and save us both any more unnecessary small talk. But I was enjoying the mounting sense of anticipation. I took a second sip before returning the glass to the table.

Out of nowhere, he stifled a yawn.

"Sorry, am I boring you?" I said, with a hint of mischief.

"No, far from it," he said. "And please excuse me. It's been a busy couple of days. On the contrary, I find you quite stimulating."

"Really?"

"Very much so."

"Interesting." I left it there. I was trying to play the femme fatale but I couldn't stop myself from laughing. I leaned forward. "So tell me, Steven. Does your wife know you're in Cologne, talking to strange women in hotel bars?" I let my eyes fall to the wedding ring on his left hand. There was no point in him denying it.

"She, um ..."

"My turn to guess. She doesn't understand you? She has a lover of her own, and has given you permission to stray?"

"Does it bother you?"

I thought for a moment. Of course it bothered me. Not for my own sake, but I didn't want to do anything that caused hurt for anyone else. There'd been more than enough of that already. But then, if it wasn't me, it would be someone else. He didn't look like the faithful type. Of all the crimes I'd committed, this would barely even register.

"I could be persuaded to turn a blind eye," I said, dropping my voice to little more than a whisper.

"Are you staying at the hotel?"

"I am. Are you?"

He nodded. I leaned back and finished my drink, then stubbed out the cigarette. He did the same. It was now or never.

"I could show you my room, if you like," I said. "See how it compares to yours."

His eyes were alight with possibility.

"I would be very interested to see it," he said. "Shall we?"

I nodded, then collected my bag from the floor. He did the same with his small leather holdall, and I led him in the direction of the lift. As we waited for it, a man strolled in from the lobby, joining us. I gave him a sideways glance. It was Steven's companion from the bar. The younger man was tall but his slightly dishevelled appearance looked even more out of place in the brightly-lit hotel lobby. I expected Steven to acknowledge him, and maybe continue their conversation from before, but there was only the faintest nod of recognition. All three of us entered the lift in silence.

We arrived at the second floor. Thankfully, the other man turned in the opposite direction. I took Steven's hand.

"Follow me," I said, my heels sinking into the opulent carpet. As we arrived at my room, I reached into my bag for the key card, then turned to him as I inserted it.

I was shocked by the change in his appearance. His skin looked pale and sickly, sweat beads running off his forehead. And before I'd even opened the door, he'd collapsed unconscious at my feet.

Chapter 3

I DROPPED to my knees, trying to stay calm. It had the makings of a crisis, but I'd been in worse. And yet there was still a gnawing sense of panic. How could I explain this, when the whole point of being in Cologne was to keep a low profile and stay out of trouble?

I checked for a pulse. He was still breathing, but he was out cold.

Perhaps alerted by the noise of the fall, the man from the lift was running towards me from the end of the corridor.

"What happened?" he asked as he dropped to the floor beside me, his voice urgent. He was maybe late twenties, and had a German accent but spoke in English. How did he know to do that?

"I don't know, I ... He just collapsed."

"Let me help." His eyes looked kind and full of concern.

"Are you a doctor? Do you know him? He just came over all weird."

He shook his head.

"Is this your room?" he asked. I nodded. "We can't leave him here. Can we lie him on your bed?"

"Of course."

"Come on, give me a hand."

The man propped up Steven from behind, lifting him beneath both arms, then started to reverse into my room. I lifted Steven's legs, the door closing automatically behind me. Even with someone taking the bulk of the weight, it was a struggle to lift him up to the bed, but eventually we managed it. Between us, we arranged him into the recovery position. Then I remembered Steven's bag, and brought it in from the corridor, putting it on the chair by the desk.

"Thank you," I said to my saviour. "Sorry, I don't know your name?"

"Henning," he said.

"Henning, I'm so pleased you were there. I'll phone down to reception and ask them to call an ambulance."

I should have seen the signs. Had I not been preoccupied by Steven, I would have noticed the way he'd moved between me and the door.

"An ambulance won't be needed. He'll wake up," he said.

"I hope so, but we need to get him checked out."

"No," he said, his voice getting ever-less compassionate.

"Okay, well thank you again for your help, I can take it from here," I said, taking a step towards the door, suddenly keen to get rid of him. But Henning moved to block me. His expression made the unconscious body on the bed seem like the least of my worries.

"What do you want?" I asked, my voice hard and defiant. "Money? Jewellery?"

He shook his head.

"No, I want to speak to you, Clare."

"Who's Clare? My name is Charlotte Sadler."

"No it isn't."

I'd heard enough. I tried to push past him, but he grabbed

both of my arms, then took a step back so he was flat against the door. I was trapped.

"Who are you?" I snarled. Then I noticed the shoulder holster under his jacket, and my breath stopped.

"I'm not here to cause you harm. But we know who you are, and we know what you've done."

"Who's we?"

"The people I work for."

"And what have I supposedly done?"

He laughed, but it sounded spiteful.

"Do you really need me to remind you? You were an investigative journalist in London. You masterminded an art fraud, then killed your colleagues and faked your own death. How much detail do you want?"

He still had hold of my arms, but his grip had loosened. I shook myself free and took a step backwards.

"I think you're getting me confused with someone else," I said, knowing it was futile.

"Let's not play that game," he said. "I've just saved your life."

"*What?*"

He nodded in the direction of the man who lay prone on my bed.

"Check his jacket."

I'd been hoping to give my brain a rest, but suddenly it was in overdrive. I did as directed. I found Steven's wallet. And his BKA warrant card.

"The BKA is the *Bundeskriminalamt* – the Federal Criminal Investigation Office," said Henning. "And his bag."

Again I followed the instruction. There were handcuffs and a gun. I thought about grabbing the weapon and using it to save myself, but there was a significant risk I'd take a bullet in the process.

"He was here to arrest you," Henning continued. "I slipped

something into his drink. If I hadn't, you'd now be on your way to prison, if you ever made it that far."

I sat down on the edge of the bed. This was all a bit too much.

"I'm on your side," said Henning.

"You've got a funny way of showing it."

He took a step towards me, but it wasn't threatening.

"I have a proposal for you."

That sounded ridiculous.

"What sort of proposal?"

"I need you to come with me."

"Where to? I don't even know who you are."

"You don't need to worry about that."

"Forgive me for sounding traditional, but I'm not in the habit of going off with strangers, whether they've allegedly saved me from the police or not."

He took another step towards me, then stopped.

"It's in your interests to do so," he said. "I told you, I'm not here to hurt you. We're aware that you recently had something of a career change. That you might be looking for new opportunities. My boss is impressed and would like to meet you, and make you an offer. To come and work for us."

"That's deeply flattering, but I'm not actually looking for anything at the moment."

He laughed again and shook his head.

"So what are you going to do? Call reception? Get an ambulance? Call the police? Wait till they discover you've drugged one of their own? Tell them your name and give them your address, and wait around until they speak to their colleagues in London?"

"I haven't drugged anyone."

"What will you say, then? Sex game gone wrong?"

I looked back at the man on the bed. It wasn't supposed to be like this.

"Because even if you think you can talk your way out of this,"

Henning continued, "it's only until he comes round. And even if you think you can go on the run after giving a false name and fake address, they'll find you again. It's what they do. I can help you disappear properly."

I let out a deep breath, struggling to comprehend exactly how things had gone so wrong, so quickly.

"Ask yourself how come I'm here, in your room right now," Henning continued. "You can't hide on your own. But my boss is a reasonable man and he merely wants to meet you. He sent me here to do you a favour, so now you need to do me a favour in return."

"And where is he?"

"Paris."

"*Paris*? How am I supposed to get to Paris? If you know anything about me, you know I'm going to struggle to get around for a while. I'm red hot. As you've quite clearly pointed out, people are looking for me. I turn up at an airport and I might as well wear a badge saying '*arrest me*' in flashing lights."

"We have a helicopter waiting. I'll drive you there."

What sort of person had a helicopter waiting? It was all so surreal.

"And what about him?" I nodded in the direction of Steven.

"He'll be unconscious for a couple of hours. We can clean this up for you."

I didn't dare to ask what that meant. It was madness, but it was becoming apparent that I really didn't have a choice.

"Can I at least pack my suitcase?"

"Put whatever you want in hand luggage. There's no need for anything more. You won't be staying long."

"But I can't just leave everything here."

"I'll sort all that out for you."

"For God's sake."

I sighed. I wasn't overburdened with options. It was a risk, but in the circumstances, probably a smaller risk than doing nothing.

I emptied Steven's bag onto the bed and packed a few essentials into it. Henning took the gun before I had a chance to grab it. A few minutes later, I was ready.

"Don't try to run," he said, as though reading my mind. "We found you once, we can do it again, and it would not look good if you fail to return our courtesy."

"Okay, I'm not running." I was still alert, though. Looking for a means of escape at the first opportunity, because that was far from the most reassuring thing he'd said.

The door closed behind us. Henning checked it was locked. Then we took the lift to the ground floor and headed out to the nearby private car park. I was still wearing heels. Why hadn't I thought to change? I wasn't thinking straight.

We reached the car park, then Henning nodded in the direction of a black Audi 100.

I didn't see his assailant approach, but I heard a sickening crunch as the baseball bat connected with his skull. Before he'd even hit the ground, I was being bundled into the back of a people carrier, its tyres squealing in revolt as the driver floored the throttle. And for the second time in the last few minutes, I was looking at a gun.

Chapter 4

MY first instinct was to fight, but the weapon persuaded me otherwise.

"Sorry about that," said the man with his finger poised on the trigger, in a surprisingly refined English accent.

I guessed he was somewhere in his mid-forties, but he was dressed young for his age, in dark combat trousers and a white hoodie under a black leather jacket. The impressive physique, rugged stubble and piercing blue eyes all helped give him the aura of an ex-SAS hero, and definitely not someone I was going to beat in a fist fight.

But that didn't mean I was going to go quietly.

He seemed to sense that, and shot out his left hand, ramming it over my mouth with rapid and unnecessary force. I feared a cut lip at least, and possibly an urgent need for dental realignment.

"Please don't scream or shout, and I'll explain everything," he said, in a voice that was far more polite than his hand gesture.

My eyes narrowed as my brain tried to process every possible scenario. Eventually, though, realising my chronic disadvantage, I nodded. His grip loosened. I pushed his hand away, and then replaced it with my own to check for signs of blood.

"My name's Matthew Sommer," he said. "Friends call me Matt."

"I'll stick with Matthew," I spat back, edging away from him, as far as the car door would allow. We were still powering through the streets to God-knows-where.

He lowered the gun.

"It's not loaded, by the way," he said with a shrug, putting it in the side pocket of his jacket. "But we couldn't let you be taken by the Pencil."

"What do you mean, *the Pencil*?"

"Henning Bierstadt. HB. That's his nickname. It's a type of ..."

"I know what an HB pencil is, for God's sake. Who was he? More to the point, who are you?"

"He was a local lowlife. A sub-contractor. He'll have a headache for a few days, but I'm pleased to say you won't need to worry about him again."

"Evidently." I waited for him to answer the second part of my question, but instead his next comment scared me.

"Clare, we know you. We know what you've done."

Was there any point protesting?

"I've just had this exact conversation with the man you knocked unconscious," I said, still struggling to regain my normal voice.

"I expect you have. And what did he tell you to make you go with him? Are you comfortable by the way? I'm sorry I had to grab you, but needs must."

I took a deep breath and turned to look out of the window. We'd progressed to an autobahn, and the city streets had given way to wide open fields. The driver hadn't spoken. I hadn't even noticed him look in his rear-view mirror. He was like a robot, completely uninterested in the abduction behind him.

There didn't seem to be anything to be gained from lying.

"He said his boss wanted me to go to Paris. Something about

a job offer," I said. "And I'm fine, assuming I don't need dental reconstruction."

"Sorry. I don't know my own strength sometimes. And you agreed to go along with that?"

"He didn't leave me much choice. There was an unconscious policeman in my room. If you know what I've done, you'll also know that's probably not a good position for me right now. And on balance, he'd already had the chance to kill me, if he wanted to. So, I thought it worth giving him the benefit of the doubt."

Sommer shook his head and smiled. His expression was part-friendly, part-pitying.

"Clare, I hate to say this, but you have a lot to learn."

The tone of condescension was infuriating. As if I didn't already have enough to be livid about.

"Are you actually going to tell me who you are and why you've just kidnapped me?"

"I am. But first, let's fill in the things Henning didn't tell you. Don't take this the wrong way, but there wasn't a job offer. It's true that he didn't want you to get arrested, but only because you owe his boss a lot of money. And if you were behind bars they'd have no chance of reclaiming it."

"What do you mean I owe his boss a lot of money? I haven't borrowed anything from anyone." But I had a sickening feeling that I knew where this was headed.

"Henning was working on a contract for Nicolas Thiel," Sommer continued. "Do you recognise the name?"

"Should I?"

"Maybe." He reached into his inside pocket and then passed me a small colour photograph. There was a sharply-dressed man with slicked-back hair. In his late forties, I'd have guessed, and tall, judging by how far he towered above the woman standing next to him. "He runs a strip club in Paris, and he's pivotal in the local drugs trade. And he bought paintings from Dominique Chernin."

I looked away but could feel his eyes on my face, testing for a reaction.

"Where's this going?" I asked.

"And again, excuse the imposition, but you dealt in stolen art. Agreed?"

I refused to acknowledge the accusation, even though I knew it was true.

"Thiel was one of your leading customers," he continued. "But since you've been exposed, all the paintings you sold to him are going to be repossessed, leaving him hugely out of pocket. And he wants you to repay him. But not by going on the payroll. If I hadn't stepped in, you'd have been whisked off to Paris, probably tortured until you made a bank transfer equalling whatever he gave you, plus punitive interest, and then almost certainly killed. So, yes, Henning might have prevented you from being arrested, but believe me, that would have been infinitely preferable to what Thiel had lined up."

This was all a lot to take in. Today was supposed to be the start of my new life. Calm, quiet, and out of the public eye.

"So, who are you, and what do you want with me? Did your boss buy pictures too?"

He laughed.

"No, far from it. And even if she had, I think she'd have applauded your ingenuity."

"She?"

"Indeed. But believe it or not, I've genuinely been sent to protect you. Because unlike the others, I really do have a proposal, and I really would like to offer you a job."

Chapter 5

I STILL had no idea where we were going, but the driver pulled off the autobahn, then, after a short drive up another main road, turned onto what looked like a farm track. He stopped, with two wheels on the grass verge, and killed the engine. But still he didn't look round.

"A proposal?" I said, wondering if the doors were locked. As if to answer my unspoken question, the driver pressed a button on his dashboard, and the locks popped open. The message was clear. I was free to leave if I wanted to. But whether I'd get very far was a lot less certain.

"I'm going to be honest with you," said Sommer. "There's a lot to admire about what you've done. Your career on the newspaper. The ruthless way you conducted recent activities when you went rogue. The way you planned your escape. I'm a big fan. It's genuinely an honour to meet you."

That sounded unlikely.

"But?" I turned to face him.

"But, like I said, you've got a vast amount to learn. I'm offering to teach you."

"And why would you do that?"

"Because you're good. And I'd like you to work with us. Not for us, with us. There's a clear distinction."

I laughed and turned back to the window. I just wanted to be left alone.

"I appreciate the offer, but I'm fine, thanks. I've retired."

He grabbed my shoulder, and turned me towards him. Again, I was impressed by the strength of his grip, but this time the movement itself was gentle.

"Clare, unfortunately when you've done the things you've done, you don't get to make the decision on when you retire," he said. "You can stop operating, but you can't just walk away." He paused, giving me a moment to assess his expression. His eyes looked almost pleading. "In the last hour alone you've nearly been captured twice. Three times if you include me. You've made a lot of money, and I applaud you for that, and I'm not squeamish about how you did it, but you've got to understand that you've crossed a line. You've pissed off some seriously dangerous people, if you excuse my language. So you're very far from fine."

"And so you're what? A bodyguard? And I pay you in kind with stolen art? Or newspaper exposés? Because I'll warn you now, my supply of both has dried up of late."

His face cracked into a smile. There was an almost boyish enthusiasm.

"No."

"What then?"

"Let me tell you how I see this, and stop me if I'm wrong. Okay?"

I nodded.

"You don't trust anyone but yourself, right?"

"In essence," I said.

"And you're fiercely independent. Always have been. A bit of a loner. You want to be left by yourself, to disappear. As far as you're concerned, you've done one bad thing, and have no intention of doing any more. In fact, I'd go so far as to say that part of the reason you did it was the intellectual challenge. How am I doing so far?"

I didn't want to give him credit for the accuracy of his assessment.

"Go on," I said instead.

"Let's save ourselves a lot of time and effort. I'll earn your trust eventually, because I'm never going to lie to you. And I know you probably think that's the biggest lie of all, and I have no way of proving otherwise at the moment. But all I ask is that you give me the benefit of the doubt."

He reached across me and rested his hand on my door handle.

"I'm not stopping you from leaving," he continued. "I'll open the door now, if you think you're better off walking away and trying to survive on your own. We can even turn around and drop you back in Cologne. And if that's your decision, you'll never hear from me again. But I think you understand that's not as straightforward as perhaps you thought it was this morning."

He let go of the door, but the symbolism had been noted.

I closed my eyes, trying desperately to stop tears forming. This whole thing was ridiculous. I had no idea what had happened to my bag. I was technically wealthy, even if most of the money was in a bank account in Switzerland. But here I was, sitting in a stranger's car, wearing my only clothes in the world, and even they were entirely inappropriate for my current situation. There was a limit to how far a dress, laddered tights and high heels were going to take me. And I was listening to a man who both impressed me and terrified me, who seemed incessantly polite for a kidnapper, and yet who was explaining that my life was a nightmare. The worst of it all was that I knew he was right. And I only had myself to blame.

I'd had one moment of madness, frustrated by office politics, dreaming up the perfect crime, almost, as he'd said, purely because of the sheer intellectual thrill of it. But somewhere in the execution, things had become seriously derailed. People had been hurt. Others had been killed. I'd hurt them. I'd killed them. And for what? Nothing other than greed and a moment of insanity.

And it was so unlike me. So out of character. Until that point I'd always tried to fight corruption. Taking the side of the little person against the might of big corporations. I'd built a career and won awards by exposing wrongdoing at the heart of government, and uncovering exactly the kind of scam that I'd subsequently attempted to mastermind. And all for what? Money? Freedom? Yet here I was without so much as a change of underwear, being told that for the rest of my life I'd never be free again.

And the very worst of it all? I knew, in my heart, that I deserved it. I'd got carried away. A massive mental failing. I had no desire to be arrested and spend the rest of my life in prison, but equally I knew that I had to accept whatever other punishment the world sent my way, and I could have no complaint if it was merciless.

No amount of introspection was going to help me now. I was somewhere in rural Germany, at the mercy of a stranger. I opened my eyes, and looked at him.

"You're right," I said. "I don't trust you. I have no idea who you are. And yes, I acknowledge you just saved me, but I only have your word for any of this. As far as I know, the whole thing could have been a set-up, to make it look like you were coming to rescue me, and maybe you paid Henning to take a crack on the head so it looked like you were my saviour."

"But you're not running?"

"Not yet. But I might. I still don't know what you want with me."

"Let's say, we have a common interest in wanting to stay under the radar, common enemies, and - believe or not - a common set of values."

That sounded even more ridiculous.

"Have you got a cigarette?" I asked.

Without a word, the driver passed back a nearly full pack of Marlboro Lights. They'd have to do. So he was listening then, even if he was resolutely refusing to look at me. Was I really that much of a mess? I didn't dare to imagine the state of my make-up.

I opened the car door, then got out and closed it behind me, before leaning on it and lighting up. The outside air was cold. The low sun was doing its best to provide a thin sliver of warmth, but not achieving much success.

A moment later, Matthew joined me. I offered him the cigarettes, but he shook his head. Instead, he took off his leather jacket and wrapped it round my shoulders. I was grateful for the kindness, even if the jacket itself drowned me.

I was wearing heels that added four inches to my natural five foot seven, but he still towered over me. His stubble and short hair added a hint of military menace, but again I was drawn to his eyes. I wondered about all of the things they'd seen.

"You know a lot about me," I said, inhaling deeply, and looking out across the fields.

"I've done my research."

"That worries me."

"It shouldn't. Because I'm on your side. It would be more of a problem if I wasn't."

I raised my eyebrows, then flicked ash before continuing.

"And what exactly do you want me to do?"

"I want to take you to a safe house. Then we'll meet with a colleague, and we'll explain everything to you in detail. Answer any questions you have. Show you what we can offer and explain what we do and why. How you could fit in. What you stand to gain and what the risks are."

"Again, I'm pretty much done with taking risks."

"I get that, but our risks are managed and moderated. And you're taking a far bigger risk if you walk away on your own.

Without wanting to over-dramatise, or keep going on about it, I've saved you today from torture and a very painful death."

I smiled, despite myself, then shivered, aware of the goosebumps forming on my arms.

"You're right, that did sound over-dramatic," I said.

"But it's true. These people aren't going to give up and I might not always be there, much as I wish I could be, because I meant what I said, I'm a big admirer. But they knew exactly where you were this morning, and they'll have people looking for you in any city you turn up in next. And next time they won't give some bullshit excuse about protecting you from the police. It will be a swift and brutal abduction: carted off in the back of a car, and nobody will ever see or hear from you again."

"A bit like what you've just done?"

"Exactly like that. Except I'm not going to kill you."

"Glad to hear it."

"And I hope it wasn't too brutal, was it? I apologise if so."

"Can you stop being so bloody nice?"

I flicked the cigarette away, then got back into the car, grateful for its relative warmth. Matthew followed on the other side. I kept hold of the jacket for now. I could feel the gun in the pocket. He'd said it wasn't loaded, but that might have been a lie.

"Look," he said, "I know this is all a lot to take in. But if you agree to work with us, then from that moment onwards we can start to protect you. We can give you somewhere safe to stay until you get yourself sorted. You can be paranoid or you can trust me, it's up to you."

"But if you know me as well as you think you do, you'll know I'm not an impulsive person," I said. "I didn't write stories based on the first lead that came across my desk. I like to gather the evidence, consider the implications, and make rational decisions based on a thorough evaluation of the facts."

"And you're perfectly entitled to do that. But by the morning you might be dead. It's completely up to you."

Put like that, he had a point. But there were so many unanswered questions.

"I still don't have any idea about what you actually do."

"Part of it is making an awful lot of money."

"I don't care about making an awful lot of money. I've already done that."

"Okay. But we also like to think we have a strong code of ethics and we do the right thing, which was always your forte, too. Investigating and uncovering corruption, identifying those who are responsible, and bringing them to some form of justice. The money is a factor, but we also do it to protect those who are weaker than us. But take your time. This isn't a pressure sell. I'll give you my number. We'll take you back to your hotel. Go to sleep, think about it and call me tomorrow."

The display of faux impatience was quite endearing.

"Or I come with you to a safe house now?"

"Precisely."

"Which is where?"

"Koblenz."

"*Where?*"

"It's on the Rhine, about an hour away."

I swore internally. This was yet more insanity. But I was making a habit of that. What else did I have to lose?

I nodded in resignation, mixed with trepidation. The driver fired the engine. And still without looking back, he turned the car and set off in the direction of my destiny.

Chapter 6

NICOLAS Thiel stood in the hallway of his chateau on the outskirts of Paris, watching the police forensic team carefully remove the last of the paintings and load them into the waiting armoured van.

It was pointless protesting, but that just made his fury even more intense.

Saskia joined him, and put her arm round his waist in comfort, but he shook it off. He didn't want comfort. He wanted revenge.

Once the police had driven away, he walked through to his office, and slammed the door. The police hadn't been in here, but he wouldn't have put it past them to leave listening devices in any of the rooms they'd occupied. He'd arrange a sweep. It was one more irritation, but far from the worst.

He picked up the desk phone and pressed the speed dial. The call was answered on the third ring.

"So?" he barked. There was no need for introductions.

"You will get her. But there has been a problem."

"What kind of problem?"

"Our man was attacked. She got away."

"For God's sake, Thorsten."

So much for German efficiency.

"I'll deal with it. It won't happen again."

"You'd better make sure you do," Thiel said, before throwing down the handset, veins popping in his neck. Somebody was going to suffer for this.

———

Standing in the shadow of a disused barn, on deserted farmland on the edge of Cologne, Thorsten Stötzner ended the call on his Nokia mobile phone and turned to the much taller man next to him.

"My boss is not very happy with you," he said, in a voice that was calmer than he was feeling inside.

Henning Bierstadt winced, and touched the bandage that had stemmed the bleeding on the side of his head.

"They jumped me. I'm sorry."

"Who did?"

"I don't know."

"You don't know?"

"What can I say? They hit me with something. I was knocked unconscious."

Stötzner snorted.

"And you didn't see them coming?"

"No."

"But they clearly saw you. Which means they knew what you were doing. *Which means you were getting followed and didn't spot them doing that either.* It's not good enough."

"I know." The man looked pitiful, eyes sinking to the ground.

"How many more chances do you need?" asked Stötzner.

"Just one. I'll find her again. And next time I'll be more careful."

"You think there'll be a next time?"

"I'll find her."

"No." Stötzner shook his head and took a step away, turning his back for a moment. When he turned around, his hands were behind his back.

"*This* was your last chance," he said. "It's one fuck-up after another. It can't go on."

"I've told you, I'm sorry."

"It's not good enough being sorry. You're making me look incompetent. Now I've got to clear up your mess and I don't like to see myself as a mere cleaner."

Henning looked up, his eyes pleading. And that's when he noticed the gun.

"No! Please!" he screamed.

But it was too late. The first bullet entered just below his left eye. The second and third were delivered purely out of spite.

———————

My preconception of a safe house was an anonymous mid-terrace, or maybe even a flat. But when our car finally stopped, it was outside a huge stone building that looked more like a mini castle. It was grand and opulent, and far from discreet.

"We call it the Schloss," said Matt. I'd decided to call him Matt ever since he'd lent me his leather jacket.

"German for castle? I can see why," I said. "But it's not exactly inconspicuous."

"You don't need to worry about that. The security means nobody would dare come anywhere near."

He'd said that to reassure me, but the effect was quite the reverse.

"What sort of security?"

"You'll see. Let me take you in and I'll introduce you to the staff."

What kind of safe house had staff?

The minute we were out of the car, the driver powered off, back down the track that ran through the grounds, in the direction of the main road.

"I'd offer to carry your bags," said Matt, "but ..."

"Very funny."

He led the way across a gravel courtyard to the huge wooden front door. It was opened by an elderly man with thinning grey hair, and smart but casual clothing rather than a butler's uniform. He extended his hand in welcome.

"This is Walter Lorenz," said Matt. "He looks after the place."

"Hello, I'm –" I hesitated, while accepting the handshake. What name to give? "Pleased to meet you."

"It's okay, he can't hear you. He's deaf," Matt continued. "He was an elite sniper in the German army until standing too close to a Russian bomb, in Lviv, in 1944."

I quickly did the calculation. If he was about seventy now, he'd have been around sixteen when war broke out. Twenty-one in 1944. No age at all.

"Where's Lviv?"

"Ukraine. Near the Polish border. The Eastern Front."

Walter stood back for us to enter the impressive wooden-panelled hallway. There was genuine warmth in his smile. I'm not sure why, but I found that more reassuring than the thought of intense security. A woman of a similar age appeared from a room to the right.

"And this is Birgit Lorenz," said Matt. "Walter's wife. She does most of the catering and housekeeping."

I smiled and offered my hand, which she took with something approaching a bow.

"Pleased to meet you, too," I said.

"She doesn't speak English, unfortunately," said Matt.

They had a brief conversation in German, after which Birgit nodded, and then turned towards the impressive central staircase.

"Birgit will show you to your room," Matt explained. "I'll give you an hour or so to freshen up, then we'll meet downstairs and I'll give you the guided tour."

"Perfect." I wasn't sure if I'd need an hour, with no clothes or toiletries, but there was little point in rushing things.

Birgit led the way, up two flights of stairs, and then along a wide landing that led off to either side. It was like the most amazing country house hotel, albeit with the faintest aroma of something delicious wafting up from downstairs. Suddenly I was overwhelmingly hungry. Everything was immaculate, despite the age of the place. The wooden bannisters were freshly polished, and the thick pale green carpets on the landing looked like they'd never been walked on.

We turned left, and then stopped by a large wooden door. Birgit gave me a key and gestured to the lock, making a turning motion with her hand. I opened the door and she followed me inside, then retrieved two luxuriously thick, soft towels from a wardrobe and handed them to me. With a nod, she turned and left me on my own, closing the door gently behind her. It was reassuring to know the door could be locked, even if it was ultimately meaningless when I didn't know who else had a key.

But what a room. It was dominated by a huge limed-oak four-poster bed, with equally outsize sash windows along one wall. In the dying embers of daylight I could just make out the Rhine, far below, and a couple of fields away. I flicked on the bedside lamp, and a beautifully warm glow replaced the gathering gloom. A full-length mirror dominated one wall. I hardly dared look in it, but when I did, I was relieved to notice I wasn't as much of a mess as I'd feared.

There was a knock at the door.

I padded across and opened it to find Walter standing next to the two suitcases I'd left behind in Cologne, together with the holdall I'd stolen from the policeman. He carried them in for me, and then smiled as he turned to leave. I thanked him, even though I knew he couldn't hear.

How had they managed that?

I laid the first suitcase on the floor and popped the catch. Everything was immaculately folded. Then I did the same to the second, with similar results. Any sense of intrusion that someone had gone through my underwear was supplanted by the sheer relief of actually having fresh clothes to change into. And toiletries and make-up and even the copy of Douglas Coupland's *Shampoo Planet* that I'd left on my bedside table.

It really did seem like a luxurious hotel. I locked the door, hung up my clothes in the wardrobe, even if it was just for one night, arranged everything else in the bathroom, and then stripped off and headed to the shower. The powerful jet worked its magic, reinvigorating me. An hour later, it was pitch black outside, but I was ready, in a charcoal grey dress, fresh tights and a pair of new, dark red suede shoes that matched my temporary hair dye, ready to face whatever they threw at me.

Chapter 7

THERE was another knock at the door. I unlocked it and came face to face with Matt.

"How are you finding the room?" he asked.

"Very impressive."

"I love the outfit. It suits you," he added, taking a step back and appraising me.

Was he flirting? That was all I needed. He'd changed into a formal navy suit that emphasised his broad shoulders, with a white shirt, unbuttoned at the neck. It made me wonder if he lived here too. By any reckoning he was handsome, and in any other situation I'd have allowed my imagination a brief detour into a dark world of wild debauchery, but now really wasn't the time.

I picked up a small clutch bag containing the driver's cigarettes and a tube of lipstick, and then followed him onto the landing, taking care to lock the door behind me.

"I won't ask how you did the thing with the suitcases," I said. "But for the record, I did appreciate it."

"My pleasure," he said, with a smile. "Follow me and I'll take you down to meet Anders. We can have dinner and wine, and then we'll talk you through everything."

He led the way downstairs and into a grand drawing room. Everything about the place oozed character, from the exposed thick stone walls to the giant open fireplace in which a couple of logs were burning. A man in perhaps his late fifties or early sixties rose from a leather armchair to meet us. His grey hair and close-cropped beard gave him a serious look, which was accentuated by the round, horn-rimmed spectacles, but there was a warmth in his greeting.

"Clare Woodbrook," he said, with a noticeable German accent, offering me yet another handshake. "Anders Hagström. It's an absolute pleasure to meet you. I trust the hospitality's up to standard?"

"Everything's very lovely indeed," I said, feeling I should sound grateful. "It's an amazing house."

"Matt will give you the full tour later. But for now, would you care for a drink? There's a choice of wines, or anything else you fancy." He oozed self-assurance.

"A white wine would be good. Do you have a sauvignon blanc?"

He nodded.

"Take a seat and I'll be back in one moment."

I was just sinking into one of the large leather sofas when he came back, with Birgit a couple of paces behind. She was carrying a tray with a bottle of wine in an ice bucket, together with three crystal glasses.

Matt settled down on another sofa opposite me, with a deep red rug between us, while Anders poured three generous measures.

"Frau Lorenz said dinner will be five minutes," he said, retaking his position in the armchair. "Cigarette?"

It didn't seem like the sort of room you should smoke in, but he offered me an open packet and there was an ashtray on the table. And after the day I'd had, I didn't think one more would do any harm. Again, Matt declined, but Anders offered me a light and then took one for himself.

"You must be wondering why you're here," he said.

"It has crossed my mind."

"How are you finding Germany?"

"I've had an interesting welcome." I looked around as I said it, and noticed Matt grinning. I took a sip of the wine. It was magnificent.

"Different to the London Docklands I expect," Anders continued.

"You have done your research."

He shrugged.

"For your information, my flat in the Docklands is rented out to a complete stranger and likely to stay that way."

"Matt tells me you had a run-in with Henning?"

"I made his acquaintance."

He looked as though he was about to say something else, but was interrupted by Birgit, presumably announcing that our table was ready. Matt led the way across the hallway into an equally impressive dining room. Three places had been set at one end of a large table, with candles arranged beautifully between them.

Matt pulled out a chair for me, and then offered me a basket of bread. A moment later, Birgit reappeared, with the first plate of what became an exceptional three-course meal.

Anders was clearly in charge. He made it plain that we shouldn't discuss business over dinner, but instead asked questions about my former career, showing a surprising depth of knowledge about some of the stories I'd worked on. The wine continued to flow. Occasionally I had to stop and remind myself that I was still potentially the victim of a kidnapping, but if they were attempting to put on an impressive display of charm, they were doing it with aplomb. And if they were trying to relax me to the point where they could strike unawares, they were doing a pretty good job of that too. I was going to need to be on my guard.

When dinner had finished, Birgit cleared the plates away, and we headed back to the drawing room. The men had brandy, but I opted for another glass of wine. And that was when it all became clear.

"So let me put this simply," Anders began. "We're a kind of trade and development organisation. A network of people who recognise and exploit opportunities, on an international level." He paused, as though to check I was following so far. I nodded. "But at the same time, as Matt has probably already mentioned, we use our position of influence and intelligence-gathering skills to try to stop corruption when we see it, and to prevent exploitation of people who aren't in a position to look after themselves."

"He did, and it all sounds very noble," I said. I don't know if he detected the cynicism. "Obviously that tells me virtually nothing, but I'm thinking a kind of German Robin Hood situation."

That caused Matt to laugh and Anders glanced in his direction before continuing. For my part, I felt emboldened by the wine. At least they hadn't drugged it. Yet.

"We work on exciting projects," Anders continued. "And yes, we occasionally push the boundaries, but let's just say, we have a good working relationship with law enforcement agencies throughout Europe. We do things for them that they couldn't do for themselves."

"Such as?"

"Supply them with information where they would struggle on their own. Call it a happy collaboration. We help them, they help us by turning a blind eye."

"But you're still a criminal outfit?"

Anders appeared awkward, while Matt was reluctant to make eye contact with me, but finally looked up and took over.

"That depends on your perspective," he said. "Occasionally we have to do things that stretch the definition of legality, but the deals we work on are strictly above board. Just occasionally we have to take the law into our own hands to ensure that bad people don't prosper."

Anders nodded in agreement, as though relieved to be let off the hook.

"Such as hitting people over the head with a baseball bat?" I said. "But who are you? What's your background? How many of you are there? Where did you come from?"

"You've heard of the Blood Angel?" asked Anders.

"No."

"Maybe in the original German? *Blutengel*?"

"Still no. It sounds like some sort of vampire. Who is she?"

"You assume an angel is a she?"

"Isn't she? Or he?"

He shrugged. Of all people, I should have been alert to the dangers of casual sexism, and mentally scolded myself.

"She is, or was, indeed female and a notorious East German spy and crime boss," Anders continued. "Her real name was Angelica Schröder, but in the grand tradition of spies, mobsters and criminal legends from Mata Hari to Carlos The Jackal, she became known by her pseudonym."

"She sounds charming."

"Don't judge yet. I'll give you the bad things first, although bear in mind some of the facts are open to interpretation, and others might purely be part of the legend, and not real facts at all."

"Go on." He had my attention.

"As far as we know, she was born in 1929, just as the Great Depression hit. She grew up in Leipzig and prospered under the communists, once she hit her twenties. Up until that time, and especially during the Weimar period, the German equivalent of the mafia was the *Ringvereine*."

"Ring clubs," added Matt.

"Exactly," Anders continued. "Members wore identical signet rings, followed a set of rules and had a code of conduct. They looked after each other, providing alibis on demand, and had a big network of underworld contacts. The Nazis tried to outlaw them, but they continued until the communists successfully managed to suppress them."

"Good old communists, eh?" I said.

"Quite. But East Germany, as you know, was far from idyllic." That was an understatement. "There was still crime, but there was a culture of fear and secrecy, not least because of the brutal effectiveness of the Stasi. Which brings us back to Angelica."

"She was part of it?" I asked.

"To an extent." It was hard to read his expression. "At its height, there was one Stasi officer or informant for every sixty-three people in the GDR. Imagine that. They also had male *romeo* spies, who were sent out to the West to seduce women, often secretaries in the ministries and government offices in Bonn. Which as you know, I presume, was the capital of West Germany."

"Of course."

"The romeo spies were extremely successful because there were far more single women than men. But I digress."

"Angelica was a beautiful woman," said Matt, taking over. "There are rumours that she acted as a female romeo, if that's not a contradiction. A kind of a femme fatale for special ops. And other rumours that she had relationships with several high-ranking Stasi officers, as well as being an informer. She was uniquely effective, ruthless, and got things done. But as you could imagine, it was a different era. She managed to create a niche, and operate under the radar, building her own criminal network."

Anders lit a cigar, which was my cue to have another of the driver's Marlboro Lights. I felt guilty that I'd stolen them, but thought it was probably a small crime compared to those of the people around me.

"Doing what exactly?" I asked.

"Smuggling, mainly. There was a powerful black market," said Matt. "And the occasional assassination." He made that sound like a trivial afterthought.

"She didn't look like a typical gangster," added Anders. "In fact, far from it. As she rose to prominence, her connections and experience helped her stay out of trouble, for the most part. But she divided opinion, and eventually time caught up with her."

"As it does with us all," I said. I was acutely aware that I was now in my thirties.

"Indeed. By the mid-seventies she was established, with a phenomenal underground network, but her influence with the government had started to wane. And suddenly, almost overnight, her former masters turned on her. They started to see her as a threat and an embarrassment, and they decided she had to be stopped."

"Which was when she disappeared," added Matt. "And when the legend of the Blood Angel began. You don't pick a fight with the Stasi and expect to win. But she did, meeting fire with fire, and earning her reputation for merciless revenge. Every time one of her network was killed or captured, she'd strike back with more of the same. An eye for an eye, and all of that."

"And a body for a body," added Anders, adding little-needed emphasis.

"So what happened to her?" I asked.

They exchanged a glance before Anders continued.

"Well, that's where things start to get interesting."

Chapter 8

THE black BMW 7 Series pulled up next to the kerb, outside a large art nouveau block close to the Frankfurt *Hauptbahnhof*, the city's main train station. The small gang of men who were gathered on the corner dispersed.

From the front passenger seat, Florian Straub made a mental note. Very little escaped his attention.

"Keep an eye on them," he said, nodding in the direction of the now-empty junction.

"Want me to follow?" asked Michael Eidinger, his driver and henchman.

"Just watch for now. See if they come back. If they do, I want to know what they're up to."

"Understood."

Straub got out of the car and crossed the road, then walked through an entrance with a flashing red Eros Centre sign. He made his way past the garish neon tubes of the lobby and took the stairs to the first floor. While most of the building's visitors continued further upstairs, to sample the delights of the working girls, he unlocked the padlocks on the door that ultimately led to his office.

He didn't bother to remove his coat. He didn't intend to stop long, but he straightened his bow tie out of instinct. He had a call to make.

"Nicolas," he said, once the connection to Paris was made. "Florian. I hear things didn't go well."

"News travels fast," said the Frenchman.

"I make it my business to know things."

"I'm sure." There was an awkward silence for a moment, before Thiel continued. "I made the mistake of relying on a German. Did you call to gloat or do you have anything practical to add?"

"There's no reason to gloat. But I can add it to the list of things I can help you with. I'll put the word out. Wherever she is, I'll find her."

"Maybe get your English policeman to help."

Florian laughed.

"He'd love nothing more. How's Saskia?"

"She's fine. Although she advised me against dealing with you."

"That's families. She'll come round. But you need to come to Frankfurt. She doesn't need to know about it. I'll introduce you to some of my favourites. On the house."

"In Paris we have the finest showgirls. The very best. I'm insulted by the suggestion you think I would be interested in some German *Hausfrau*."

Florian laughed again.

"We have the best of Poland. Of Ukraine. Think about it. The offer is there. And in the meantime, I'll call you with progress. On Clare Woodbrook and the other issues. Expect news very soon."

"You do that."

Florian ended the call, then poured a small shot of vodka before making his second call. Maybe it wasn't such a ridiculous idea.

In London, Detective Chief Inspector Graham March picked up his phone.

"And to what do I owe this unexpected pleasure?" he asked.

"We have a little problem with your English friend," said Florian.

"I assume you're using the term 'friend' in its loosest sense? What has she done now? Robbed a bank?"

Florian chuckled.

"If only. No, an associate of mine very much wants to speak to her."

"I'm not casting aspersions on your associates, but why would he want to lower himself to that?"

"She owes him money. For some paintings."

"Ah."

"Ah indeed."

"Very interesting. And does this associate want to extract the repayment with disproportionate amounts of brutal violence? Please say yes."

"He does. I think it would be an extremely uncomfortable meeting for her."

"Excellent news. Now you've got me interested."

"You're just sore because she exposed you."

Florian thought he could detect March's rising blood pressure at the far end of the line.

"For your information, and as you very well know, some tabloid hatchet job, based on largely manufactured and equally fanciful evidence, does not constitute what I like to call an exposé. And I will be cleared, once the hearing takes place, as you also know."

"Graham, I think you forget who you're talking to. I have intimate knowledge of the things you've done."

"Yeah? Well, remind me not to call you as a witness."

"I wouldn't dream of it. We need you back in action."

Florian noticed a document that had been left on his desk, and started to scan it. It was an inventory of an incoming shipment of outerwear from Turkey. He was more interested in the accompanying cargo that wasn't listed on the manifest. His attention snapped back to the call.

"Joking aside, I need you to come back to Germany," he said. "I've promised we'll help. And I want to include you in the plan. I think it will be in all our interests."

They made arrangements to meet and then Florian ended the call. He finished the vodka and headed back out into the night.

Chapter 9

I STILL wasn't sure where all of this was going, but I half expected an East German assassin to walk in, introduce herself as Angelica, and shoot me. She didn't, but the night was young.

"Don't tell me, she's also looking for me?" I said.

"No. If she's still alive, I expect she already knows exactly where you are," said Anders.

I didn't like the sound of that, on several levels.

"How do you mean?" My eyes shot to the door. If I made a sudden move, I could be out of it before they had a chance to stop me. Although I doubted I'd be able to get far, with no transport, and no real idea where I was.

"She's our boss," said Matt.

"In a manner of speaking," added Anders.

I was beginning to like the sound of this even less.

"Like I said, don't judge yet," he continued. "I told you I was going to give you all the bad things first. Because that was then, and times are different now. We knew things would change once the Berlin Wall came down, but no one could have predicted how much would transform in just four years: Germany reunified, and the Stasi disbanded."

"And that presents new challenges and opportunities," Matt continued. "The good news is that in the last few years, the Blood Angel has evolved from one person into a movement. And developed a conscience."

"What do you mean a conscience?"

He turned to Anders, who continued.

"I don't know if you can imagine what it was like to live in East Germany, but it was tough. Really tough. And I am not going to - what's the phrase? Add sugar?"

"Sugar-coat," said Matt. Anders nodded.

"I'm not going to sugar-coat any aspect of it. But some things were simpler. And now we're back, reunited with the rest of Germany, the rest of Europe and the rest of the world, and we've seen - and been shocked by - some of the corruption and exploitation that takes place in the West."

"So, hold on, just so I get this straight, you grew up in East Germany?"

Anders nodded. "In Dresden."

"And now you work for this Blood Angel woman?"

He shrugged. "In one sense." I surmised there was a lot more to it than that.

"Okay, well, can I stop you there?" I extinguished my cigarette. "I don't know who you think I am, and what you think I've done, but I'm really not sure why I'm here or why you're telling me all of this."

"We're telling you because we want you to come and work with us," said Anders.

"I kind of got that. But that's also my point. I'm not sure I want to become part of some violent former East German mafia, if it's all the same with you. No offence intended, obviously."

They both laughed.

"That's not what we're suggesting," said Matt. "We were just getting onto the good part."

Despite my reservations, the investigative journalist in me was curious. Even though, to my increasingly heartfelt regret, my newspaper days were over.

"Go on," I said, reaching for the wineglass, regretting finishing the cigarette early.

"I'm sure you don't need me to tell you about organised crime," started Anders. "But all around the world, there are gangs, families, and all sorts of other networks and organisations. There are the big ones like the Camorra in Naples, the Sicilian Mafia, the Hong Kong Triads, the Jamaican Yardies and the Japanese Yakuza. But some of those are lazy labels. Even within the bigger organisations there are different factions, and sometimes they're at war with each other."

"Alongside those there are states, churches, police forces and corporations that use the techniques of organised crime," added Matt. "They derive their power from their status as social institutions. And there are lots of different types of crime: white-collar, financial, war, state, political. And alongside all of those there are the independents and small-scale operations: from freelance terrorists right down to street gangs within every city and town across Europe, the USA and beyond. You're with us so far?"

"It's a dangerous world," I said.

"It is. But Angelica was different," Anders continued. "To her mind, everything she did had an element of fair play. She could be deadly, and certainly had many enemies, but she never preyed on poor people. She ran various scams and systems that involved corruption, but it wasn't always for personal gain. There were many normal East German people who benefitted from her ability to break the rules."

"She was rumoured to be shocked by how cruel some of the Western groups could be," added Matt. "Running drugs, exploiting the vulnerable, trafficking people, extortion of those who work hard building legitimate small businesses. She didn't want any part of that. It was against everything she stood for."

"Really?" I said. "You are aware you just told me how she regularly murdered people?"

"But that was different," Anders continued. "There was always a political motivation. In the early days she thought she was doing things for the love of her country. Then, when she fell out of love with East Germany, she did it to fight against an oppressive totalitarian regime. But her victims were never innocent. She never exploited the public."

"So she *was* like a German Robin Hood?" I said.

Matt laughed again. "Kind of."

"She would argue that she always tried to look after her own people," said Anders. "It's just that her own people are now under threat not from the State, but from criminal gangs from all of the rest of Europe, and the rest of the world."

"So she's still active now?" I asked.

Anders shrugged.

"She hasn't been seen in over a decade."

"But you said she was your boss? You must know her. You must have seen her."

"That's not how these things work." He stood up, and refilled both their glasses of brandy, then offered me a top-up of wine. Once he'd poured it, he retook his seat. The only sound in the room was the gentle ticking of a grandfather clock and the occasional crackle from the fire.

"Okay," I said when I realised further elaboration would not be forthcoming. "But I still don't understand why I'm here."

"You've heard about the Schengen Agreement?" asked Anders.

"Of course." That was an abrupt change of direction.

"So you know that it'll soon be possible to move freely around much of Europe without showing a passport?"

"In the Schengen countries, yes. I'm from England. We don't get involved in that kind of thing."

Matt smirked. I think he knew what I was referring to, but I clarified it for the sake of Anders.

"There's a significant proportion of the British population who read the *Daily Mail* and are scared of foreigners, think that Europeans can't be trusted, and want nothing to do with the French and Germans especially," I said. "Some of us embrace the ideal of a united Europe, but there's plenty of xenophobia and bigotry. So yes, I know of the Schengen Agreement. And I'm very excited at the prospect of the Channel Tunnel and look forward to using it, but I doubt we'll ever be part of the treaty."

"I feel the same," said Anders. "And Schengen will be a wonderful thing. But it also brings problems as well as opportunities."

"Such as?"

"There will be no border controls. So let's just say, that while it opens up opportunities for an organisation from the old East Germany to extend its business into other territories, it also means it's possible for less fair-minded organisations in other countries to move into ours. There's likely to be a jostle for position."

"Okay."

"Which could get very dangerous," he added.

"I told you it's a dangerous world."

"It is," said Matt. "And like it or not, you're now a part of it."

"I'm really not. I did one bad thing and retired."

"You did one thing, but now you've got a target painted on your back." Matt appeared to like reminding me my life was at risk. It was one of his less endearing qualities. "Your problem is that you don't know who's taking aim at you. You met a couple of them today, but there could be more. There'll be those who want revenge. Those who want to inflict punishment. And you don't know who they'll outsource it to. It could be a local kid on a pushbike, given twenty Deutschmarks to put a knife in you."

"You've made your point."

He didn't take the hint.

"It could be a professional hitman. And it doesn't even matter, really, who you ripped off. Other people could be out to get you to try to win favour from elsewhere. It's not a question of running, but how long you'll be able to run before someone catches you. And believe me, they will. You've seen that already. Because people talk and there are networks of informers who'll supply information about you, whether for money or just to save their own skin."

I didn't want to think about the truth behind his comments, but a terrified part of me knew it was probably all true. Just not something I'd ever considered before.

"And so, what? I come and work for you, committing to a life of crime, and you protect me?"

"No," said Anders. "Because they were the old days. We don't really do crime any more. As my colleague told you, the Blood Angel developed a conscience."

Chapter 10

LOGS shifted in the hearth, sending a shower of sparks shooting up the flue. I adjusted my position on the sofa, and then recrossed my legs, aware that Matt kept glancing in their direction. I pulled my hem down slightly, to give him a subtle reminder that some things were off-limits, special forces dreamboat or not.

"What do you mean those were the old days, and she's developed a conscience?" I asked. "And are we talking about the Blood Angel as Angelica, or the organisation as a whole? You're confusing me."

"Both," said Anders.

"And you claim you no longer do crime, but you mentioned opportunities? Presumably to extend your activities, however noble, into other areas." Again, I don't know if he detected my sarcasm.

"Exactly that."

I tried not to smirk. This all sounded ridiculous.

"So if not crime, what?"

"We look for other legitimate opportunities to make money," said Matt, taking over. "And at the same time, as Anders said, we work with law enforcement agencies, in a very informal way, where our contacts, and our network, can provide information that they would struggle to get through more conventional means."

"So all squeaky clean, with a side order of espionage?"

"Squeaky-ish, but yes."

"And what sort of 'legitimate opportunities'?"

"I'll give you an example," said Matt. "In Bulgaria, the first free elections took place shortly after the Wall came down, but the Bulgarians don't like to create a scene, so they re-elected the communists. Friends of the Communist Party were given large amounts of cash to buy factories, but as it stands, they have no idea how to run them."

"So, the economy is a mess, and it wouldn't surprise me if it's heading in the direction of hyperinflation," Anders continued, taking over. "There's an opportunity to broker deals between people who own the factories in Bulgaria and other people from elsewhere in Europe who have the expertise in running them. Or to put it another way, if you want to be more, what's the word? Cynical. If you want to be more cynical, there's an opportunity for entrepreneurs to acquire factories in Bulgaria very cheaply by Western standards. We help put those deals together."

"And you're the only ones doing that?"

Matt shook his head.

"No. A lot of people are aware of this kind of thing. But other groups have other agendas, like using it as a front for activities such as money-laundering, drug distribution, counterfeiting ... the list goes on. We don't do any of that. We try to ensure that those deals are done properly, that nobody is ripped off, that the factories end up in safe hands, and the Western entrepreneurs get very rich in the process."

"So effectively, you're competing with, for example, the Italian Mafia or corrupt corporations. But you're doing it in a compassionate, albeit money-making way?" I found it hard to stifle a laugh.

"Kind of."

"It sounds very dangerous. You must be very brave."

"It can be," said Matt, not rising to the bait. "The problem is that it's a competitive market and sometimes we have to adopt a slightly no-nonsense approach."

"Hence squeaky-ish?"

"Exactly. Which is where we occasionally push boundaries. But we have to be careful, because with some of these groups, the police are on the payroll. And when we can't trust the police, we sometimes go higher."

"Like government intelligence?"

Matt shrugged, avoiding the question.

"But Bulgaria is only one example," he said instead. "There are lots of opportunities all over Europe. Last week I was in Bratislava, Anders was in Budapest. And at the moment I'm also dealing with a situation in London. But we can't say too much about those at the moment. Not until you decide if you want to join us."

"Of course." This was a lot to take in, if any of it was true. It sounded far-fetched, but then I looked around, and thought about the events in Cologne, and began to think that maybe they weren't just making up stories. I never like to make assumptions. Had I still been a journalist, this would have been gold dust. But I wasn't, and I was aware that if this was a trap and they told me too many secrets, my chances of escaping alive would be seriously diminished. "I'm deeply flattered that you think I might be of some use to you. But while I wish you well, I've got lots of plans of my own. Starting with going home."

"And home is?" asked Matt.

"I'm working on that."

They both laughed.

"I'll tell you what we see in you," said Anders. "We see

someone bright, brave, and with a ruthless determination to get what they want. Someone who doesn't always play by the rules."

"And someone who's done good work fighting corruption, until a recent lapse," added Matt with a charming smile. "And who needs our protection, whether or not she admits it, because you defrauded some people and murdered your associates along the way."

"I think murder is a bit strong," I said. "I prefer to call it self-defence."

"Let's not bullshit. But like Anders said, we know what you're capable of. Concocting and executing elaborate plans. And setting aside recent developments, it seems that you have a track record of doing good things for the right reasons, and that you have the right kind of connections and contacts. Information can be vital."

"But you're forgetting, I'm officially dead," I said. "You presumably heard about the helicopter crash? So my contacts from the newspaper world will most likely be turning up at my funeral in the next few days, assuming that I'm not already a figure of public disgrace. I did one bad thing. I'm not brave. I got away with it."

"But you didn't get away with it," said Matt. "You're now a target. If you want to stay safe and wipe the slate clean, you can turn yourself in, do your time, and emerge an old woman, and if you're lucky you'll qualify for a council house on the basis of being a vulnerable member of society. But I don't think that's what you did it for. I think you did it because you wanted something better, because you were sick of playing by the rules."

He had a point, but I refused to acknowledge it.

"I'll tell you why I did it," I said. "My job was largely writing about corrupt people who made millions, but they weren't very intelligent and kept getting caught. I was worn down by the corporate bullshit and office politics, and I thought that if I could do what they did and just be clever about it, then I wouldn't be caught. As I said to one of my former colleagues recently, I'd lie awake at night, making up stories, trying to imagine little scenarios where I could mastermind something brilliant. I never thought it'd happen. And then it did. I deeply regret that people got hurt in the process, but really it *was* self-defence. But that was then. It was a one-off."

They exchanged a glance.

"Excuse me, then," said Anders, standing up. "I understand what you're saying. It has been a pleasure to meet you." He offered me his hand to shake. I stood up, confused. "I wish you a safe onward journey."

Without a second glance, he turned and left the room, closing the door behind him. I was shocked by the sudden change in mood. I think Matt noticed my discomfort. But if I was expecting an explanation, I was to be frustrated.

"We don't want to waste any more of your time," he said, standing up too.

"You're not wasting my time. I appreciate the chat," I said.

"You're welcome to stay the night. Where would you like me to drop you off in the morning?"

I had no idea.

"We appreciate what you're saying," he continued. "And we're not like Henning, and we're not going to threaten you. I think you've made your point. Like I said at the beginning, you need never see or hear from us ever again."

"But?"

"But nothing. I understand that you want to get on with your life. I get that you're clever, and brilliant at what you do, but I still maintain you've got a lot to learn. Not about how to do your job, if we're talking of being an investigator. Your reputation is there. But how to survive. I really do wish you the best of luck."

"Thank you."

He didn't move. I looked away, but I could feel his eyes burning into me.

"So that's it?" I said.

He didn't answer immediately. I knew the tactic: leave a silence and wait for the other person to fill it. I was determined not to be the first to crack.

But I was even more determined to not be drawn into some elaborate gameplay.

"What exactly did you want me to do, and what do I get in return?" I said at last.

Chapter 11

F

AR off a door slammed, and a moment later came the crunch of tyres on gravel. The engine note faded into the distance. Suddenly, the thought of Anders leaving filled me with dread.

"Is there any point discussing it?" asked Matt. He looked annoyed, and that unsettled me too.

"Humour me."

"Okay." He sat down again, and I retook my position opposite.

A moment later Anders reappeared.

"I've sent Walter to get more wine," he said. Despite everything, I had to smile. They'd played me brilliantly. "What have I missed?"

"Clare was asking what it involves," said Matt.

Anders nodded.

"So, you'd work with us, occasionally negotiating in different countries throughout Europe, and benefitting personally when deals are done," he said. "At the same time, you use your skills as an investigator to find out things and help gather evidence against those we wish to bring to justice."

"Including Graham March," said Matt.

That got my attention, in a way not un-akin to somebody sticking a knife in my eye.

"What do you know about Graham March?" I asked.

"We know he's a Detective Chief Inspector back in London. We know you were investigating him for all sorts of corruption. And we know you left a dossier of evidence for one of your colleagues, Danny someone?"

"Danny Churchill," I said.

Matt nodded.

"We read Danny's exposé, and we know that as a result of that, March has been suspended."

"But we also know March will probably talk his way out of it because he has power and connections," added Anders. "What I don't think you had in your dossier was all of the information on his German interests."

"And his more recent interest in sex trafficking," said Matt. I think he could tell by my expression that he'd caught me unawares with that one. "Anyway, you'd go undercover when we needed you to. You'd gather information and report back. At the same time you'll get involved in making deals, and the rule then is that you pay ten percent of your commission into a central bank account that we use as a fund to cover organisational expenses."

"That reporting is up to you," added Anders, pouring the last of the wine into my glass. "There's an element of trust. But you would be well advised not to breach it."

I took the moment to light another cigarette, and drew deeply before blowing smoke in the direction of the fireplace. I was desperate for thinking time. This was beginning to get serious.

"Effectively you want me to be a spy?" I said at last.

"There's certainly an element of that," said Matt. "But it's just what you've been doing for the newspaper, except on a much larger scale, without any of the office politics."

It was unnerving, the way he knew how to push my buttons.

"I'm not saying it doesn't come with risks, but that's why we'll train you," added Anders. "Our network is there to alert you to any danger, but on top of that we'll give you extensive training to give you the skills you need to spot threats for yourself, and then deal with them before they become a problem. We'll teach you self-defence, both in terms of unarmed combat and elite-level firearms training, just in case you ever need it, although obviously we hope that is purely precautionary."

"And we'll give you a personal trainer who will sort you out with a fitness programme," said Matt, his eyes dropping to the smouldering cigarette. "We'll teach you German. You'll learn about technology, get to travel all over Europe, and sometimes further afield. We'll give you a new identity and a passport. You'll have access to properties in several countries that you can treat as home. Some, like this one, come with staff. Others are more basic, but you'll have the freedom to move around. You're familiar with the internet?"

"To an extent."

"It's increasingly at the core of everything we do, so we'll train you on that too. We'll teach you how to use Archie to find specific files and show you Usenet newsgroups for exchanging coded messages."

"Once you've done the basic training, we'll cover your expenses for travel and hotels if you need them," added Anders. "And you can know that wherever you are in Europe, within reason, help is not too far away."

"And who do I report to?"

"I'll be your main point of contact initially," said Matt. "But in reality, once you're up and running, you'll be left to your own devices. You'll be able to check in with me if you ever need to, but you'll develop a network of your own. Effectively, you're self-employed. There'll be times when someone approaches you, to call upon your specific areas of expertise, but that works both ways and if you need specialist help at any stage, you'll never be short of people to call."

This was all so much to take in. Despite my obvious reservations, it was beginning to sound breathtakingly exciting, but there was still so much I didn't know.

"How big is the organisation?" I asked.

"It's a network," said Anders. "There's no linear flowchart of organisational structure. There are cells that communicate with each other, and work in collaboration, but on a day-to-day basis everyone is independent."

"But all answering to the Blood Angel, Angelica, wherever she is?"

"In a manner of speaking."

"Presumably you've met her?"

"Nobody knows who she is or even if she's still alive. She might have passed control and the name on to somebody else. As far as you're concerned, and as far as anybody is concerned, it might be me. It might be the barman of a hotel in Bavaria. There are sophisticated structures of communication and ultimately there's somebody at the heart of it. But we don't have official staff meetings and Christmas lunches and corporate away days playing golf. It all comes down to pixels on a screen and knowing who you can trust."

I stubbed out the cigarette and immediately fancied another. Alcohol has that effect. I reached for my wineglass instead and took a big sip. My head was starting to spin. I hoped the alcohol might steady it. Which was a symptom of already having had too much.

"Is there a monthly salary?" I asked.

"You said you already had enough money," said Matt.

"That's hardly the point."

"No, there's not a salary," he said. "You'll have the opportunity to become very wealthy, but there's a strong element of altruism underpinning everything. You earn on a case-by-case basis."

"I don't suppose I'd get a trial period to see if I'd like it?"

"As I said, you're free to leave any time."

"Okay."

I took a deep breath. Both of them were looking at me expectantly. I decided to stop drinking the wine as it really wasn't helping.

"I have some conditions," I said at last.

Matt laughed.

"Do you?" said Anders.

"I think I'm entitled to that, at least."

"On what basis do you think you're entitled to make conditions?"

"On the basis that you approached me, and therefore it's clearly in your interests for me to say yes. And I get the sense that this is my best opportunity to negotiate."

A glance passed between them.

"Go on."

"Number one, I want to know your real names, because you already know mine."

"And what makes you think that we haven't already given you our real names?" said Anders.

"The fact that there's absolutely no reason why you should have done, and I'd be disappointed if you had. And unless I'm wrong, or my hearing is off, you're calling yourself Anders, which is Swedish rather than German. The German version is Andreas."

I looked for any reaction from Matt, but his expression was inscrutable.

"Okay," continued Anders. "The second condition?"

"I want the right to say yes or no to any proposal. And I don't want to kill anybody. Despite what I might or might not have done in the name of self-defence, I'm not some sort of assassin."

"Okay. But you have shown you can make tough decisions, and take whatever action is necessary."

"In extreme circumstances. But I don't want to do anything that's morally reprehensible. And I want the freedom to work and live where I choose."

"Okay."

I frowned at him.

"You keep saying okay. Do I take that to mean yes, okay, you agree, or that you're just acknowledging the request?"

He sighed.

"It's okay in as much as you can do anything you like. You're not reporting to anybody. As Matt said, you'll be asked to help with various projects, but whether you choose to get involved is completely up to you. But it's only fair to say that if you always say no, you'll stop being asked, and gradually you'll find that the network starts to fade away and concentrate on other assets. And as for my real name? I haven't used that for so long, I can hardly remember it myself."

I badly needed a moment to collect my thoughts.

"I'm just popping to the bathroom," I said. "I'll be back in a moment."

Once I'd left the room, it occurred to me that I had no idea where the bathroom was. I could have gone to my room, but I'd left the key in the clutch bag by the sofa. I could hear noises coming from the kitchen. Birgit was there, clearing things away, and I managed to ask her, via a combination of made-up words and sign language. I was tempted to take the opportunity to explore the house further, but several glasses of wine meant I had a rather more pressing concern.

Chapter 12

SO, this was madness. I leaned on the sink, looking at myself in the mirror, wondering if everything was a dream. Or a nightmare.

Everything they'd said made perfect sense. They made me feel safe, even though I knew there could be danger. It was exciting, and I felt flattered to be given the opportunity. It solved the immediate problem of where to live and what to do with my life, and if they were speaking the truth, it gave me a chance at some form of redemption. So why wasn't I rushing back in to grab it with both hands?

I thought of my old life, and particularly Danny and Anna. What would they say if they could see me now? I loved Danny. I loved the way he came to me, so full of wide-eyed innocence and wonder, wanting to learn to be the best investigator on Fleet Street because he shared my innate sense of justice. And I loved his flatmate Anna because she was funny, and brave, and self-deprecating. Even if I got the very strong impression she couldn't stand the sight of me. I thought of how they'd put their own lives on the line to search for me when they thought I was in danger. And, once they found me, how awful I felt when I looked into their eyes and had to admit that I was a fraud. Because I didn't want to be a fraud. I only ever wanted to do good. But it was a moment of madness that spiralled out of all control, brought about by stress and exhaustion and ...

And who am I trying to kid? It was greed. Plain and simple. That wasn't me. And yet it was me. I'd done it. I couldn't excuse it. I couldn't justify it. But I certainly couldn't wind the clock back and repair everything, and undo the hurt.

I'd killed people. Me! The girl from Sunderland who only ever wanted to make her father proud because he'd worked so hard to give me the best start in life before being taken by cancer. It made me aware of my own mortality. Turning thirty made that worse. Every tick of the clock is a step closer to the end. And what do we become when everything is over? What legacy do we leave? All I really wanted was to do good and make a difference, and try to enjoy myself while helping others. And somewhere along the line, I'd fucked up about as dramatically as anyone ever could.

So that left one question. Did I believe them?

It sounded plausible. I couldn't see an obvious trap. If they'd wanted to kill me, they could have done it already.

And above all else, when they'd described the Blood Angel, I wanted to put up my hand and say it was me! Someone who'd done bad things, but was genuinely concerned about the darkness they see in the world, however hypocritical that might sound. Someone who wants to repent. Wants to put things right. Can't do it by traditional means, and therefore is willing to take risks to make a difference.

Curiously, for someone becoming increasingly obsessed by the fragility of my own existence, the thought of danger didn't scare me. Suppose I said yes and got killed in the process? At least my life would have regained some meaning. At least there would have been some justice. I was aware of the irony that all of these thoughts were going through my head as nicotine was coursing through my veins, but that was just one more symptom of my inner turmoil. Every time I drew on a cigarette, it was a reminder that I was punishing myself, because I could never now achieve what I always felt it was my destiny to strive for.

Why would they lie to me? Why would they make all of that up? I couldn't see any possible benefit, and that made me nervous. Because either they were telling the truth, or they were so far ahead of me, I really wasn't the person I thought.

And that meant it was true. Or at least that I should believe it was. And if that was the case, what were they offering me? It sounded like everything I could have ever wished for, and an opportunity I knew I didn't deserve. The chance to put things right. The chance to use my instincts again. A chance at redemption. Not taking it would be a mixture of greed and cowardice. Well, I'd had enough of greed. And I'd never been a coward.

I washed my hands, and looked deeply into my own hazel eyes one last time. There was only one possible outcome. I headed back to the drawing room to start my new life as a spy.

Chapter 13

The next day. Wednesday, February 24th, 1993

NICOLAS Thiel woke late after a long night, having taken out his frustrations at the club. Yes, he'd caused misery for the staff, but what could they expect? The place was looking shabby. The cleaning wasn't up to standard. And the private rooms would have never passed a hygiene inspection, not that they were ever likely to get one. Normally it wouldn't have bothered him, but he'd been in a filthy mood and didn't care who knew it.

And yet taking it out on work-shy employees hadn't really made him feel any better. So when his driver finally took him home, he'd hit the brandy until the early hours. It was only Saskia's incessant bloody phone calls that had broken his sleep. And he'd be sure to let her know his opinion on that.

The shower helped clear his head, but he couldn't face breakfast. Instead, he went to his office on the ground floor of the chateau, unlocked the desk drawer and tapped out a line of fine white powder. Just to take the edge off. When it was done, he returned the rest to the drawer and made sure it was locked. The sound of his phone made him wince.

"Nicolas Thiel," he snarled. Only his closest confidants had his private number, but even so, it was a stretch to be civil.

"Nicolas, it's Matt Sommer," said the voice, in a natural, refined English accent. "How did you get on yesterday?"

"Don't ask."

"I heard it hadn't gone well."

He let out a deep breath.

"Thorsten gave it to some *espèce de con* who lost her."

"I heard that too," said Matt. "But I've got some news that might cheer you up."

"Really? Amaze me."

"She's here."

He hadn't been expecting that. He sat up straighter, and started to give Matt his full attention.

"Right. Just like that?" he said.

"Just like that."

"And?"

"And let's have a discussion."

"You're claiming the reward?"

"No."

"So what then?" He wasn't in the mood for any more games.

"It's still the same. I want to prove we can work together," said Matt. "When you've seen that, I'll hand her over to sweeten the deal."

"You're expecting me to wait?"

"It's the best way. If we give her to you now, you'd have no incentive. The longer the wait, the bigger the prize. She'll come gift-wrapped eventually. I promise you."

"And Anders agrees with this?"

"You don't need to worry about Anders. Nothing changes. This is strictly between you and me, and I trust we'll keep it that way. Did you speak to your cousin?"

"Florian Straub? He's my wife's cousin, not mine. I've never been able to trust the bastard."

"So I gather. But you should. He'll be working for me. I'll be there to watch over him and make sure he does what he says. And in the meantime Clare's safely where I can keep an eye on her."

Nicolas paused for a moment. His brain was hazy, but he could see the potential. Was it worth waiting for? A bit of time would give him longer to think of more ways to make her suffer.

"I'll need proof," he said at last, taking a deep sniff.

"I'll send you a picture."

"Anyone could take a picture, for God's sake."

"She'll be holding today's newspaper. Is that good enough for you?"

"I'll let you know when I've seen it."

He ended the call. Sommer could be useful. Very useful indeed. But it was never safe to take things at face value. He stood up from the desk and went to find Saskia.

She was still in her dressing-gown, sitting on the bed, laughing away on the bloody phone again. He'd soon put a stop to that.

He pressed the hook switch to end the call and grabbed her by the arm, pulling her up.

"What the hell did you do that for?" she shouted, trying to shake free. But Nicolas wasn't in the mood to explain his actions.

"Who are you bloody talking to all the time?" he spat.

"Friends. That was Claudette. We're organising our weekend away. I thought you'd be pleased."

What was the point? He let go, then pushed her back on the bed.

"What are you in such a mood for?" asked Saskia, in a more conciliatory voice.

"You know bloody well," he said, lowering himself onto the

foot of the bed. Saskia lifted up her legs and propped herself up on the pillows, facing him. He could never maintain his anger long when she looked at him with those eyes. At thirty, she was fifteen years his junior, and in spectacular shape, with long wavy brunette hair.

"But there might be progress," he continued, also in a calmer tone.

"That's good news."

"Possibly. It may involve dealing with Florian."

Saskia pursed her lips and let out a deep breath, then rearranged the neckline of her dressing-gown.

"Don't blame me if that all goes wrong."

"I'll lose him as soon as I can."

"You'd do that? You'd betray your own family?" Her smile was mischievous, and infectious. "You're ruthless."

"It's why we get on."

"It's kind of sexy."

She reached out her hand to him, but he brushed it away.

"So, what's the news on Clare Woodbrook?" she said, with a pout, looking disappointed.

"She's with a group in Germany. Not Florian, but someone else who has dealings with him," said Nicolas.

"Can you go and get her?"

"Not yet. But they're willing to deal."

"Do you trust them?"

"As an organisation? No. But I have a man on the inside."

"Do you trust *him*?"

"For the moment. We'll see."

"And if they realise he's working for us?"

"It gets messy. But they won't."

"You're sure?"

"Positive."

"I like your confidence. That's also kind of sexy."

She sank back deeper into the pillows, loosened the dressing-gown, and slightly parted her legs.

Nicolas was glad of the cocaine. He had a busy morning ahead, but there was nothing that couldn't wait half an hour.

Chapter 14

I DIDN'T set an alarm, and it was nearly 10am before I finally came to, in the unfamiliar surroundings. It took a moment to adjust, and remember everything that had happened. Anders had said he would be gone, but Matt had agreed to stay for a few days, to help me settle in.

The wine had left me with a headache, but I eased myself out of bed, opened the curtains, and took my first proper look at the view. It was spectacular. Sunlight glinted off the surface of the Rhine; a large riverboat was cruising past a much smaller vessel, causing great ripples in the otherwise calm water. In the distance I could see a real castle. Maybe that was why they called our house *the Schloss,* in the hope that if anyone came to attack us, they would go there instead. Who knew? I had so much to learn.

I quickly dressed in casual clothes and set off in pursuit of pre-shower coffee, passing Walter at the bottom of the stairs, and exchanging a nod of recognition. The kitchen was huge but empty, so I started to look through cupboards. The first held a ridiculous number of wineglasses, but before I got to the second, Birgit appeared, as if from nowhere.

She smiled at me, and I wondered what she made of her strange new house guest. How much they'd told her about me.

"*Hätten Sie gern ein Frühstück?*" she said, I think. I have no idea really. I didn't know what it meant either, but my blank expression didn't seem to discourage her. "Breakfast?" she added, with a heavy German accent, as though it was the only English word she knew. I felt embarrassed by my typical British ignorance of other languages.

"*Oui, merci,*" I said, and then immediately felt worse, because that was French. Christ. "*Danke?*"

She nodded and laughed, then pointed in the direction of a table at the far end of the room.

"*Kaffee?*"

Even I could work that one out.

I watched in silence as she bustled around the room, preparing something for me, making me feel immediately both grateful and unworthy. It felt rude not to ask how she was feeling, or attempt to make polite conversation, but I hoped she understood why.

Before long, there was a pot of coffee, but I then had to do an elaborate hand gesture that involved miming the action of teasing a cow's udders.

"*Milch,*" she said with a chuckle, leaving me feeling even more stupid for at least not giving it a go. Croissants followed, then she offered me a selection of various meats and cheeses, but I made another gesture that said the pastries would be fine on their own. I didn't want to put her to any extra trouble, but in truth she had such a cheerful demeanour, I don't think she would have minded.

Birgit left me alone after that, which then gave me the conundrum of what to do with my plate and cup. I didn't like the thought of leaving them on the table, but equally had no idea where to put them once I'd finished. I was saved, not for the first time, by Matt.

"Good morning," he said, as he entered the room. "Did you sleep okay?"

"Beautifully, actually," I said. "Once the adrenaline wore off, I was out immediately."

"That's great news. Leave those there," he added, sensing my discomfort with the crockery.

"Are you sure?"

"Yes, of course. Have you been in the shower yet?"

I think he was being polite, and giving me the benefit of the doubt. Given the way I looked, he was probably having second thoughts on the whole arrangement, if this was the best I could do.

"Not yet. I just came down for coffee."

He nodded.

"Okay. Should we say to meet in the drawing room in an hour? I'll give you the tour and we can discuss the plan."

"Perfect."

His face broke into a rather enchanting smile. Not for the first time, I wished I'd met him in other circumstances. He had a bewitching effect on my insides, but I had to put any thoughts of unprofessional behaviour aside.

"It's good to see you," he said. "Thank you for staying. I don't think you'll regret it."

An hour later I was back downstairs, dressed in the same casual clothes as breakfast, but with slightly better hair and a basic amount of make-up.

"Tour?" asked Matt, then led the way, starting with the ground floor, and a whole other wing of the building with even bigger and better appointed rooms than the drawing room and dining room I'd already seen.

"What happens here?" I asked. "And how many people live here?"

"It's used for entertaining occasionally. Feel free to use any of them, watch TV, relax, or have meetings if you need to. And only you at the moment, aside from Walter and Birgit."

I didn't know whether to be excited or nervous. The rooms were stunning, but I didn't see evidence of the promised security.

"Not you then?"

"I travel around a lot. I stay here occasionally. There will be others from time to time."

At the end of the hallway, there was a stone staircase, leading to a floor below. It was lit by gentle tungsten wall lamps, and had a dark red carpet runner.

"The dungeon?" I asked.

"Kind of," said Matt, with a grin. "You could think of it as a torture chamber."

With a leap of faith, I followed him down. I was glad I did. It led to a fabulously-appointed gym, with a treadmill, upright and recumbent exercise bikes, a rowing machine, free weights and lots of resistance machines - all pointing in the direction of a bank of TV screens. Four of them showed CCTV images of the grounds and main entrance, while the other four were blank.

"You've got a choice of satellite channels, or there's a VHS machine," said Matt. "There's a CD player too. It can get quite loud down here, if that's what you want, but the walls are thick enough to keep the sound in. Impressed?"

"It looks fantastic."

He pointed at a door on the far side.

"That's a training room with floor mats and all of that kind of thing, if you ever feel the need to do yoga. But you haven't seen the best bit yet."

We walked past a couple of changing rooms, and then came out to a deliciously-inviting swimming pool. It wasn't huge, but the crystal clear blue water, lit from below, looked breathtaking.

"Wow," I said, and meant it.

"I told you you wouldn't regret it."

Against one wall were a row of sun loungers, and next to those a jacuzzi that looked big enough for at least ten people.

"There's a sauna and steam room on the far side," Matt continued. "And there are always fresh towels in the changing rooms. Essentially, treat it all as your very own upmarket private health club, although obviously other people might use it when they're staying here."

Back upstairs, we walked past the main staircase that led to my bedroom.

"You've seen upstairs, obviously," said Matt. "There are fourteen en-suite bedrooms in total, across two floors, and most of them are empty at the moment, so if you'd like to swap, feel free. Birgit or Walter can show you round them. Take your pick."

"I can't help thinking you're going to hit me with a huge bill when I come to check out," I said.

He grinned.

"You're our guest. Make use of it all. Treat it like home. You can be here as long as you like, and I'd definitely recommend staying at least till the end of the basic training. But I'll tell you about that when we've walked round the outside."

It took nearly fifteen minutes to complete a full circuit. Aside from the house itself there were several outbuildings, including a workshop and garages for around a dozen cars. Since the Schloss was perched on a hill, the views were spectacular too. Were it not for the nagging doubts about what they expected of me, I thought I could be very happy here.

Eventually the tour was over and we made our way back to the drawing room.

"First thing first: I need to take a picture of you," said Matt.

"Really? Why?"

He handed me a copy of that morning's *Süddeutsche Zeitung*

newspaper, told me to hold it up next to my face, and then picked up a Nikon camera from the coffee table.

"It's just a record for you, really. And for us. So we can look back and see if your appearance changes. Plus a note of today's date, in case we forget."

"I'm not going to forget."

"You never know what might happen."

"Is my appearance likely to change?"

"It's up to you. You might want to change your hair, if you go undercover. I'm not recommending plastic surgery." He laughed and fired off a couple of shots before I could protest any more. And then, before I had a chance to press him further, Birgit arrived with a tray of tea things, followed by another woman, who I guessed was in her mid-fifties. She was stylishly dressed, with short grey hair and an engaging smile. Matt made the introductions.

"This is Sabine Cosker," he said. We shook hands. "Sabine is from Vienna, and she's the very best German-language tutor in the business."

The plan was for two hours of lessons every weekday morning, with daily homework that would double up at weekends. I didn't envy Sabine's task, but I was determined to master the language, even though everyone I'd met in Germany, with the exception of Birgit and Walter, spoke perfect English. It was primarily a question of respect, and, of course, wanting to know what was being said about me if I caught anyone talking behind my back.

Sabine left, and we spent the rest of the morning discussing my agenda for the next few weeks, all of which was to be spent at the Schloss. After a break for lunch, Matt offered to take me into Koblenz in case I needed to do any shopping, and to show me my new home town. In normal circumstances, Walter was supposedly always available if I needed transport, but Matt suggested I should think about buying a car for added freedom of movement.

I saw enough of the town to know that I'd thoroughly enjoy exploring it more, but this was just a flying visit. When we arrived back, Matt went on to explain the catering arrangements: Birgit would cook for me, and would be happy to accommodate any requests, but I also had free use of the kitchen if I wanted to do anything on my own. And after that, and an hour or so showing me how the televisions worked, where the various phones were, and how to log on to the computers and connect to the internet, he left me for my first evening alone.

Everything I'd seen looked spectacular. I found it hard to believe how much my life had changed in less than thirty-six hours. But as I went to bed, I couldn't shake the feeling that one day there would be an almighty price to pay.

———————

Florian Straub kicked his office door closed and picked up the phone.

"Matthew," he said, recognising the caller's voice. "And how is Clare?"

"She's settling in. I think she'll have fun there, while it lasts."

Florian laughed to himself, while removing his tweed jacket.

"I'm impressed by your technique. She believed everything you said?"

"She had her doubts at first. But I can be very persuasive," said Matt.

"I'll bear that in mind. And our French friend?"

"Still very French."

"He's prepared to wait?"

"If the prize is big enough, he'll do anything. I've made him see Clare as part of a package. He gets her when we say, not before, and it opens up a world of new opportunities in the process."

There was knock at the office door. Florian told Matt to hold for a moment. He opened the door and found his driver, looking stressed.

"A word, boss?" Michael said.

Florian sighed. One thing at a time.

"Give me ten minutes," he said. The hired muscle nodded, then Florian closed the door and returned to the call.

"Sorry about that."

"Everything okay?" asked Matt.

"We've had a few problems with a bit of unauthorised dealing, but nothing we can't handle."

"I'm glad to hear it."

"It happens. Anyway, what does Anders make of all this?"

"Who?"

Florian laughed again.

"I assume you're keeping him fully on board with it all?"

"No, let's just say, Anders has different priorities right now," said Matt. "I don't need to bother him with things I'm not sure he'd understand."

"You're a bad person."

"I resent the implication. I'm the good guy." Florian could hear the chuckle. "At least in comparison to some people."

"You know, I look forward to things getting back to normal. I much prefer loathing everything about you," he said.

"And Graham March?" asked Matt.

"There are problems with Graham. But we'll fix those."

"In relation to the Polish girls?"

"In relation to nothing you need to worry about at the moment."

Florian ended the call, and then opened the office door and called for Michael. It was time to show the local lowlife who was in charge.

Chapter 15

ON day two I met my personal fitness trainer, Rüdiger Heutmann. He was huge but athletic, and I had my suspicions that he'd been enrolled on an experimental performance-enhancing drug programme, back in his youth, in his native East German city of Rostock. He was bald and intimidating, with a goatee beard that only added to his aura of menace.

Rüdiger clearly disapproved of my smoking, but to his credit, he didn't try to make me stop. He made me pay for it over the ensuing weeks, though, with a relentless programme of running and gym work, and occasionally he'd watch from the side while I pounded lengths of the pool. It was agonising at first, both in terms of the pain during the actual sessions and the lactic acid burn that followed. But once I realised he was there to help me, rather than kill me, I grew to enjoy our time together, and I felt fitter than I ever had before.

He didn't like to talk about himself, and brushed off all questions about his background, family, and outside interests. In return he didn't ask about me either, and I was happy to leave it that way.

"How many people are you doing this for?" I asked at one point.

"Just you," he said.

"So what do you do for the rest of the time?"

"Think of ways to get you fitter."

Sabine turned out to be every bit as good a German teacher as promised, and she showed endless patience with me. I found the basics of the language quite straightforward, but once we got into genders, cases, and irregular verbs, my head began to spin. Matt offered me a French tutor too. I knew a little bit of French, from my time at school, but wanted to master German first. There was no rush, or so I thought at the time.

Matt, however, was an enigma. I decided he was definitely ex-services, even if he wasn't actually Special Forces. I pictured his parents as minor aristocrats, sending him to a prestigious boarding school. Once he'd finished there, he'd perhaps attended a lesser Cambridge college before army officer training at Sandhurst, or more likely joining the Royal Marines at the Britannia Royal Naval College in Dartmouth.

But then how did he end up in Koblenz? That was when my mind went off at real tangents. He didn't look old enough for retirement, so that left the option of release on medical grounds, or perhaps a dishonourable discharge, which was much more exciting.

I didn't have any evidence, of course, but that didn't stop me wondering. Maybe he hadn't done any of that. What if he'd had the tap on the shoulder walking across Parker's Piece in Cambridge, and gone straight into MI5, or better still MI6? That was proper James Bond territory. Perhaps he'd been a double agent, and that's how he'd met Anders, and Angelica, the former Stasi femme fatale. The possibilities were endless.

"Did you see much action, back in the day?" I asked him, one evening, when he'd popped into the Schloss to pick up some paperwork.

"With women?" he replied, either missing the point entirely, or deliberately trying to derail me. He changed the subject before I had the chance for a follow-up.

After the first four weeks, Rüdiger started my unarmed combat training, which largely involved throwing me around on a padded mat in the yoga room until it hurt too much to continue. Eventually I learned how to defend myself, how to punch for maximum impact, and how to destabilise an assailant long enough to run away.

Next, he started showing me how to attack. How to take out an opponent twice my size, through a combination of surprise and technique. That was harder to practise, but I worked hard on the theory and we simulated the practical side on blow-up sex dolls. It looked ridiculous, but the laughter kept us entertained.

Throughout all of this, experts would occasionally turn up at the Schloss to give me lessons in the dark arts: how to pick locks, bypass security systems, defeat computer passwords, and basic hacking techniques. I was shown advanced surveillance methods, including how to follow someone and avoid being followed myself, and then how to detect intruders and sweep for listening devices. At the same time, I was shown an array of bugs that were at my disposal, with cameras and microphones that could be hidden in items as mundane as an electrical mains socket, a plug-in air freshener, or a smoke alarm. I was shown a system of passing messages and information that involved hammering a hollow spike into the ground in a pre-determined location.

Other people turned up at the Schloss too, occasionally staying for a couple of days, hosting meetings, sending faxes, or to use the gym and computer facilities. I tried to keep out of their way, always aware that they knew what they were doing, and I was still a guest. They were friendly enough when I bumped into them in the kitchen, though, and occasionally they'd invite me to join them for dinner as a colleague, even though work itself was never discussed.

Eventually Rüdiger moved on to teaching me about weapons.

"We have no shooting range," he said. "We shall go into the woods."

Far away from civilisation, he introduced me to all sorts of handguns. He was patient with me as I learned about the different levels of recoil, even more patient as my first attempts to hit the targets were laughably inept, but then encouraging and reassuring as his words sank in and I started to make progress.

By week fourteen, I was almost able to keep up with him on endurance walks, as he went marching off into the distance, my smaller size and agility nearly making up for what I lacked in muscle and bulk. I felt like a different person. Sharper, more resilient. But then he started my survival training and it was another whole world of pain. Hiking for miles, sleeping outdoors, my body pushed to its absolute limits, followed by the realisation that this was just for starters.

Four gruelling months after first meeting Matt, in the car park in Cologne, I felt I was ready to take on anything. My German was still rudimentary but in every other respect I was transformed. That was when my training intensified, moving up several notches again.

"Rüdiger tells me you're doing very well," said Matt one night.

"He's very kind," I said, sensing an opening. "Obviously it's probably nothing compared to what you're used to."

"I've never had the pleasure of training with him," he said, before changing the subject again.

Matt would disappear for weeks at a time, but on the days he was at the Schloss, aside from avoiding my questions, he would coach me on the practical aspects of my role. Teaching me about people I might get to meet, showing me how he undertook negotiations, and, of course, further in-depth tuition on the technology at my disposal and the communication networks I was expected to master. He asked me about my newspaper investigations, and then showed me techniques that were legally questionable, but which undoubtedly had potential to yield results.

Parts of the training were brutal. To prepare me for potential interrogation, they tried to catch me unawares and disorientate me, deprive me of sleep, cover my head with a hood, and subject me to incessant white noise interspersed with the sounds of someone screaming. There was physical torture, too: being forced to run through the night with someone chasing me, through woods, water, and even at one point having to choose between capture and jumping off a bridge. I chose the bridge, winded myself as I crashed into a river far below, and was then immediately picked up, restrained, and thrown into the back of a van before another mock but brutally intensive interrogation, this time at gunpoint. I was shouted at, manhandled, and occasionally genuinely feared for my life. The bruises and cuts disappeared over time, but the emotional scars took much longer to heal.

There were physical and mental tests throughout. Nobody ever mentioned a pass mark, but I threw myself into everything to ensure that I always emerged with impeccable scores.

It wasn't all work, though. For the first few weeks, Walter regularly drove me into Koblenz to go shopping, or I'd head out to explore my new surroundings. Nearby towns, like Boppard, were quite beautiful, and I felt safe and anonymous, even though I could never take my security for granted.

We always travelled in silence as a result of his deafness, and I often wondered what he made of me. Eventually, though, I started to crave my independence, so I bought a car. Actually, not just any car, but a ridiculously indulgent red Mercedes 500 SL. It was extravagant, but in my defence, I never knew when I might need to make a quick getaway, and my living expenses were minimal. It was the first car I'd owned since abandoning my Lotus Esprit on the hard shoulder of the M25 round London, as part of my escape from my former life, and I immediately fell in love.

A couple of times I drove to Frankfurt, about ninety minutes away (or significantly less when the roads were clear and I could let the full five litres rip on the unrestricted autobahns) and then explored the boutiques and department stores on the Zeil and Goethestraße. I had a lot of shopping to do. Before going on the run, I'd left all of my most emotionally-important possessions in storage. Everything else fitted into a couple of suitcases. I'd planned on travelling light until I decided where I wanted to set up home. Now that the decision had been taken for me, I had an entire new wardrobe to acquire.

Heading out on my own wasn't without risk, so I was always cautious to obscure my identity. I dyed my hair again, going for brunette this time, and adding a slight curl, which gave me something else to maintain and an excuse to buy gadgets. Several times, though, I thought I was being followed. But whenever I turned, there was nobody there. Occasionally I'd see a car that looked familiar, perhaps overtaking me on the autobahn or parked up close to mine when I returned with bags of shopping. Of course it could have been a coincidence. Nobody ever approached me.

Even when Matt was absent, I was able to call him, should the need arise.

"Do you think I'm being watched?" I asked him on the phone one night.

"What makes you think that?"

"I don't know. Maybe I'm just being paranoid, but I keep seeing a black Porsche."

"You're in Germany. It's where they're made."

"I know but they're not very common."

"More so in Germany than England. But I don't think there's anything to worry about. We've got a very good grapevine and I've not heard any new whispers."

Occasionally, we'd have a night off together, and head into town and watch a film (which only clarified how much of the language I still had to learn) or visit a restaurant, to give Birgit a break. Again I tried to find out more about him, always aware that everything he told me could be a complete fabrication.

"Look!" I said, one night, as we came out of the cinema. There was a black Porsche parked on the opposite side of the road, but no sign of the driver.

Matt inspected it, looking through the windows, before returning to me, shaking his head.

"It's got Koblenz plates," he said, "and a parking permit for the hospital on the windscreen. My guess is it belongs to a surgeon, but I'll make a note of the registration if it'll make you happy."

"No, ignore me. I think I'm just naturally jumpy." That said, I quite liked the thought of having my own former commando/former Royal Marine/former MI6 bodyguard. Delete as appropriate, if indeed any of them were.

Throughout all our time together, Matt was never less than the perfect gentleman. Much to my dismay, because with his impressive physique, polite manner, and general air of reassurance, I was beginning to look forward to our time together in ways that weren't always purely professional.

But then there were the monthly parties. My God, the parties.

They took place at the Schloss, on the penultimate Saturday of every month, with anything from twenty to forty people in attendance, many of whom stayed over. There were some regulars, but each time there were plenty of new faces from elsewhere in the Blood Angel network - along with others that I suspected were hired in for the occasion. Activity at the house intensified before each event, as people began to arrive to use the gym or communication facilities a day or two in advance.

Nominally, the parties gave me the chance to meet and mingle with some of my potential colleagues, but before the first, Matt phoned and warned me to approach the event with an open mind.

"Try not to be shocked," he said.

"Am I likely to be?"

"Quite possibly. But have fun. That's what they're there for."

It was hedonism in the grand tradition of the last days of the Weimar Republic with lashings of debauchery as recompense for the absence of a normal, secure life and the ability to form conventional relationships. If we were going to go down, we'd go down in style. In the main, I tended to avoid the narcotics. They weren't really my thing. But once I was able to shed my British inhibitions, I embraced the more physical aspects of team bonding, and discovered a side of myself that I never knew existed. It was not for the faint of heart, but deeply pleasurable in utterly degenerate ways.

After five months of intense training, I needed a break, so took myself to the Lake District in north-west England. I was Kaarina Mäkinen from Finland, at least according to the details on my newly-acquired passport. But rather than spending a week relaxing, I found an urge to run up hills, breathing in the beautiful clear air, admiring the scenery, and coming to terms with an enormous sense of achievement and liberation. It was a glorious, life-affirming time, but by the end of the week, I couldn't wait to get back. I missed my new German home and the security of routine.

I had a desperate urge to speak to Danny and Anna. To tell them I was okay. To apologise to them for all the trouble I'd caused. I asked for regular copies of my old newspaper, the *Daily Echo*, to be delivered to the Schloss, so I could keep an eye on

Danny's career. He seemed to be doing well, writing the kind of articles that we'd previously worked on together. He was still young. Still had a lot to learn. But I was immensely - even if silently - proud of him.

Work on my fitness and language skills continued through the summer. Early one evening, at the start of September, I saw Matt standing at the edge of the pool, watching me. I finished the length and then swam across to him.

"Dry yourself off," he said. "Anders has come to see you."

Chapter 16

Tuesday, September 7th, 1993

I HADN'T seen Anders since my first evening at the Schloss, so I had that weird sensation of recognition tinged with surprise at the way he wasn't quite as I remembered. I'm not sure if he'd put on weight over the summer, but I was struck by his portly build, far more than I had been in February. Back then, I suppose, I had far more important things on my mind. At least the grey hair, neat beard and horn-rimmed spectacles were the same.

Birgit was arranging tea and coffee on the table as I entered the drawing room. I was freshly showered, and wearing a mid-grey Balmain knee-length dress, sheer black tights and a pair of beige suede Casadei ankle boots. I wanted to look businesslike, but more than that, it was a chance to try on some of my new clothes. It felt strange but refreshing to be dressed formally after seven months spent mainly either in gym kit, or jeans, sweatshirts and a baseball cap. I've never really felt at home with the casual look.

Birgit and I exchanged smiles as she passed me on her way

out. Again, I wondered how much she and Walter knew. They saw everything, but said very little, and people like that fascinate me. I'd love to see inside their minds to really understand how they're wired. But there again, I also have an urge to look out of every window in the relentless quest for the perfect view.

"How is our star pupil?" asked Anders, warmly, indicating to a sofa by his armchair. I also wondered how much Anders knew about the parties, and some of the outrageous things I'd witnessed in this room. I hadn't seen him at any of them, but that was probably for the best.

"Doing well," I said. "Although I'm still glad you asked me that in English."

"I hear your German is excellent now."

"I'm not sure I'd say excellent, but it definitely helps to be living here. It's coming on. *Langsam*."

He smiled at my use of the German word for *slowly*.

A moment later, Matt arrived, and took the sofa opposite mine. We were exactly where we'd been on that first night, although a table had been placed on top of the dark red rug.

Anders, in turn, stood up and poured the drinks, then handed me a cup of tea. Just that small gesture made me think of Anna again. Danny often mentioned that Anna had particular standards when it came to tea, and she would not have approved of the weakness of the one Anders passed over.

After a few minutes catching up on pleasantries, it was down to business.

"We have a situation," said Anders.

"That I can help with?" I was determined to sound strong, rather than the junior, subservient partner. I'm not sure I succeeded. I'd always been so confident in my career, but as in February, I found myself thrown slightly off balance by his authoritative demeanour.

He nodded.

"It will involve going to your old – what's the phrase? Stalking ground?"

"Stomping ground," I said, although immediately wondered if that was indeed correct. In isolation it sounded wrong. But the biggest worry was what he meant. Back to Sunderland? To my old newspaper? As far as I knew, everyone thought I was dead. I couldn't exactly walk back in and say "surprise!" and pretend everything was normal. At least not without being arrested and quite possibly certified insane.

He pushed a manila envelope across the table towards me. I opened it and withdrew about a dozen ten-by-eight-inch monochrome photographs.

"But first, do you recognise anyone?" he asked.

I immediately recoiled.

"Yes."

They both waited for me to elaborate.

"I don't know the others, but that is Graham March," I said, pointing to one particular, hauntingly familiar figure. He was in his mid-fifties, but hadn't aged well, and was as overweight as ever. I remembered we'd discussed him on my first night. "Where are these from?"

Matt deferred to Anders, who took a sip of his drink before beginning.

"The ones with March were taken in Cologne on various days over the last few months," he said. "He's been having meetings with representatives of Florian Straub." He pointed to a large, strangely-dressed middle-aged man who appeared in several solo shots, wearing a tweed jacket and bow tie. He put those to one side and went back to the ones with Graham, pointing out the person he was standing next to. "This is Michael Eidinger, Straub's right hand man."

Eidinger looked a typical thug, with an immensely stocky build, a shaven head, and a tattoo on the back of his left hand. I couldn't make out what it was supposed to represent.

"Who is Florian Straub?" I asked, but Anders hadn't finished.

"Of more immediate concern to you is this one." He pushed a different picture back towards me. Graham was standing outside a hotel shaking hands with another man I didn't recognise.

"That's Thorsten Stötzner. He works for Nicolas Thiel."

Immediately, my blood ran cold.

"Right," I said, in lieu of anything more constructive. I picked up the picture and studied it. Stötzner was significantly shorter than March, and wiry, with a side parting and narrow-set eyes behind wire-rimmed glasses. He was dressed in dark trousers and a long black leather coat, as though he was going for the full SS commander look, albeit on a smaller scale. I kept that observation to myself. I'd have guessed at late thirties but he could have been older. Something about him was intrinsically creepy.

"I thought the pencil man, Henning or whatever he was called, was Thiel's man in Cologne," I said.

Matt shook his head.

"He was a local contractor, appointed by Stötzner, but he hasn't been seen since the day he failed to capture you."

"You don't think he was ..." My voice trailed off.

"Most likely," said Matt. "Stötzner is ruthless. Henning failed a simple mission, so I expect the punishment was swift and almost certainly lethal. Stötzner's own reputation was at stake."

"Jesus. And you think Graham March was meeting him because Thiel is after me?"

Matt nodded. "You know how to pick your enemies."

"Which means March is now well aware I'm still in existence." I sighed deeply and reached in my bag for my cigarettes. That was the very last thing I needed. If he knew I was alive, he'd make it his mission to bring me to justice, suspension or not. Although he was deviously, irretrievably corrupt, he knew people in authority who could make things extremely uncomfortable for me. And if he decided to take it out on Danny and Anna in the meantime? It didn't bear thinking about. "How do you know all of this?"

"It's our business to know things."

"But following Graham March?"

He didn't answer that, but shrugged and looked back to Anders.

"Okay, I'll try a different way," I continued when Anders didn't answer either. "Why is March meeting this other one? What's the deal with Straub?"

"It could be as simple as March leaning on him for information about you," said Anders, doing little for my racing heartbeat. "Or vice versa."

"What do you mean vice versa? What have I done to piss off Florian Straub, whoever he is? How does he even know me?" I hoped my voice sounded calmer than I felt, but I doubted it. I took a cigarette from the packet and offered one to Anders, before reaching deeper into my bag for my lighter. Which, annoyingly, didn't seem to be there.

"Straub is a gangster based in Frankfurt," said Anders, accepting one. Matt offered us both a light. It was odd that he had a lighter when I'd never seen him smoke. "He runs a chain of brothels, or *Laufhäuser*, in various cities from Frankfurt to Dortmund, plus Bielefeld and Stuttgart, and an increasing number of FKK clubs. Do you know what they are?"

"No idea."

"*Freikörperkultur*. Nudist clubs, which are also brothels. With a few other things on the side. We don't get on."

"I've never heard of him."

"Thiel and Straub have family connections," Matt elaborated. "But as far as we're aware, there's a lack of trust on both sides and they don't talk often."

I drew deeply on the cigarette before continuing. I was calculating the risk. March was an idiot. Despite his potential for causing problems, I wasn't scared he would physically hurt me.

Nicolas Thiel, on the other hand, sounded like a psychopath, and appeared to have me very much in his sights. Having an ally looking for me in Germany, with March at the centre of it all, made me extremely nervous.

"I understand why Thiel is after me, but just to reiterate, I've never met him," I said. "I didn't have any dealings with French buyers. That was all Dominique."

"Who you killed," said Anders, bluntly.

"Let's not go there," I said. "But I still don't understand Straub's interest. Is he violent?" I picked up one of the photographs. Despite the tweed jacket and bow tie, he looked a picture of uncontrolled aggression.

"He's generally our nemesis," began Matt. "As well as the brothels, he's heavily involved in organised crime. Behind the scenes he's a fixer, dealing in drugs, guns, whatever you fancy. Every so often he rears his head trying to get involved in something more respectable, but always with an agenda."

Anders nodded and took a sip of his tea, then returned his attention to me, which was curiously unsettling.

"We've come up against him regularly on competitive tenders," continued Matt. "And it's always been feasible that he'd go into partnership with Thiel at some point. They're in a similar line of business."

"Thiel runs strip clubs in Paris," added Anders. "Again, it's also primarily a front, but we think he's looking at Germany as a route through to Eastern Europe. France only has borders with us, Belgium, Switzerland, Italy, and Luxembourg. But if you can open up trade routes through Germany you get Austria, the Czech Republic and Poland, and from there, Slovenia, Hungary, Slovakia, Ukraine, Belarus, Lithuania, and all of the rest of them."

"And by trade routes, you mean?"

"It comes back to Schengen," said Matt. "Once all the borders are open, you'll be able to smuggle anything in both directions, whether it's drugs, guns, people or anything else you want."

I flicked ash, took one last drag, then stubbed out the cigarette, before turning to the tea but wishing it was something considerably stronger. As if reading my mind, Anders stood up and walked to the door, then called out for Birgit and asked her to bring a bottle of wine and three glasses.

"Okay, so that's the set-up," I said, when he returned to his chair. "It goes without saying that we need to do our best to disrupt it. And I need to be careful, obviously. But you said we had a *situation*. Was it just that? Or something more specific?"

"More specific, although the timing is coincidental," said Anders, then turned to Matt.

"Alongside all of that, we had a property deal in London," said Matt. "Or at least we thought we did. We were working with a contact called Colin Medland over there, and all was looking good, but at the last minute he's pulled out on us."

"Okay. Because?"

"That's what we don't know. But we need to go over to find out. Medland is no longer returning our calls, so we'll have to go and find him."

My mind was working overtime, making connections.

"You said Straub competed with you. Do you think Graham March is helping him? Has he put in a better offer?"

"It might be completely unconnected, but no, he wouldn't have put in a better offer," said Matt. "That's not how he works. But that doesn't mean he hasn't applied a bit of pressure to someone. And if Graham March is his new best friend, then there's definitely a link with London."

Birgit arrived. Anders took the bottle of wine, then uncorked it and poured us each a glass.

"March wouldn't be capable of that," I said, reaching out to take one. "He's a corrupt policeman. He runs scams, intimidates people, manages to turn a blind eye if you're up to no good and pay him for the privilege. But he's very far from a criminal mastermind."

"But historically Straub showed no interest in London until March came on the scene," said Anders.

"Okay." I let that sink in while my brain caught up. Eventually, I continued. "I could easily believe March promised Thiel he'd be able to help find me, although on what basis I have no idea. On top of that, I could imagine a scenario whereby he overstates his influence to Straub, although it would be a short term arrangement, because he'd be found out as soon as he was asked to deliver. But in any case, he's suspended at the moment, pending an investigation into all of his corruption."

"That makes him more dangerous in some ways," said Matt.

"How come?"

"Because he's off the leash. He's not bound by the conventions of the day job, and he'll be forging a new career for himself in case he gets thrown out of the Force."

I'd had a wonderful, carefree summer, having fun, getting fit, learning new things, and loving my new life in Koblenz. But I knew that one day it would come to an end. This was it.

I looked again at the pictures of Graham March. Thiel's henchman Thorsten Stötzner really was giving me the creeps. Perhaps it was small man syndrome, but he looked evil.

"So what now?" I asked, partly fearful for the answer, but also excited about finally heading into action.

"We fly to London tomorrow," said Matt. "You and me. I'd suggest an early night because we've got a busy couple of days ahead, and we're definitely going to need to keep our wits about us."

"You don't need me to tell you," added Anders, "but if there's a connection in all of this, we aren't sure what it is. But we're dealing with people who want to kill you. Do you feel up to it?"

I thought for a moment, then nodded. I couldn't imagine ever feeling better prepared.

Chapter 17

IT was over a decade since Suzanne Köppen had been for dinner in a Parisian restaurant, despite living in a large country house close to the French capital. The last time was shortly before her husband died, on the day of his diagnosis.

"I've got something to tell you," he'd said. She'd thought, perhaps, that he was finally going to announce his retirement, and had been physically and emotionally unprepared for such a heartbreaking revelation.

Despite growing up on the outskirts of Trier, nestled in the Moselle wine region of south-western Germany, close to the border with Luxembourg, she'd decided to remain in Paris in her twilight years. The loss of her husband had hit her hard, but she loved the home that they'd renovated together. The sale of the family engineering company, together with the substantial life assurance payout, meant she was able to give up her career as a counsellor, and live there in comfort, without any financial concerns. It also prompted an interest in speculative investment, not just on the Paris Bourse, but on other stock markets across the world. And her considerable success at spotting emerging trends before they became mainstream had subsequently funded a lifestyle in which she was now able to regularly indulge her passions of travel and collecting art.

In almost every respect, she moved in different circles to Nicolas Thiel. But they had one big thing in common. And that was why they'd spoken to each other by telephone over the last few months, and why she was now sitting opposite him, under the glittering golden cherubs, cornices, chandeliers and spectacular painted ceilings of Le Train Bleu - a favourite restaurant of Coco Chanel, Salvador Dalí and Brigitte Bardot in years gone by.

After their plates had been collected, and Nicolas had settled the bill, attention switched from their opulent surroundings to the real reason they had agreed to meet.

"I'm not at an age where I want to play games," said Suzanne.

"Your best years are ahead of you," said Nicolas, running a hand through his hair, then lighting a cigarette, and wafting the smoke away.

"I am also not at an age where I am likely to be seduced by your Gallic charm. Have you made any progress?"

"I have, but we're being forced to take our time."

"I want my money."

"As do I."

"She owes me for three paintings."

"Madame, she owes all of us."

Like Nicolas, she'd bought art from Clare Woodbrook's colleague Dominique, but it had been repossessed. Other equally fine works now hung in their place, but that was hardly the point. Clare was responsible, and she needed to pay for her deception.

"So what are you doing about it?" asked Suzanne.

"We'll get her when the time is right."

"Is the time not right now?"

"No."

"Because?"

"Because the handover is complicated. But once all of the

details are in place, she will be given to me, and I assure you, I will make it a personal priority to ensure that you are repaid in full."

"And if she doesn't have the money?"

"Then there'll be justice of a different kind."

Suzanne was aware of Thiel's reputation. Normally she wouldn't dream of trusting him. But there was little chance of recovering her losses through legal means, and that meant that on this occasion she was willing to give him the benefit of the doubt.

"And in the meantime, the man on the inside ..." Her voice drifted off.

"Exactly," said Nicolas. "Everything is under control. But it's all about timing."

Suzanne drained the coffee cup and checked her watch. Her driver had been waiting for nearly forty minutes longer than she'd told him to expect.

"I'm running out of patience," she said.

"We're all running out of patience," said Nicolas. "But I assure you, it won't be long now."

Chapter 18

Wednesday, September 8th, 1993

ATT was supposed to pick me up at 10am for the drive to the private airfield, just south of Bonn, but he was late, and when he finally arrived, about forty minutes later, he didn't offer an explanation. Despite my growing admiration, it irritated me that I never got a glimpse into his personal life. I had my theories, of course, but I'd known him for seven months and still had no idea where he lived, nor whether he had a wife or children. I like to be in control. I don't like secrets. At least not those belonging to others.

As directed, I'd packed a small overnight bag, with enough for three days away. I wasn't sure what to take in terms of equipment, but settled on a small camera and miniature voice recorder, plus a couple of other things that I thought might prove useful. I got the impression I was primarily eyes and ears on this one. Anders had explained it was purely reconnaissance: find Colin Medland, then find out why he wasn't returning our calls, and what had prompted him to back out of the deal. We weren't supposed to intimidate him, but instead try to discover the root of the issue, so that we could subsequently deal with whoever had caused it.

I wrapped my long, stone-coloured trench coat around me, and followed Matt to his Mercedes E Class.

"Everything okay?" I asked, as he navigated back down the winding single lane track to the main road.

"Yes. Why do you ask?" he said.

"Because you were late and you seem quiet."

"I had a very early start, and don't really do mornings."

I didn't believe that for a moment, but it clearly wasn't the time to press him further. If, as I suspected, he had a military background, an early start would mean nothing. Instead I attempted to find out more about the other main man of mystery.

"It was good to see Anders again," I said.

"Yes, he thinks highly of you."

"That's good. I hope I live up to expectations. What's his background?"

That killed the conversation. Matt made a show of looking in his rear-view mirror, even though the private track behind us was obviously empty.

"I know so little about him," I persisted. "He exudes an aura, though. I get the impression that people know better than to get on his wrong side. Have you known him long?"

Matt sighed, and I left him in peace while he navigated to the autobahn, heading north. But as we reached cruising speed, I made a further attempt.

"How did you meet?"

"You're full of questions this morning," said Matt.

"I like to know what I'm dealing with. Who I'm working for."

"We told you at the beginning. You're working for yourself."

"Kind of. But under his guidance. And yours. For the moment, anyway."

Matt floored the accelerator, as though trying to hasten the journey and avoid any further probing. But I wasn't going to be discouraged.

"Does he live locally? How old is he?"

I could sense the exasperation from the driver's seat, but I felt I had a point to prove, if we were supposed to be equals.

"He grew up in Dresden," said Matt at last.

"Which was East Germany?" I turned towards him, and saw him nod.

"Okay," I continued. "Although, to be fair, he told me that himself back in February. I was kind of hoping for information a bit more recent than that."

Maybe Anders was ex-Stasi too. That would possibly explain the link to Angelica.

To my surprise, Matt finally opened up.

"He was three when the war broke out. Eight when the British dropped nearly three thousand tons of bombs on the city in a single night. He was the only one of his family who survived."

"Wow." I hadn't expected that. I couldn't even begin to imagine how terrifying that must have been.

Who knew the horrors that other people had witnessed? No wonder Anders didn't like to talk about it. That trauma would have shaped everything, forever more.

"What did he do then?" I asked.

"He grew up in foster care. Eventually got married, had two children, and started working in the semiconductor industry."

"So he wasn't a spy then?"

Matt gave a short, derisive laugh.

"No. Although he got to a management position, which opened up all sorts of opportunities on the black market. And there would have been pressure to be an informer."

"I can imagine. And his family?"

A police car powered past us in the outside lane, lights flashing and sirens blazing. I was immediately jumpy.

"They're not coming for you," said Matt, as though sensing my discomfort.

"That's good."

We lapsed into a momentary silence while we navigated past a coned-off section of roadworks.

"His wife and family were shot trying to escape to the West in 1976," Matt said at last.

"Jesus." I hadn't expected that either.

"It should have been flawless. He planned it, but it went wrong and he blames himself. He turned to drink for a while, lost his job, fell in with a bad crowd, but then eventually realised his life was going nowhere."

"Bloody hell." I genuinely didn't know what to say, but felt immediately guilty for asking. "Poor man. As if he hadn't already dealt with enough."

"Quite. So as you can imagine, he was very anti-government. The rest is a bit vague. As far as I know, he met someone in the mid-1980s who put him in touch with Angelica, or at least her associates, and he became a kind of enforcer. But I think now, like her, he's decided he's seen enough tragedy and brutality, and turned his back on it. And he's not been in the best of health for a few years, so that's slowed him down too."

It put my own problems into a humbling kind of perspective. I couldn't imagine how anyone could deal with all of that, and not be prone to irrational bursts of rage. Maybe he was, and I just hadn't seen it yet.

"He might seem distant at times," Matt continued, "but trust me, he has a good heart. He's seen more than you or I ever will, hopefully, so if he speaks, it's always wise to listen."

Thankfully, I was saved from making any further comment by our arrival at the airfield. On the way to the aeroplane, Matt gave me a mobile phone that would work in England.

It had been an enlightening conversation. But of course, I only had Matt's word for any of it.

Chapter 19

T HE tiny, seven-seat Cessna Citation II/SP was slower and noisier than a commercial airliner, but the absence of the traditional airport experience made up for it. We flew to a private aerodrome in Essex, north of London, in less than an hour and a half, and once we'd safely landed, the pilot handed me the key to a Honda Accord that was waiting for us in the car park. I was impressed by the smooth-running logistics. I was not so impressed by the British weather, although the strong winds and lashing rain reminded me of happier times.

Matt navigated while I drove to a small hotel on the outskirts of London, just inside the M25, not too far from where I'd abandoned the Lotus. Having gained an hour due to the time difference with Germany, it was still only mid-afternoon. Our rooms weren't ready, but we were issued with key cards for later. I didn't want to leave our bags behind, anyway. It would be safer to keep them in the car, out of sight, and close at hand in case there was a sudden change of plan.

Next stop was the Docklands. And very, very close to home.

"Are you okay?" Matt asked, as I steered through Enfield in silence. I nodded.

"Are you sure?"

I took a deep breath then sighed. How could I explain my emotions? This had been my home city for many years. We were heading to an address in the Isle of Dogs, barely five minutes from the seventh floor apartment in which I'd lived, and in which I'd planned my downfall. It was now owned by a deliberately-mysterious offshore company, of which I was the only shareholder, albeit not in a way that could ever be easily traced. Although there was a tenant, who was presumably unaware of its history, I had a huge urge to visit, not least to say hello to the concierge who I liked to think wondered what had happened to me.

So, the familiar sights were causing an intense feeling of homesickness, but it was more than that. It was a sense of loss. The realisation, again, that I'd given all of this away. And shrouding everything was the acute awareness that I was a fugitive. The planning for my disappearance had been every bit as complex as the crime itself, and now I was potentially jeopardising everything by reappearing in a city in which I was still on the wanted list.

"Just ... memories," I said.

"Good ones?"

"Some."

"But others?"

I shrugged, keen to change the subject.

"It's like a VHS tape of an old TV programme. You watch it back, years later, and part of you gets nostalgic for the good bits and part thinks it hasn't really aged well."

"That's quite the metaphor." He laughed. I had no idea where all that had come from. It wasn't even true.

"Tell me where we're going and tell me about Colin Medland," I said, keen to keep my eyes on the road, in case Matt could detect the sadness within them.

"First call is his office," he began. "The main objective is to speak to him, and find out what made him pull out of the deal."

"And try to resurrect it?"

"That would be a bonus."

"And the deal was?"

"We were looking to buy a disused warehouse on the river. Partly as an investment, partly as a strategic hub for anything that we needed to bring into London in the short term, and for residential development over time."

"Bringing in what kind of thing?"

"Anything."

I didn't pursue the point. In retrospect, perhaps I should have done.

"And he owns the building?"

"No," said Matt. "But he's acting as the sole agent and decision-maker on behalf of the company that does. You don't need me to tell you, the whole area is undergoing regeneration. We wanted to be part of that."

"But he pulled out."

"Exactly," said Matt. "Everything was on the verge of being signed, then we got a letter telling us the site was no longer for sale, and he hasn't responded to any communication since."

On the face of it, it didn't sound too sinister.

"But surely it could just be the case that somebody offered better terms?" I said. "Or they decided to keep it and redevelop it themselves."

"Possibly."

"But you don't think so?"

"No."

"Because?"

"Something about the way it happened. We got the sense that someone was leaning on him."

The traffic was heavy, and progress was slow. That was the one bit of London I didn't miss. Matt suggested stopping for a late lunch, then pointed out a McDonald's that was coming up on the opposite side of the road. I pulled off onto a side street to park.

"You know how to treat a lady," I said, with a smile.

"Everywhere else will be shut," he said, in mock protest.

"Even so, though."

"Actually there is a KFC if you prefer."

"I'm spoilt for choice. But no, McDonald's it is, if that's your idea of a hot date."

Why did I say that? Why even broach the subject? Luckily, he appeared to ignore me, but I made a mental note to avoid being reckless in future. I couldn't afford to take risks. There was a time and place for innocent flirtation, but this wasn't it.

The restaurant was busy, but I found a table while Matt collected the order. It was strange being out in public, hearing everyone speak English. Nobody paid us any attention, but that didn't stop a creeping paranoia. I was glad to get back to the car.

It was nearly 4pm by the time we reached the Isle of Dogs. Matt guided me to the site we'd apparently been trying to buy. From the metal gate I could see an old, fairly ramshackle building in a big yard, all protected by a wall with razor wire running across the top. It didn't look much in itself, but given the location and the way property prices were going in this part of London, it could be a gold mine. The yard and building looked deserted. An old, peeling sign mentioned a presumably long-defunct trading company. There was nothing to indicate that the site was up for sale.

"How did you hear about this place?" I asked, over the noise of machinery from an adjacent building site. I was glad of the trench coat. It was cold down by the river.

"Through somebody Anders knows, I believe," said Matt.

There wasn't much more to see. A few minutes later we pulled up on a quiet backstreet, outside a nondescript concrete office block that itself looked ripe for demolition.

"Nice place," I said. "Presumably he doesn't know we're coming?"

"Let's hope not," said Matt.

We got out of the car and crossed over to the main entrance. The front door wasn't locked, and inside, things were bleak. The floor was a patchwork of ageing linoleum tiles, aside from the ones that were missing. There were two offices on the ground floor, either side of a concrete staircase that led to the first floor. We paused, listening. Voices came from one of the offices, although they were too indistinct to make out any words.

Upstairs, the layout was the same, but both offices appeared abandoned. The letterbox of one had been screwed down, and the door reinforced with a couple of padlocks. Colin Medland's was on the opposite side. Matt knocked, but I wasn't hopeful.

As suspected, the knock wasn't answered. We waited and he knocked again, more forcefully. Nothing.

"I thought that might happen," said Matt.

"It doesn't mean he isn't there. Just that he's not answering," I said.

We returned to the car to wait, keeping an eye on the front entrance. Just past 5pm, a man and a woman emerged, and then set off in opposite directions. We watched while the man walked across to an ageing Ford Escort, got in and drove away. The woman was still on foot, but she turned the corner at the end of the street and disappeared from view. A few minutes later, another man came out, but this time paused to lock the main front door. He was carrying a white helmet, and walked across to a waiting motor scooter, mounted it, and set off as well.

We gave it another twenty minutes, but it was clear that the building was empty.

"We didn't come all this way to try again tomorrow," I said. "Come on."

I retrieved my lock-picking kit and strolled over to the building. It was good to be able to put the theory into practice.

Within a few minutes we were back inside the lobby. And within a few minutes of that, I'd successfully opened the door of Colin's office upstairs.

A pile of post got jammed under the door as I pushed it open. Inside was spartan, with just an old wooden desk, a chair and a couple of filing cabinets. Separate doors led to a small bathroom and an equally tiny kitchen. I opened the fridge. There was milk, but it was long past its use-by date, and had separated in the bottle.

"Any luck?" I asked, returning to the main room. Matt shook his head then asked to borrow my kit. He opened each filing cabinet in turn, but both were empty.

"I think it would be fairly safe to say he's moved out," I said. "Do we have a home address?"

"I'll make a call," said Matt.

I felt bad leaving the doors unlocked, but my lock-picking skills didn't extend to doing them back up again.

Colin's address was in nearby Stratford, East London. Matt looked up the address in the A-Z book from the glove compartment, and offered to navigate again.

We arrived shortly before 7pm. Lights were on. Somebody was home. We exchanged a glance before making our way to the front door.

"Mrs Medland?" asked Matt when a woman opened it. He flashed an impressive-looking ID card. "Is your husband home?"

"Who wants him?" she asked.

"It's nothing to worry about. We're just making enquiries about an incident near his office and wondered if we could have a quick word?"

A young girl appeared from a doorway further down the hall, presumably coming to see what her mummy was up to.

"He's not in, I'm afraid." The woman looked upset, and made a move to close the door.

"When will he be back?" I asked, with a hopefully-encouraging smile.

She shook her head.

"Sorry, he's away at the moment."

"Mummy," said the girl, in a tiny voice. "Are they looking for daddy?"

"They are, my darling," she said, turning to the child, who in turn wrapped her arms around her mother's legs.

"Look, I don't know where he is, and I don't know when he'll be back," she said, returning to us. "And if you don't mind, I've got to go."

She closed the door.

"That wasn't stellar," I said, as we made our way back to the car.

We'd reached a dead end. It was time to start being creative.

"She didn't look happy," I said, rather stating the obvious, as we set off for our hotel.

"Very nervous, I thought," said Matt.

"How old do you think the girl was?"

"Five? Six?"

"Old enough to go to school?"

"Just about."

"That's what I thought." I paused while I navigated a roundabout, looking for signs pointing in the direction of the North Circular road. "Let's have an early night. We've got to be up very early tomorrow."

We had dinner at the hotel. It was far from the first time we'd been to a restaurant together, but it was the first time that there'd been a convenient hotel room just a short lift ride away.

I can't say I wasn't tempted. But then I remembered the last time I'd attempted to seduce someone in a hotel. That hadn't gone according to plan. And I still knew virtually nothing about Matt's relationship status. It was time to come out and ask.

"So, is there a Mrs Matt?" I asked as we finished eating. It was a touch route one, but justified, I thought.

"Why do you ask that?"

"I'm curious. I don't know much about you."

"You know lots about me."

"I know you don't get up to mischief at the parties. In fact I think I've only ever seen you at one of them. And even then you kept your clothes on."

"I travel a lot. I'm not always anywhere near. What about you? Have you ever been married?"

I laughed.

"That's avoiding the question. If you don't tell me anything, how do I know I can trust you?"

"By definition that means you can trust me all the more, because you know I'm not lying."

I suppose he had a point, of sorts.

"No, for your information, I've never been married and I doubt I ever will be," I said.

"You don't want children?"

Now it was my turn to be deliberately vague.

"You can't ask me questions like that unless you're willing to answer them back. I don't even know how old you are. Fifty-two?"

"Are you taking the piss?"

I was, but I was enjoying it.

"Well, are you?"

"No, I'm forty-bloody-three."

"Well I never. Tough childhood?"

As expected, he saw the funny side.

"You're outrageous," he said, with a grin. "So how come you don't think you'll ever get married?"

"Look at me."

"I'm looking at you. You're young, gorgeous. Great legs." He winked. "And not shy, based on your enthusiasm for our monthly team bonding sessions."

"Yeah, right. I mean look at my situation. I'm eternally damaged."

"The right person would overlook that."

"Really? Knowing I might go mad again at any point, and execute them?"

"Some people would find that exciting."

"Like who?"

"Like people who appreciate living dangerously. Or would see it as a challenge to tame you."

"Haha, is that what you think? That I'm wild but ultimately controllable?"

I reached for a post-dinner cigarette while we finished our drinks. I was fascinated to hear his opinion.

"No, I think a bit reckless, possibly. But you're very intelligent, stylish, you work hard and you mean well. You're a nice person."

"*Nice?*"

"What's wrong with nice?"

"It's a bit damning with faint praise, isn't it? You could say admirable, lovely, well-mannered, kind, amiable, sexy, decorous, intriguing, captivating, and possibly sexy again, for emphasis. But no, no. You went with nice. It's fine. I know where I stand."

He reached across the table, ran his finger over the central sapphire in my ring, then squeezed my hand.

"I think you're all those things," he said, with a smile. "But it got downgraded to nice when you said I was fifty-two."

I wasn't going to get any more out of him this evening. We finished up, then made our way to our adjoining rooms.

"Be ready by six," I said, as I took out my key card. I nearly moved in to give him a goodnight peck on the cheek, but held back just in time.

"Sleep well," he said.

"And you."

Once I was alone in my room, I stripped off and headed to the shower, submitting to the warm jets of water. I needed to control myself. Because unless I could do that, what chance did I have of controlling others?

Chapter 20

Thursday, September 9th, 1993

BY 7.30am, we were back in the car outside Colin Medland's house, watching the rain fall, and drinking styrofoam cups of coffee from a local cafe. If Colin appeared, that would be a bonus. If not, we'd wait for his wife.

By 8.30 I was getting nervous, wondering if we'd had a wasted trip. But ten minutes later she emerged, holding a school satchel in one hand, and her daughter's hand in the other.

"Game on," said Matt.

We'd wondered if they'd get into a car, which in turn could have made things difficult, but thankfully they set off on foot.

I got out of the Honda, leaving Matt behind to make some phone calls, and started to follow, close enough to keep them in view, but far enough away that I could lose myself if, for any reason, they decided to turn around. A much-needed umbrella gave me an extra prop to hide behind.

A couple of streets later, in front of a small parade of shops, they fell into step with another mother and child, heading in the same direction. And shortly after that, a primary school came into view. Colin's wife and daughter walked through the playground and up to the main entrance, while I waited at the gate.

I was ready when she returned.

"Oh, hi again," I said, with a smile.

She looked up and frowned, as though trying and failing to place me.

"It's Mrs Medland, isn't it?" I continued, allowing my latent northern accent to the surface in an attempt to sound approachable, then extended my hand, moving the umbrella to protect her from the worst of the weather. "Charlotte Sadler. I came to your house last night, looking for Colin?" She didn't accept the handshake but I could tell that at least she now knew who I was. Kind of. "Does your daughter come to this school?" I laughed, feigning embarrassment at my own ridiculous question. "Of course she does, or you wouldn't be here."

"Can I help you?" she asked, voice cold, looking ready to walk straight past me.

"Sorry," I said. "I don't even know your name."

"It's Ella."

"Ah, Ella. No, not really. I've just transferred to the area and I'm looking at schools. I've got a son who should be starting this year but it's all been a bit last minute, so I thought I'd pop in and have a word with the Head. How is it?"

"How's what?"

"The school?"

"It's a school. They teach things. What do you expect? It seems friendly but she only started on Monday."

"Of course."

She made another attempt to move past me.

"And in terms of good areas to live?" I asked.

She shrugged.

"Ask the estate agent. If you don't mind, I've got to go."

I took a step back so she could pass, then spoke again as she did so.

"Are you okay?" That caused her to pause. "I appreciate you don't know me, but you look kind of hassled, and what with Colin being away ..."

"I'm fine," she said. She didn't look fine. She looked nervous.

"Can I buy you coffee?"

She stopped and glared at me.

"Why would you want to buy me coffee?"

"Because I don't want to sound needy, but I'm new to this area. I don't know anybody. And if my son comes here we're probably going to end up seeing each other every morning." I sighed. "Sorry, I'm from the North. Forget I asked. It's probably not the done thing in London. I've got so much to learn. Although in fairness to myself, that's all the more reason to buy you coffee." I smiled, and finally I saw a crack in her cold veneer. If I was right, she'd be desperate to talk to somebody, if I could just get her to open up. "Listen to me. I'm useless. I don't even know where the nearest coffee shop is."

That was a lie. We'd passed two on the way from her house.

"I understand if you're busy," I continued. "But I just thought it might be nice to get to know one of the mums. You probably know what it's like. It's all a bit new and daunting. And a bit scary if I'm honest." I smiled again, deciding it was time to turn up the frivolity, to look less threatening. "I literally don't know anyone round here, apart from my sergeant, and I'm desperately keen not to talk to him, because strictly between you and me, I'm developing a bit of a crush, and if he tells me he's married I'll be heartbroken. I mean, you've seen him, so you can't really blame me. Of course, if you don't like coffee, I could stretch to tea."

She looked at her watch and then down the street in the direction of the parade of shops.

"I suppose I could. Just for ten minutes," she said.

"That would be fantastic, thank you."

She set off, and I followed.

"So, you work with the police?" she said as we walked. "What are you? Some kind of detective?"

"Yeah," I lied. "But I don't want to bore you with work stuff."

"And what did you want with Colin?"

"Oh, that? It was nothing really. We're following up on an incident on CCTV near his office, so we're trying to speak to people who might have seen something."

We reached the coffee shop. There were plenty of free tables. The windows had steamed up, through a combination of steam from the kitchen and rainwater evaporating off the dozen or so customers. I ordered the drinks at the counter, and was told they'd be brought over in a moment.

"Are there any streets to avoid?" I asked, bringing the conversation back to my original query.

"In Stratford? Most of them."

I laughed.

"Is it that bad?"

She frowned.

"It's like anywhere in London. Good people and bad. The Railway Works closed a couple of years ago, so there's a lot of unemployment. But it's like anywhere else, it'll get all gentrified I expect. If we don't get murdered before then."

I feigned shock.

"Wow, are you saying it's dangerous?" I asked, as the waitress put the drinks on our table.

"Nah, no more than anywhere else really. There's the odd fight and burglary. But you're in the police, you probably know about crime prevention and all of that."

"Exactly. I can get you a discount on a burglar alarm if you want one." I smiled, taking a sip of the coffee, but it was still too hot to drink.

After a few more minutes of small talk about schools, amenities, local transport and shopping, I managed to get the conversation back round to Colin, in what I hoped was a natural way.

"I'll probably be back to see you, actually, whenever Colin gets home, unless we've solved it by then," I said. Perhaps it wasn't all that natural. She suddenly went very quiet. "How long did you say he was away for?"

"I didn't."

"But is it like a day or two or is he away somewhere?"

"Your guess is as good as mine."

I did my best to look concerned and sympathetic.

"Is that normal? Does he go away often?"

"Sometimes," she said.

"Business, or?"

She shrugged. I could sense the shutters coming down with alarming force.

"Do you have a number for him? Then we wouldn't need to bother you again."

"A number?"

"Like does he have a mobile phone or anything?"

She shook her head, and frowned as though the question was ridiculous. It was time to backtrack.

"I've done it again, haven't I?" I said. "I promised not to talk about work."

But it was too late. She stood up.

"Thanks for the coffee," she said. She hadn't touched it. "I've got to go. Places to be."

"It's my pleasure. I'm sure we'll be seeing a lot more of each other. And thanks for all the information, it's been a huge help."

I'm not sure she heard me. Before I'd finished the sentence, she was already on her way out of the door.

"How was it?" asked Matt, when I got back to the car, glad to be back in the dry.

"She's spooked about something," I said. "I was getting her to open up, but as soon as the conversation came round to Colin, she clammed up and made a run for it."

"Did you get the impression she was hiding him?"

"I got the impression she was scared. Like she genuinely doesn't know where he is. But if I had to put money on it, I'd say she's more scared about his safety than the thought that he might have run away with his secretary. Fundamentally, this should be quite straightforward, but I'm getting the impression it runs far deeper. How did you get on?"

"Good news," he said, waving a notepad in my direction.

"Excellent work." He was clearly very pleased with himself. "Are you going to tell me?"

"I spoke to somebody who knows a man who knows Colin socially. He said he'd spoken to him a couple of days ago. Something about a motel."

"That sounds promising. Where?"

"On the Essex/Hertfordshire border, about an hour or so from here."

"And he said Colin was staying there?"

"The contact doesn't know him personally, but according to the person he called, Colin stayed there in the past when he fell out with his wife and needed a couple of days away."

"Ella."

"Is that her name?"

I nodded.

"So it might be nothing, but it's worth a look," Matt continued.

It sounded a long shot, but with Ella stonewalling and the office a dead end, it was our only hope of picking up his trail. A trail that was growing colder by the minute.

Chapter 21

THE motel reminded me of one I'd stayed at on a road trip through northern Florida and Alabama a few years before, somewhere between Tallahassee and Pensacola. Except, as you'd expect in the Home Counties, on a much smaller scale, and considerably less warm.

Colin drove a dark grey Saab, according to our research, but there was no sign of one outside the motel. That didn't mean he wasn't there, but it would have been quite a time saver if we'd seen one. In fact, less than a third of the parking spaces outside the single-storey apartments were occupied. I wasn't sure if there was ever a peak holiday season on the Essex side of the Essex/Hertfordshire border, but if there was, this wasn't it.

Matt led the way to reception, and flashed his fake ID at the young blonde woman behind the counter before starting to speak.

"Excuse me, we're looking for someone we believe might be a guest here," he said. "A Colin Medland. Do you know if he's staying at the moment?"

The woman's name badge said Susan. She looked no more

than twenty, and appeared nervous. I gave what I hoped was a reassuring smile.

"Erm, I'm not sure," she said, her face flushing red. "I don't think I'm supposed to talk about the guests."

"I know," I said, trying to play the good cop. "You probably aren't, really. But it's nothing to worry about. He's not in any trouble, and you're certainly not. We're just investigating something that happened near where he works, and need to know if he saw anything. It's routine, really. But it would save a lot of time if you knew him."

Her eyes flicked between us, as though she was trying to work out what to do, and who to trust. And coming up with neither of us.

"I'll ring my manager and ask if I'm allowed," she said.

Matt sighed.

"Could you just look on the computer quickly? We're in quite a rush. It's Colin Medland."

"I ..." She hesitated.

"Thanks Susan," I said. "That really is a very big help."

"The thing is, we don't actually have a computer," she said. I was beginning to feel sorry for her.

"Registration cards, then?" said Matt.

"Or if you pass them to me, I'll have a look through, and then that gets you off the hook anyway," I added. Much as I liked Matt, his sheer size could be intimidating.

She started to protest again, but then gave in, and passed me a small red box of index cards.

"Thank you," I said. "I'll be quick."

There were only eleven, and none of them said Colin Medland.

"And this is everyone?" I asked. She nodded. "I wonder, if we show you a picture, would you be able to recognise him?"

"I'll try," she said.

I turned to Matt.

"Do you have a picture?"

"In the car."

"Pop and get it then."

While he was away, I engaged Susan in small talk, trying to make her feel more at ease, but primarily to stop her from going back to the original plan of calling her manager. The weather, obviously, is always a classic. By the time Matt reappeared, I knew that she'd started there after finishing A Levels in June, and was therefore only eighteen.

Matt passed her the picture. Again, her cheeks flushed, but she shook her head and passed it back.

"Sorry," she said. "I don't know him."

"Okay, not to worry. Many thanks for your help, anyway," I said. I gave one last smile, and wished Matt would do the same, before we headed back to the car.

"She was lying," I said, once the doors were closed.

"How do you work that out?" asked Matt.

"Did you see her face? She obviously knew something, but she's not letting on, for some reason."

He went to speak again, but I raised my hand to stop him. Instead I pressed my finger to my ear. Matt looked confused.

"That was interesting," I said, a minute or so later, removing the tiny earpiece.

"What's that?"

"I left a little bug under the counter. She just made a phone call."

"And?"

"Pop back in and retrieve it for me, without making it obvious, and then I'll tell you."

When Matt returned, I drove off into a nearby side street, made a three point turn, then stopped the car so we were out of sight, but still had a view of the entrance to the car park.

"Well?" said Matt.

"She called him," I said.

"Colin?"

I nodded.

"Obviously, I could only hear one side of the conversation, but the clue was in the way she said 'I've just had two people in here looking for you'."

"Interesting."

"There's more to it than that. First, she didn't introduce herself. There was no 'hi, this is Susan from the Travelstop'. She was straight in, which means they know each other, and he was probably expecting the call. Second, she described us, although you probably don't want to know the specifics of that."

"God. What did she say?"

"One was a woman with brunette hair, pretty, well-dressed, seemed nice. The other was a big ugly bastard. He was horrible. I'd like to say I paraphrased, but that was pretty much word for word."

"Charming."

I struggled to stop myself laughing. I had no idea he could be so gullible.

"Anyway, more important was how it ended. Something like, *'no, they've gone now, what time are you coming back, excellent, I'll see you soon'.*"

I gave a nonchalant raise of the shoulders, very pleased with myself.

"So we wait?" said Matt.

"We do. And hope that when she said soon, she was being specific rather than just using it as a turn of phrase. Although there's also a chance that she meant coming back to somewhere else, so if she leaves, we need to follow her."

Several hours passed, during which we lapsed into a companionable silence. We'd missed breakfast, skipped lunch, and I was beginning to have very enthusiastic daydreams about dinner, when Matt nudged me. I looked up. A dark grey Saab 900 was turning into the motel car park.

I turned the key in the ignition and edged forward to give us a better view.

It was definitely Colin, but the way he parked at an angle and then ran from his car to the door of his apartment gave me the impression he wasn't stopping for long.

"Let's go," said Matt.

A minute later, I parked the Honda across the back of the Saab, so there was no way he could drive it away. We knocked on the apartment door. There was no answer. We knocked again. Still no answer.

Matt looked at me, then shouldered the thing off its hinges.

Chapter 22

COLIN looked terrified. Which was understandable, really, given the abruptness of our arrival. He backed away, but couldn't go further than the wall. He grabbed a desk chair, as though he could use that to protect himself. But if he'd hit Matt with it, the chair would have unquestionably come off worst.

"Hi Colin," I said. "We've been looking for you."

"What do you want?" he asked, his voice broken in fear. He swallowed, but it seemed awkward, as though his mouth was dry. He was smaller than I'd expected. About five foot five, with nondescript fair hair, and metal-framed glasses. He didn't look like the kind of person who'd be key to a multimillion-pound property deal, but there again, I hadn't met many by which to judge.

"We're not here to harm you," said Matt. "We just want to know what happened. You were working with a friend of mine who was looking to buy a warehouse in the Docklands."

"So?" said Colin.

"So, you pulled out at the last minute. We wondered why."

"That's business. These things happen."

"Do they?"

Matt took a step forward, which scared even me. I sat down on the edge of the bed and crossed my legs, waiting in case I was needed.

"I was offered a better deal," said Colin.

"Hmmm," said Matt. He took a deep breath, which made his chest even more imposing, and if anything, his shoulders look even wider. I really hoped he wasn't going to hit him. I hadn't signed up for violence. This was the first big test.

"My boss is not very happy, and would like the opportunity to renegotiate if there are any points of the deal that need to be addressed."

"It's too late for that," said Colin, his eyes ever wider.

"You look worried," said Matt.

"Obviously I look worried. I know who you are. I know your reputation. You turn up here unannounced, smash your way in and start threatening me."

"We're not threatening you." Matt turned to me. "Have you heard any threats?" I shook my head. "Believe me, we're the good people here. We just want to know what happened. Who made the better offer?"

"I can't tell you that."

"That makes things more difficult."

Matt took another step forward. There was nowhere else for Colin to go. For a split second, his eyes shot towards the desk. At first, I thought he was looking for something to use as a weapon. But then I saw the envelope.

I stood up, walked over, and picked it up.

"You can't look in there," he said, clearly panicked. I raised my eyebrows, then returned to the bed and opened the flap. Colin was sweating.

"Oh dear," I said, when I started looking through the pictures. "Oh Colin, these do not look good."

"It's not what you think," he said.

"I should hope not. Because I met your wife this morning. She seemed lovely. I don't think she'd approve of these."

Colin had been photographed in colour in various states of undress, surrounded by even more scantily-clad women, and in a few, his hands and face were where they really ought not to have been. The others were far worse.

"Who took these?" I asked. Colin didn't answer, but swallowed again, and nearly choked. He coughed. His eyes were watering. I doubt it was the cough.

"Let me put it another way," I continued. "I think you're getting blackmailed. Am I right?" Again nothing. "We can help with that. We can make all of this go away. You need to tell us who's behind it, and we'll have a word with them."

"I ... I can't," he said.

"Let me guess, because they'll kill you?"

He nodded.

"Okay."

I stood up, put the pictures back in the envelope, then bent the envelope just enough so it would fit in the pocket of my trench coat.

"I'll tell you what we're going to do," I said. "You're going to come with us. We can put you up in a safe house. We'll look after you until all of this is over, and then we can go back to Germany and tell our boss the deal is back on and everyone is happy. All right?"

I waited for a response but it wasn't forthcoming.

"That was actually more of a statement than a question," I said. "We don't approve of the way that business has been done here. So we'll sort it out for you."

"If I even get caught talking to you, they'll kill me," he said at last.

"And we'll make sure that doesn't happen. Come on."

Matt stepped forward again and grabbed his upper arm, guiding him towards the hole where the door used to be.

"Let's not make a fuss," he said.

As Matt brought Colin out of the apartment, I went ahead to open the back door of the car for them.

I hadn't fully registered the sound of the motorbike. By the time I did, it was nearly upon us. And by the time I'd looked up to see why it was getting so close, the rider's bullet was already smashing its way through Colin's skull.

Chapter 23

MY heart nearly stopped, but Matt knew exactly what to do. He took control, grabbed the keys, and powered us away with all the calm panache of an experienced getaway driver. I hated the thought of leaving Colin's body behind.

"We've got to call somebody," I said, after a few minutes, aware my voice was nearly hysterical, but unable to control it. I glanced behind as Matt floored the accelerator again, looking for any sign of a motorbike, or blue flashing lights.

"And do what? Hang around to answer questions? Give a statement? *'My name's Clare Woodbrook and I saw everything, so let's keep it to that rather than discussing all the other stuff.'* Jesus."

"But we can't do nothing!"

"We're not going to do nothing. But for the sake of your liberty, we've got to put as much distance between here and there as possible."

I knew it made sense, but it sounded so wrong. So heartless. A man had just been killed, less than a minute after I'd promised him that wouldn't happen. Less than a minute after I told him he'd be safe if he came with us. A man with a wife and a young daughter, who had been perfectly safe in hiding until we turned up and interfered. I wound down the window to let in fresh air. It was either that or throw up.

Matt took the first available turning, then stopped as soon as he saw somewhere wide enough to park.

He killed the engine, then turned to me, and took hold of my hands.

"Clare, you cannot blame yourself for that," he said.

"*What?*"

"You didn't pull the trigger."

"I might as well have done."

"No."

I had to get out of the car. I was going to be sick. I'd seen dead bodies before, but never seen someone so brutally executed by a stranger.

Once out, I leaned against the side of the car, my arms folded on the roof, taking deep lungfuls of air. When I was confident the nausea was under control, I tried to light a cigarette, but my shaking hands made that impossible. Matt joined me, took my lighter, and produced a flame. The nicotine did its best to calm me, but it was a losing battle.

"What I don't understand is how it happened?" I said, when I was confident of making a coherent sentence. "How did they know we were there? Are they watching us?"

Matt put his arm around my shoulders and pulled me towards him. There was blood on his jacket, and I was nervous of it transferring to my trench coat, but the hug was worth the risk. I hated the thought of needing a big strong man to protect me, but simultaneously was bloody glad I had one.

"I need to make a call," he said, after a few moments of silence. "We can't stay at the hotel. I'll organise a safe house."

"What about our bags?"

"We'll pick them up on the way, but we'll do it discreetly. Trust me on this. I'm good at not being followed."

"Really? You really think that?" I probably sounded on the verge of hysteria. "How can you say that when we've just been followed to the bloody motel?"

"Because we weren't followed to the motel. Whoever did it was already there. Already watching it. You've *got* to learn to trust me."

I took one last drag of the cigarette and dropped it, grinding it into the gravel.

"Of course I trust you. But you've got to make allowances. I'm not experienced with this side of things."

"I know."

He gave me one last squeeze, then waited for me to get back into the car. We continued driving in the gathering gloom of the evening. At some point he asked me for my key card, then eventually stopped in an unfamiliar street. He told me he'd be back within ten minutes.

———

"Trouble?" asked Florian Straub.

"The worst kind," said Matt.

"I don't want to ask."

"You don't need to. You'll hear all about it. I've got to be quick. I just thought I should let you know, in case you heard it from anywhere else."

"And how's our golden ticket?"

"She's safe. Shaken, but she'll come round."

"That's good. Keep it that way. You can't let anything happen to her yet."

"It's my number one priority."

Matt was as good as his word. And when he returned, he was carrying my overnight bag, as well as his own.

"I've got an address," he said. "Are you up to driving so I can map-read?"

I nodded.

Half an hour later we were in a mews at the back of a row of terraced houses, and outside a large wooden gate that reminded me of my old flat, back in the golden days, in Sunderland. Matt got out, spent a few moments adjusting the dials on a heavy-duty padlock, then opened the gates so I could drive through and park in the rear yard. He closed the gates behind us, and fastened the padlock to the inside.

The house was an unremarkable Victorian two-up, two-down terrace, with a kitchen extension at the back. I didn't see where he got the key from. Maybe he'd had it all the time. But once we were inside, he locked the door and closed all the curtains before turning on the lights.

"Sit down and I'll make us some food," he said.

"I honestly don't think I could eat anything."

But as soon as I'd said it, I had a sudden, sharp hunger pang. I'd had nothing all day. Thankfully, he ignored me, and a few minutes later, an appetising aroma started to fill the air. Ten minutes after that, he produced two freshly cooked pizzas, and a bottle of chilled white wine.

"Wow," I said. "Where did you get all this from?"

"Pizzas from the freezer, wine from the fridge," he said, with a smile. "Come on, this'll do you good."

We ate in near silence, but at one point Matt looked at his watch and then flicked on the TV. We were the lead story on the local news bulletin. A reporter was already at the scene. Police wanted to speak to a man and a woman who were in the vicinity, and gave a compelling description of us, presumably from discussions with Susan. And no doubt Ella would be able to provide even more. It all felt surreal. It should have been such a simple task, but trouble followed in my shadow.

"It's not a question of who pulled the trigger," said Matt at one point. "It's who issued the order."

"But I don't understand why. It was a straightforward property deal, wasn't it? Am I missing something?"

He shrugged.

"It should have been. I genuinely don't know. But we'll find out. Obviously it's going to be harder if the police are looking for us."

I nodded, then thought for a moment. Then had an idea that I'd been trying to suppress. The risk was huge, but it was time to play my trump card.

Chapter 24

Friday, September 10th, 1993

WHEN I was a journalist, I frequently came across corruption, and developed good relationships within the Metropolitan Police. Obviously, I'd burned those when I went rogue and crossed to the dark side, but there was one particular person I'd been very close to, and who I thought would at least give me the opportunity to explain myself before slapping me in handcuffs and escorting me to a cell.

Detective Superintendent Joe Leyland had become a friend as well as someone with whom I shared a professional understanding. And when I'd worked on the exposé of DCI Graham March, it was to Joe that I'd turned with my concerns, first and foremost, and then later my evidence, as more of it came to light.

As a DSI, Joe was in a powerful position and cut an imposing figure. He was removed from day-to-day investigations, but held a senior management role, and had a well-deserved reputation as someone capable of inspiring intense loyalty within a team. He'd been horrified by the evidence I'd compiled against March, but was personally as well as professionally grateful.

Although his loyalty was to the upholding of the law, and he had to play by the rules, I had to hope he had a certain amount of discretion. Even so, it was a huge risk to even think about calling him. As far as he, and everyone else, was concerned, I'd died. If I suddenly reappeared, there was a significant chance he'd be extremely keen to make sure I served time for my crimes, no matter how close we'd been before.

So, it was dangerous. But desperate times sometimes call for radical solutions.

"But you could get sent down for twenty years," said Matt, who seemed horrified at the suggestion when I'd made it, after the pizzas, and emboldened by two glasses of wine.

"Yup."

"I can't let you do that."

"I get the risk, but what can we do? They're looking for us. If they've got us on CCTV we're screwed anyway. And it's better that they spend their time looking for the killer, rather than us."

"So let's get out of here," he said. "Get back to Germany. Call it off."

"And walk away from finding out whoever killed Colin? Sorry, but I'm not programmed like that."

"You can't do it."

The more he objected, the more determined I became. It was almost as though he had some other agenda. What the hell did he mean, "I can't let you do that"? Who did he think he was?

But nonetheless I was aware that we were colleagues, and although it was still early days, we were here to do a job together. He'd been good to me. I really didn't want to fall out with him.

So that was why I made the call early the next morning, while he was still fast asleep.

"DSI Leyland," said the voice. I knew his mobile phone number off by heart.

"Joe, hi," I said, my voice conveying BAFTA-nomination levels of meekness and pleading.

There was silence at the far end of the line. My overriding emotion was a deep sense of shame that I'd betrayed him.

"Can I talk to you?" I said.

"Where are you?" he asked. There was sadness in his voice, rather than anger. I was aware that I'd caused both.

"I can't tell you that. Not yet."

"Then no, I can't talk to you," he said. "Unless you want to turn yourself in."

"I don't want to do that, Joe. I want to apologise, though."

"Apologise? For committing fraud and killing people? I'm sure the jury will bear that in mind."

"Not apologise for what I did. I know that's unforgivable. But apologise to you, personally. I know I've let you down."

"That's one way of putting it. A bit like calling a hurricane a light breeze, though."

"Hey, I'm the one who does the metaphors." I thought for a moment. "Actually, is that even a metaphor? I'm not sure it is."

The silence returned. I broke it after a moment.

"I know you hate me, and I understand all the reasons why, but just so you know, I deeply, deeply regret the things that happened. And I know that doesn't make a blind bit of difference, but if it's any consolation, I spend almost every waking moment hating myself too."

"I don't hate you, Clare," he said. "I'm disappointed in you. But I don't hate you."

"Really?"

"Really. I spend my working life dealing with bad people. I don't think you're a bad person. You did bad things. You deserve to be punished for them, and yet I know you did lots of good things too. But I do want to know why you're calling me. You need to come in. I can make it easy for you. I can't promise favours, but I can at least ensure it's done with a degree of dignity."

I felt like a naughty schoolgirl being sent to the headmaster, one who was benevolent, but nevertheless was duty bound to give me the cane. I try not to smoke before 9am, but I lit a Silk Cut before continuing.

"I'm not turning myself in, Joe," I said. "But I do want to talk to you. I want to propose a deal."

"A deal?"

"Yes."

"What on earth makes you think you're in any position to do a deal?"

I had to think about that. It did sound ridiculous. So I tried to stop thinking about it and just bluster on.

"Two things. I've come across evidence that Graham March is up to no good again. In Germany. And I've got information about the shooting in Essex last night."

He didn't seem impressed.

"For your information, Essex is outside my remit. And as far as Graham goes, the disciplinary action is underway. I'd much rather talk about what you did. *Why* did you do it?"

"I can't excuse it. I got carried away."

"But you killed people."

"In self-defence."

"Bollocks was it self-defence. You were getting paranoid. Were you on cocaine?"

"No."

"Sure?"

"I promise."

"So why then?"

"I can't explain it. Greed? Madness? Stress most likely."

"Oh fuck off. We all have stress. We don't kill people."

"I know. Listen, I would love to discuss this with you, and I'm very happy to at some point. But there's something a lot more pressing. You heard about the shooting?"

"Of course."

"And you've heard the description of the people they're looking for?"

"Oh God."

I knew, at that point, that I was losing him. I desperately needed to pull it back round.

"Look, it's me, okay? It's me they're looking for. But it wasn't me who pulled the trigger. I was there but I was as shocked as anyone. But I can help. I can give a statement. But I have to do it anonymously or else you know what they're going to do. I want to help you, but I don't want a life sentence for doing it."

"I told you, it's not my remit. It's Essex."

"But the victim lived in Stratford. It's all related to London."

Again, silence descended.

"Look, a lot has happened since February," I said. "Things have changed for me. I'm moving in circles where I'm going to come across a lot - and I mean a lot - of information that will be useful to you, or Interpol, or whoever. I'm working for an organisation that is hell-bent on exposing corruption and international crime. But I'm going to be a lot more use to you if I continue doing that, and can come up with a way of working with you, rather than spending the next twenty years in Holloway."

"So you want me to give you amnesty in exchange for information?"

"Yes, if you want to put it like that. You do deals with informers."

"It happens, and sometimes, if the information is good, they'll get a reduced sentence. They're not all left free to roam."

"I really can help you, though."

He laughed.

"No really," I persisted. "I'm even happy to come and meet you. I'm in London. If you promise not to arrest me, I'll take you out for coffee. Dinner even, if that doesn't sound bizarre. We can help each other. Please."

I heard him sigh. It was still early. I'd probably woken him up, and this was almost certainly the last thing he needed.

"I can't make that decision on the strength of a phone call," he said. "And it's particularly difficult because if I go into work this morning and announce that I've been speaking to Clare Woodbrook, I'll probably get fired, and you'll have SO19 knocking on every door until they find you."

"I get that. But you haven't hung up."

"Give me your number and I'll call you."

"I can't give you my number, Joe. I wish I could."

"Because you don't trust me?"

"No, because I genuinely don't know what it is. I was only given the phone on Wednesday, and I didn't think to ask."

"It sounds like you're moving in dangerous circles."

"I'm beginning to think I am."

We ended the call. I agreed I'd call him again soon. Meeting was high risk, and there was a reasonable chance he'd arrest me. But I was in this for redemption, and if that was the potential price, then so be it.

I turned and saw Matt, standing just outside the door. How long had he been there? Why had he not come in?

"Did you hear much of that?" I asked.

"Yes," he said, stepping forward.

He looked at me with an expression that I'd never seen before. And I didn't like the way he was holding a gun.

Chapter 25

"YOU went ahead with it then?" he said, taking the chair on the opposite side of the dining table to me, and putting the gun down between us, disappointment etched on his face.

"I'm not going to apologise," I said. "Unless this whole 'we work for ourselves' thing is bullshit."

"It's not bullshit. You've got to trust your instincts, and if you think that's the right thing to do, then I support you. But I do feel a deep sense of responsibility. My number one objective in all of this is to get you home safely. And that means not being shot by whoever killed Colin, and equally not being arrested by a former friend in the police force."

"And hence the gun?"

He pushed it across to me.

"It's for insurance. We don't know what we're up against here. Are you familiar with these?"

I nodded. It was a 10mm Auto Glock 20. I'd fired one under Rüdiger's supervision, but had no desire to repeat the experience. The recoil was harsh. The Danish government had authorised it for defence against polar bears in north-east Greenland, but there weren't many polar bears running wild in London.

"Is it loaded?" I asked.

"Yes."

"Be careful then." I pushed it back into the middle of the table.

I got up, headed to the kitchen, and filled the kettle. Matt joined me, then took me in his big strong arms while I waited for it to boil.

"I worry about you," he said. I leaned into him. I had no idea where that had come from, but it was deeply comforting.

I came back from the trance when the kettle flicked off. We both opted for tea. When it was made, we went back to the front room, not mentioning the hug any further.

"Have we got a plan for today?" I asked.

"We need to think and come up with one."

"Let me have this, and then have a shower and I'll be all yours."

"Sounds exciting."

I noticed the wink and smiled. I'd wanted to add "as long as you promise not to shoot me" but hopefully that was a given.

———

As I emerged, fully dressed, on the landing, I could hear Matt talking to someone on the phone, but his voice was low and the words indistinct. And by the time I reached the bottom of the staircase, the call was over.

"What I don't get," I started, when we were both back on opposite sides of the table, "is why somebody would want to kill Colin Medland. I get that they may have wanted to stop him dealing with us, but as far as I was aware, he'd already done that. So why shoot him?"

"I don't get that either," said Matt.

"So what are you not telling me?"

"In regard to?"

"This deal? This whole situation in London? I thought we were coming over here to find him, to ask him why he wasn't taking our calls, and then find out who was leaning on him, so we could get things back on track."

"We were."

"I find it hard to believe there's not more to it."

Matt paused, removed the top from a bottle of water and took a long swig before continuing.

"This isn't particularly groundbreaking," he said at last, "but all I go back to is that whoever was applying the pressure didn't want him to talk to us."

"Clearly, but why not?"

"Presumably because they don't want us to know who they are."

"But we know, don't we? It's Florian Straub."

He scrunched his face.

"Possibly, but I don't think so. It's not his style."

"Okay, so we find out who Colin was giving the contract to instead."

"It's never that easy. Firstly, it'll be a company. We could get the name, but working out who ultimately controls it is much more difficult. It'll be a shell company owned offshore, and there'll be a web of connections before we finally uncover the ultimate owner."

"So we can't just follow the money? Isn't that the phrase everyone uses?"

Matt shook his head.

"That would be much the same. If it's being presented as a legitimate UK company, it would have a UK bank account. How that money is then transferred overseas is probably just as difficult to ascertain. We're not dealing with beginners here."

I stood up, and collected the envelope of pictures from my coat pocket, then spread out the contents on the table.

"This is all we have then," I said. "Colin Medland getting up to no good, presumably with prostitutes. That sounds like Straub, doesn't it? You said he ran brothels."

"He does. But he's far from alone in that."

"Nicolas Thiel then?"

"Maybe. But this is even less the kind of thing he'd get involved in."

"Because?"

"Because we've been looking into him, and he's a scumbag, but as far as we know, all he's interested in is his club in Paris, and what he can channel through it. He's very wealthy, but I doubt he'd have the money, the motivation or the connections to buy property in London."

There was something about the pictures that was troubling me. I studied them all again, to try to spot what I'd missed.

"Maybe my perspective on life has been badly skewed of late, but I can't help feeling these pictures don't really amount to much," I said, collecting them together into a single pile. "This is 1993. They're a bit scandalous, but is that enough? It's not like he was a government minister."

"It would still be a difficult conversation to have with his wife," said Matt.

"I know that. But really? It seems too straightforward. Too obvious, too basic."

"What are you thinking?"

"I'm thinking that this is probably how they hooked him in, but if so, it's fairly flimsy. Because what's the worst that could happen? He'd split with his wife. And if that happened, the damage would be done, and they'd have no further hold on him."

"Fair point."

"Likewise, imagine that in a fit of remorse, he confesses all to Ella. He could even come up with a semi-plausible story, explaining that it was a business trip, he got drunk and it's not as it seems. They have a big blistering row but decide to stay together and work through it. Again, if someone is relying on these pictures to be their sole leverage, that sounds like a big risk to me."

"So you think they have something else?"

I drummed my fingers on the table while trying to think it through.

"It would seem logical. What if this was just the start? But then they put him on the payroll? They could set him up with an overseas bank account. We need to speak to Ella and find out how often he's been away on business in the last few months, maybe the last couple of years, and whereabouts he's been. I know a bit about Swiss bank accounts."

"Is that where all your money is?"

I cast a suspicious glance in Matt's direction, and declined to answer. He'd have to marry me before I confirmed that. And even then, quite possibly I wouldn't.

"We can't go back and talk to Ella," Matt continued.

"Why not?"

He laughed.

"Because her husband has just been murdered. She'll have been speaking to the police. And given the descriptions on the news, I suspect she thinks that we're responsible. At the very least the police will have told her that we have no connection with them. Although in fairness, we never said we were. She just assumed that when I flashed my ID card."

I thought back to our conversation outside the school, and thought it best not to tell Matt I'd referred to him as "my sergeant". Or said yes when she asked if I was a detective. God.

"I didn't say it was going to be easy," I said.

"Forget it. For all you know, the police could be keeping a watch on her house and the minute you turn up, you're going to get arrested."

"But we didn't kill Colin."

"If not for that, everything else."

"Which takes us back to Joe Leyland. If I can speak to him and get him on side, he might be able to help us."

The conversation paused as Matt suggested an early lunch. Our eating patterns were all over the place, so I was all for that. He looked through the kitchen cupboards, then asked what I'd like from a local sandwich shop. I asked for a baguette with something vaguely exciting, like coronation chicken.

He borrowed my umbrella and headed out, after I'd offered to go with him. But there was logic behind not being seen together in public while it was still all on the news.

While he was away, I lay on the sofa, closed my eyes, and tried to think. He'd left the gun behind. I hoped I wouldn't need to use it before he returned.

Chapter 26

MATT returned with a chicken caesar baguette, but I didn't complain as it was a valiant effort, especially given the weather, and he'd also managed to rustle up a Diet Coke and a couple of cream doughnuts. There's not much I wouldn't do for a cream doughnut, but I didn't say that in case he put it to the test.

While he was cleaning up (and again, there's something deeply seductive about a man spontaneously doing the washing-up; perhaps he was in the Royal Marines catering corps? And oh my word, if he offered to do my ironing I could not be responsible for my hormones), I decided to call Joe again. It went straight to his answering service. I decided against leaving a message, for obvious reasons, and instead waited for Matt to return before taking another look at the pictures.

"You're well-travelled," I said to him, "and you look like the kind of man who might spend time with ladies of the night. Does the venue look familiar to you?"

"I'll pretend you didn't say that," he said.

"Pretend all you like. But does it?"

He studied them all again, but eventually he shook his head.

"I'm not an expert," he quite possibly lied, "but that could be any strip bar in any city."

"You don't think it's one of Florian Straub's places?"

"No, he doesn't own clubs like that."

"Nicolas Thiel then?"

Matt shrugged. "Could be. And that could make sense, but equally it could be anywhere."

I started to examine them like I would a *Where's Wally* book. There had to be a clue. I just had to spot it. There were beer mats on the table, but I couldn't make out any writing. I tried to read the time on the one photo that showed his wristwatch, but again the detail was obscured. The furniture was a mixture of black leather and red velvet, but again that was hardly unique.

And then something caught my eye. One picture showed Colin entering the building. There was nothing on the outside that gave any indication of its address, but right at the edge of the frame, a car could be seen. Its headlamp was yellow.

"There you go," I said, jabbing it with a finger, and sounding triumphant.

"Let's have a look," said Matt. He turned the photograph around so it was the right way up.

"As far as I'm aware, France is the only country that has selective yellow headlamps," I said. "I know they're stopping it this year, but the vast majority of cars will still have them. I remember reading about the changeover and thinking it was a shame as the yellow was so intrinsically French. So that looks like Paris. Might not be, but it backs up the Thiel theory."

"Maybe," said Matt. "But even if it's France, it could equally be Lyon, or Marseilles or the Cote D'Azur. France has got a population of sixty million people."

"I know. And it could also be a trick of the light. And actually, all it means is that it's a French car that could have been driven abroad. So it could be Belgium, the Netherlands, or even Germany. But even so, Thiel makes sense. You said he was in discussion with Straub. So Thiel gets Colin over, gives him a night to remember, passes the pictures to our man in Germany and there's your link."

I sat back, pleased with myself. I hadn't proved anything, but it was more than we had.

My phone rang, catching me completely by surprise.

"Who's that?" I hissed, looking at it, frowning with the effort of trying to work out who might have my number.

Matt shrugged and shook his head. "Are you going to answer it?"

I thought for a moment. Then pressed the green button to connect the call.

"Hello?" I said.

"Clare, it's Joe," said the voice. "You rang me."

"Joe." I glanced at Matt who raised his hands in a don't-ask-me gesture. "How did you get my number? I distinctly remember not giving it to you."

"You didn't but it came up on caller ID anyway." He chuckled. "Always the detective. Were you calling to turn yourself in after all?"

"No." I momentarily forgot what I'd been calling him about. That was a warning. I hated the fact that I'd made such an obvious beginner's error. It was pathetic. I seriously needed to up my game. But then it came to me. I pressed the button again to put the call on speaker so Matt could listen as well. "I was ringing about Colin Medland. Can you find out if he's been on any business trips over the last couple of years? Maybe to France, specifically Paris. Possibly Switzerland?"

"Excuse me?"

"It could be important."

"I don't care if it's important. Let me just make a point here. I'm a detective superintendent. You're pretty high up on our wanted list. There's nothing in that arrangement that gives you the right to ring up and give me orders."

"Joe, come on."

Matt started laughing, albeit silently. I shot him a filthy look and turned my back on him.

"Let's put it another way," I said, undeterred. "If you haven't asked his wife already, then I think you should. And either way, it's kind of a case in point, because when I said I could be useful to you, this is exactly the kind of thing I was talking about."

"Let *me* put it another way. I'm not hands-on. An SIO will be leading the investigation. And even, on the off-chance that I found that out, there's zero chance – actually significantly less than zero – that I'm going to share details of an investigation with you. I'm retiring in a couple of years. I'm not going to throw my pension away for anyone. And least of all you. No offence."

I stuck two fingers up at the phone, which made Matt laugh again.

"None taken," I said. "But it does rather illustrate why we need to meet."

"I think that's high risk for both of us."

"Arguably more so for me. Listen, think about it. I'll ring you tomorrow."

"It's Saturday tomorrow. I'm not at work."

"All the better."

I ended the call, and hardly dared look at Matt. I knew I was blushing. I work hard to give the impression that I'm cool and in control, and blushing has no part in that.

"That went well," he said. I could hear the smirk in his voice.

I reached for a cigarette and lit one, hoping the cloud of smoke would obscure my complexion long enough for it to return to normal, then turned back towards him.

"Is it just me or is it warm in here," he continued, still finding my discomfort hilarious. I chose to ignore him.

"Paris, then," I said. "We need to go."

"That's the last place you want to go," he said, getting serious all of a sudden. "You can't just walk into Nicolas Thiel's club to see if it looks like the pictures. Unless you've forgotten, this is the number one person who wants to kill you."

"I don't think it would be a problem," I said. It was an obvious lie. It was a huge problem, but I desperately needed to restore a veneer of self-esteem. "If it needs to be done, I'd be happy to do it. I can't live my life hiding from my past."

"Although you definitely do need to do that."

"Well, yes. Kind of. But you know what I mean. I can't go on letting it define me."

"Which it does."

"God's sake. Are you trying to be awkward?"

He smiled. I didn't.

"I'm impressed by your courage. But that would be madness."

"It'll be fine. I'll go in disguise if necessary. In the meantime –" I looked at my watch, suddenly making a decision "– I've got something I want to do this afternoon. Have you got any plans?"

He shook his head.

"What do you need to do?"

"Something personal. Can I ask you something?"

"Of course."

"Are you safe in England? By which I mean you're not also on the run from the police? Or anyone else for that matter, like facing a court martial?"

"No, that's just you."

"Okay. Let me drop you off in the West End, and you can go to do some shopping or visit a gallery, or whatever you're into. I just need a couple of hours on my own."

"To do what?"

"I told you, it's personal."

I was hardly going to tell him in the circumstances. Not least because I wasn't sure how wise it was myself.

Chapter 27

IT was good to get out of the house and get some fresh air, even though I knew it was a risk. But everything in life was a risk for me, especially when I'd shown myself to be careless. At least the rain had stopped.

Matt agreed to my suggestion, although I could tell it annoyed him. But it was all about balance. He already knew far too much about me. And the longer he went on, not telling me anything about himself, the more often my intense irritation was going to flare up.

"When you get back, I want to take you out to dinner," he said, as I navigated through the late afternoon North London traffic.

"Excellent," I said. "You can tell me all about yourself. It's not good to have secrets."

He snorted, which annoyed me even more.

"I'm not even going to answer that one," he said. "I want to go to an Italian restaurant. I've had a tip-off that Graham March will be there. But it's okay, I've booked a corner table so you can keep your back to him if you're worried."

"I've told you, Graham doesn't scare me," I said, trying to

keep the surprise out of my voice. "Although if you see him making a phone call, let me know and I'll make a swift getaway. Anyway, he won't recognise me as a brunette. Who gave you the tip-off?"

"Sources."

That wound me up even more.

"I thought we were on the same team," I said, frustration evident in the increasing volume.

"We are."

"But you still keep information from me! What sources?"

"I don't know."

"Oh, come on. I don't believe you."

"Why would I lie to you?"

"I don't know. Unless you don't trust me. Or you can't see me round the side of your massive ego. Maybe you don't think I'm fully on board with this. But believe me, if you want to find out what March is up to, you could not have anyone better placed than me."

"I'm aware of that."

I took a left and headed towards East Finchley Underground station. I was buggered if I was going to give him a lift all the way into the centre. I pulled up in a side street close to the station.

"I'll drop you here," I said, without looking at him.

"Where shall I meet you?"

"You know what, at this moment, I don't care. Where's the restaurant?"

"Islington."

I thought for a moment. It was hardly worth me dropping him off at all if he was going to spend half the time travelling in, and the rest of it coming back out. He'd have no time to do anything.

"And where are you going now?" I asked.

"I was going to go to Covent Garden, but it hardly seems worth it." Evidently he'd done the same calculation. "Actually, if you drop me off near Hampstead Heath, I'll go for a walk for an hour or two there, and just come back to pick me up when you're ready."

"Okay."

Although it was dry, there was no guarantee it would stay that way, and it was cool, cloudy and breezy. I felt guilty. I was probably being childish. But I had a lot on my mind, and I badly needed to clear some of it, as I was beginning to worry it was affecting me.

I put the car in gear, then set off in the direction of Hampstead. I said I'd be back in less than two hours, and probably quicker than that. The road to Camden was filled with memories, and not all of them were good.

———

After dropping off Matt, I called Anders. I'm not sure if he was surprised to hear from me, but if so, his voice didn't show it.

"I heard about Colin Medland," he said, once we'd said hello. "Are you both okay?"

"I think so, but ..." I stopped.

"But what?"

"How do you know about Colin?"

"I called Matt. He told me."

"You called Matt. You didn't think to call me?"

"I didn't need to. Matt told me everything."

My blood pressure was rising.

"That's not the point I'm making," I said. "The point is, I feel very much like the junior partner, here. Being kept in the dark. I thought we were all supposed to be equal."

"We are. And maybe next time I'll call you."

"Oh, don't worry about it."

I nearly ended the call there, out of sheer exasperation. But I needed to say the things I was about to say. It felt like I was betraying Matt, but I couldn't go on not knowing.

"What's wrong?" asked Anders, picking up on my mood, but to be frank, it would have been hard not to.

"I don't really want to have this conversation, but can I talk to you in confidence?" I asked.

"Of course. *Auf Deutsch?*"

"*Nein.* Preferably English." One day I'd love to be fluent but there was still work to do.

"*Natürlich. Was ist los?*" He chuckled. I think it was his attempt to cheer me up. I sighed.

"Nothing is wrong, as such," I said, understanding his question, but finding it hard to smile. "It's Matt. I think there's something going on."

"In what way?"

"He won't answer any question about himself, so I know nothing. I completely get that everyone is entitled to privacy, and there's no reason for him to actually say anything. I'm sure we all have backstories. But without wanting to sound like a spoilt child, he knows everything about me, and the things I did, and I have no perspective on him at all apart from my own mad theories. It's like he doesn't trust me. And now he's arranging to go to dinner on the back of information from a source, but he won't tell me anything about that either. Only that he doesn't know the source himself, which I find hard to believe."

"But you're a journalist. You know about protecting your sources."

"Of course, but we're on the same side." I knew it sounded ridiculous. I didn't know why it was bothering me so much. But I had to persist. "Please feel free to tell me to shut up and get over it, but I just find it really frustrating. I used to think it was because he was private. But now, I don't know. It seems like more than that. We got shot at yesterday. We have to be able to trust our lives to each other. But he won't tell me anything about his background, and I really would like to know. Not because it matters, in one sense, but because until I know, part of my mind will be consumed by theorising about what he's hiding and why. Does that sound unreasonable?"

Anders didn't answer immediately. I didn't know if I'd overstepped the mark.

"Anders?" I prompted.

"No," he said at last. "It's not unreasonable. But we all have secrets. I'm sure you do too."

"I'm sure I have. And I don't want to know everything. Just a little bit more than I do."

"One moment."

I heard footsteps walking across a wooden floor, then the sound of a door closing, followed by more footsteps. Then Anders picked up the phone again.

"This is difficult, because I don't know everything and Matt is a very private person," he said. "But if I tell you why that is, will that help?"

"Anything would help at the moment."

"Okay." An ambulance went shooting past me, its sirens blazing. I was worried I wouldn't be able to hear Anders, but he seemed to be aware of the background noise, and waited till it passed.

"Matt grew up in England, in Dorset," he continued, eventually. "He was privately educated, and then ended up working for a bank in Frankfurt."

"So he's not military then?" So much for the Royal Marines theory. "And that's how he ended up in Germany?"

"*Genau.* Exactly. He met a German woman, and they got married and set up home together. But at the same time, through work, he got involved in several financial crimes."

"What kind of financial crimes?"

"I don't know all the details. But fraudulent things. Corporate scams."

I wasn't shocked. By definition, we'd all done bad things.

"And then? Did he get caught?"

"No. He got out in time. But then his wife became pregnant."

"So he has a child?"

Anders hesitated.

"Sadly, both his wife and the baby died through complications in the birth."

"Shit. That's awful."

"It gets a lot worse. One of his crimes involved defrauding the German health service and he believes that may have indirectly contributed to their deaths."

"Jesus."

"Ever since then, he's been wracked with grief, guilt and everything else you could imagine. And everything he does now is because he wants to put things right. He lives on his own but still visits their grave regularly. Understandably, he doesn't like to talk about it."

"No, I can imagine."

I felt terrible now, even asking about it.

"Anders, I am so sorry. Thank you for telling me, but immediately I wish I hadn't asked."

"That's okay. It's better you know."

I was momentarily lost for words. He filled the silence.

"My friend, all you need to know is that Matt is one of the good guys. The very, very best. He does his own thing on occasions. He has unusual methods. But I've known him a long time, and I promise you that you can trust him. I give you my word."

"Understood. Thanks, Anders."

"My pleasure. Take care out there."

I ended the call, and looked out of the windscreen at the late afternoon traffic. My view was blurred by moisture, but I wasn't sure if it was the onset of light rain, or the watering in my eyes.

There was still one more thing I had to do. My emotions were in tatters after the call with Anders. I had a suspicion they were about to get worse.

When I decided to try my hand at crime, my motivation was greed, pure and simple. I'd come to terms with that now. And although I hated the person I was back then, the thing I hated the most was the hurt I'd caused to others.

I regretted everything about what I did, but in my naive stupidity, I thought it would be clever to disappear and leave clues for Danny, my former researcher at the paper. If he could follow those and find me, he could write a piece about it for the *Echo*, and it would launch his career in my absence. It was shockingly arrogant, really. It would have been far better to not do the crime, and instead continue nurturing and training him, as I had in the years since he'd joined me as a student intern.

What was worse was that when Danny rose to the challenge, his flatmate Anna came to his assistance. And together they trailed up and down the country, looking for me, worrying about me, and getting shot at in the process. Two innocent young people, caught up in the deluded fantasy of a madwoman. And then, when they finally found me, in Switzerland, I made things infinitely worse by pointing a gun at them.

I wanted to scream at the memory. I'd replayed that moment in my mind countless times, and it never appeared any better.

The gun wasn't loaded, but they didn't know that. I took them inside and confessed everything, before making my escape in a helicopter that I knew was going to crash shortly after dropping me off. It was all part of my plan to disappear forever. And it was the most unbelievably selfish act of a horrible person that I was deeply ashamed to realise was me.

I remembered Danny's words that night. *"You're a fraud. I idolised you. And all the time you're no fucking better than the rest of them."* And I responded by trying to justify myself. Telling him to publish the story and become a superstar, and one day he'd realise that everything that had happened was for the best.

I felt physically sick every time I thought about it. He was absolutely right. I'd done unforgivable things. And in all the long hard months at the Schloss, punishing my body with the intensity of the training regime, the thought that kept coming back to me was that one day I would make it up to both of them. I'd take all of the abuse they wanted to give me, and apologise from the absolute depth of my heart. And when that still wasn't enough, I'd try and try again until eventually I found a way to repay them.

But the first step on that journey was to face up to reality. To knock at their door. Show them that I was still alive. Say sorry for the person I was, and let them know a day didn't pass without thinking of them. To give them a chance to slam the door in my face.

I parked the Accord in Rochester Square, in Camden, a couple of houses away from the one they shared. Anna's Honda Prelude was parked outside. She was home. All of the guilt I felt about what I'd done to Danny was magnified a thousand times over for the impact on Anna. She didn't deserve any of it, and yet she'd put her life on the line to help her friend and to find me because she thought I was in danger. That kind of loyalty was priceless. It deserved to be rewarded. Not thrown back in her face as I'd done that night in Switzerland, with a pathetic attempt to justify myself.

I knew what time Danny would get home from work. And, on cue, I saw him approaching at the end of the street, walking towards me. He didn't see me waiting in the car, watching him.

He climbed the steps to their front door and let himself in. I decided to give him a moment before making my approach.

I got out of the car and started walking towards their house. The lights were on. They were together in the front room, talking, laughing, having fun. They wouldn't notice me, on the street, in the gathering twilight.

As I reached the first step, Anna came to the window and

closed the curtains. And in that moment, such an innocent daily task struck me as deeply symbolic. I stopped. I'd imagined this moment a thousand times. And yet now, I saw it for what it was. I was doing this for me. Not for them. They didn't need me. I was being as selfish as ever. Maybe the ghost I'd been trying to exorcise was still deep within me.

I went back to the car, closed my eyes, and felt an overwhelming sadness. For Danny. For Anna. For Matt, his wife and their unborn child. And then I cried like I never had before.

Chapter 28

I THINK Matt was taken aback by the hug when I finally picked him up, although he'd have been even more shocked if I hadn't stopped at a chemist on the way and bought cleansing wipes and emergency replacement eye make-up, among other things.

"Have you forgiven me for whatever I did to annoy you?" he asked.

"I had to clear my head for a bit. I'm okay now. Are you all right?"

"I'm cold."

I felt bad about that.

"Let's go to dinner and I'll warm you up." It came out as more of an innuendo than I'd intended. Matt raised his eyebrows and I blushed, but it was gloomy enough in the car that I don't think he noticed. "What time do we need to be there?"

"The table's booked for eight."

I looked at my watch. There would be just enough time to go back to the safe house to freshen up. I suggested it, and Matt nodded. There was no further discussion of our afternoon apart, and I was happy to keep it that way.

Shortly before 8pm, Matt found a parking space close to the restaurant.

"Don't laugh," I said, as he applied the handbrake.

"What do you mean, don't laugh?"

And then he looked at me and laughed.

"I specifically told you not to do that."

"I've never seen you in glasses. It's very sexy secretary. Where did you get those from?"

"My pocket."

That confused him.

"I stopped at a chemist this afternoon," I continued. "They're technically reading glasses but the nearest I could get to plain lenses. I thought if Graham March was here, it might help to be a little bit disguised. You're lucky I didn't go for a false nose and moustache."

"I don't know. That could have been fun."

"In your dreams, perhaps. But bear in mind that even though they're not very strong, they're still strong enough to make my vision go funny." It was ironic, really. The trip to Camden was supposed to help me see things more clearly.

"Understood. I'll protect you."

The restaurant was noisy but warm and welcoming. As promised, our table was towards the back, in a corner. Matt sat with his back to the wall, giving him a good view. I sat facing him, so nobody could see my face.

We ordered a bottle of *Superiore Frascati* dry Italian white wine and another of sparkling water. Matt looked longingly at the former when it arrived, but it was his turn to drive. I smiled inside at the small victory.

"So you've had fun at the parties then?" he asked, with a cheeky glint in his eye, once the garlic bread arrived.

"I have."

"You weren't shocked?"

"I wasn't shocked, as such. You'd warned me, and it's good to be able to let off steam in that environment when it'd be impossible to have a normal relationship. We all have needs. But the first time, it seemed strange that all of these people were suddenly at the Schloss. I'd got used to the thought of it being my home and then lots of strangers turned up."

"That's the problem with staying there. It's a treat for most people, but you got it all from the outset."

"I need to find my own place, I suppose."

He shrugged.

"There's no rush. You can decide where you want to base yourself and find somewhere eventually, but nobody's going to kick you out. Birgit and Walter seem to like you."

I smiled. "They're sweet. I have no idea what either of them make of the parties, though. Presumably she keeps him away from temptation. I've seen her there, supervising the catering, but he keeps well out of the way."

"Can you blame him, at his age? The poor man would have a heart attack."

I laughed. Then had flashbacks of some of the things I'd witnessed. They would have tested the constitution of anyone.

"You should go more often," I said. "I'd look after you."

"Really? You think I'd need looking after?"

"There are lots of hot women, Matt. In various states of undress. I'd hate to think that one or more might lead you astray or take advantage."

"But you don't mind the thought of yourself being led astray by hot men?"

"I'm young enough to get away with it, but you're in your fifties now. You need to be taking things easy."

"I'm forty-bloody-three."

"So you say."

I laughed, but his attention was suddenly far behind me.

"He's here," he said.

Immediately my smile vanished. I wanted to look round to see him for myself, but I couldn't make it obvious. In the end I couldn't resist a glance. The glasses made everything blurry, so I peered over the top. It was definitely Graham, in all his obnoxious, rotund glory. His companion looked familiar but I couldn't quite place her. They were seated at ninety degrees to us, so we weren't in his direct line of sight.

I turned quickly back to Matt.

"Let me know what he does," I said.

"I will, but don't worry. He seems quite preoccupied."

I felt sorry for the woman, whoever she was. Why would someone want to spend an evening with Graham March? She was older than his normal type, but still definitely not his wife.

"She looks familiar," I said. "I can't think of her name, though."

"She just laughed at one of his jokes."

"Christ. She's up to something then. Have you got a camera?"

Matt nodded.

"Do me a favour. Take pictures of them, without attracting attention to yourself. Oh, and for heaven's sake make sure the flash doesn't go off."

Matt took a tiny Nikon AF600 from his jacket pocket and rested it on the table between us, behind bottles of olive oil and balsamic vinegar. Every so often, he moved it slightly to the right and pressed the shutter. For the rest of the meal, the wine flowed, and Matt asked more questions about the parties. I got the impression he might have been a little bit jealous, which was interesting. Who had I slept with? Was it just men or women as well? What was the biggest orgy? What was the most depraved thing I'd seen? I managed to swerve some, and answer others without incriminating myself, because certain things were best kept private. Again he still didn't reveal anything about himself, but for once I didn't mind.

Graham and his friend were still deep in conversation and apparently enjoying each other's company by the time we were ready to leave. I walked past them on the way to the door, passing within a few inches of Graham's back. I glanced again at his companion, but even close up, I couldn't think of her name, not that the glasses helped. She looked to be in her late forties, but had a deep tan and the premature wrinkles that went along with it. Her hair was obviously dyed black, and her leopard-print blouse and choice of outsized jewellery conveyed a victory for glitz over taste.

I stopped on the street outside.

"What's up?" asked Matt.

"Do me a favour. Go back in and find out who she is."

"How do you propose I do that?"

"Use your initiative. Ask the bar staff or the waiters. Worst case scenario, go over and introduce yourself. *'Graham, long time no see. It is you! How are things?'* He won't have a clue who you are, but that doesn't matter. I doubt he remembers lots of people. Wait till he introduces you, and if he doesn't, introduce yourself."

"Okay."

I lit a cigarette while I waited. It was the first one in hours, which felt like progress. I knew I'd have to give up one day, but in the meantime I'd try to ration myself. Apart from in times of stress or when wine was involved, and especially when there was both.

Matt headed straight for the men's toilet. After checking he was on his own, he pulled out his phone.

"Florian," he said. "I've got to be quick."

"Where are you?" asked the German.

"At a restaurant. March is here. Clare wants to know who he's with. Do I tell her?"

There was a momentary pause.

"It can't do any harm."

"Do you know who it is then? I can't exactly go over and ask."

"Describe her."

"Middle-aged. Tanned. Black hair. Animal print. Too much make-up and a bit gaudy."

Straub laughed. "Sounds like Jacqueline Glover. He said he was meeting her this week, so that makes sense."

"Okay. And she is?"

"She runs a casino. Long-term project. How are things anyway?"

Matt looked at his watch.

"Clare had a major wobble today. Something freaked her. And she keeps trying to pin Colin Medland on you."

"That's not helpful."

"Exactly. She's very bright, but I'll keep pointing her in other directions. Oh, and she wants to go to Paris."

"Paris? Why?"

"To track down Thiel."

Straub drew breath. "She can't do that. The entire point is that he gets her from us when we're ready. If he catches her on his own, the entire thing is *fucked*."

"You don't need to tell me. Hold on."

He paused as a diner entered the bathroom and headed for one of the urinals. Matt checked his reflection in the mirror and adjusted his shirt collar. Eventually the man left, but not before giving Matt an accusatory look that implied he was some kind or drug dealer or looking for an illicit sexual encounter.

"Sorry about that," said Matt, when he was back on his own. "A punter came in."

"No problem. You can't just bring things forward a few days? Go with her?"

"No, I need the next few days to finalise things." He checked his watch again.

"When are you back in Germany?" asked Straub.

"It looks like tomorrow night."

"Talk her out of Paris then."

"Wish me luck with that."

"You can't stop her?"

"Short of tying her up somewhere, I very much doubt it."

"Leave it with me, then. I'll see what I can come up with."

"I will, but likewise."

Matt ended the call, then washed his hands and went back out into the night.

When Matt reappeared, he looked slightly hassled.

"Come on," he said, turning in the direction of the car. I fell into step alongside him.

"So? Did you get a name?"

"Jacqueline something. I think she said something about a date. It was noisy so it was difficult to hear. Does that mean anything to you?"

I thought for a moment. It should have done, but I couldn't quite get over the horrible mental image of Graham March having a lover. I thought I recognised her, and "Jacqueline" rang a bell, but I couldn't place her. I was tired. It'd been an emotional day. All I wanted was to go home, and start afresh tomorrow. The only thing I was certain about was that if Graham March was meeting somebody, it was unlikely to be entirely innocent.

Chapter 29

Saturday, September 11th, 1993

IT came to me in the night. Jacqueline Glover ran a casino and gentleman's club in the West End of London, just off Berkeley Square. She'd crossed my radar while I was investigating Graham because there were rumours of illegitimate activities going on behind the scenes, and hers was one of the many businesses he was offering protection to.

But now he was no longer on the Force, what was he up to? It certainly wasn't a date if the rumours of her lesbianism were true.

Matt was already in the kitchen, cooking breakfast, by the time I made it downstairs.

"Smells good," I said.

"Take a seat and I'll bring it through."

Within a few minutes he delivered bacon, poached eggs, and toast, along with fried tomatoes and mushrooms and a cup of decent-looking tea. He was definitely back in my good books.

"I've been thinking about Paris," he said, as he joined me at the table. "I think we should wait."

"Why?"

"Because I'm going to be away for the next few days, and it would be too dangerous for you to go on your own."

"I appreciate the concern. But there is a degree of urgency."

"Because?"

"Because Colin Medland just got shot. We're in the frame until we can prove his links with Paris. And between you and me, I'd rather do that before the police catch up with me, in case there are other things they also want to discuss."

As if on cue, my phone started to ring. It was Joe again.

"You're still in London?" asked the DSI.

"I am."

"We need to meet."

That kick-started my brain.

"Okay," I said. "Where and when?"

"Do you know the NCP multistorey car park in Saffron Hill, Farringdon? Of course you do. One of your colleagues was killed there."

"Not by me, Joe." I didn't like his tone.

"Meet me on the top floor. At eleven."

I checked my watch. It was doable.

"Am I going to be safe?"

He hesitated.

"Do you mean: am I going to arrest you?"

"You, or anybody else."

"Are you planning on committing a crime?"

"Not this morning. But I was kind of referring to previous things that I might have been accused of."

"Nobody's going to arrest you for those. Not this morning anyway."

"Okay. It'll be good to see you."

He ended the call, and I went back to the breakfast.

"Joe Leyland?" asked Matt. I nodded. "Do you trust him?"

"I trust him," I said, "but it does make me nervous. I

suggested a meeting yesterday and he didn't seem too enthusiastic. I don't know that I can trust whoever he's spoken to in the interim."

"What's the deal with you and Joe?"

I thought for a moment.

"Can I give you a metaphor?"

"No."

"Please?"

"No."

"Okay."

I paused for a moment, but Matt didn't want to wait.

"When I said don't give me a metaphor, what I meant was actually explain. Just in plain English," he said.

"But it's complicated."

"All the more reason to avoid one of your metaphors, then."

"God, you're getting cheeky." I took a bite of toast before continuing. "In the simplest terms, we got on really well. He became a good friend. I spent a lot of time investigating stories and discovering crimes. There's a traditional view that the police don't like the press poking their noses in, and I get that completely, but this was the other way round. I wasn't some news reporter who was getting in the way and asking awkward questions. I was writing features and exposés, and more often than not, the police wanted to talk to me, rather than trying to avoid me."

"So it must have been a shock when you swapped to the other side?"

"Definitely. And I think it would have hurt Joe quite badly, which is not something I'm proud about. We'd really got to know each other. We went to dinner together. We became close."

"Were you sleeping with him?" I could sense Matt studying my face for a reaction.

"Wow, where did that come from?"

"It sounds like you might have been."

I sighed.

"No, for your information, not that it's technically any of your business, I was not sleeping with him. He's twice my age and as far as I know he's married. It was purely professional. He's a gentleman."

We finished our breakfasts in silence. Then Matt said he'd do the washing-up while I had a shower. I think he realised he'd overstepped the mark. He hadn't really, but coming on top of last night's interrogation about the parties, I was beginning to wonder if his interest was merely professional. And a growing part of me hoped it wasn't.

Matt drove me to the largely deserted top floor of the car park for about 10.45am and then parked close to the down ramp. If anything went wrong, and I got ambushed, I had the choice of trying to make it to the car or escaping via the stairs to a lower floor, assuming that either route was left open. If they were coming at me from all directions, I was in trouble.

"You don't have to do this," he said, for about the fifth time since we'd left the safe house.

"I do," I said. "You seem more worried than I am. And you can put that away." I nodded at the Glock he'd just retrieved from his inside pocket.

"We might need it."

"Trust me, we won't. If anything goes wrong and Joe arrests me, I'll take my chances in the courts. But I really don't want 'conspiracy to murder a policeman' on the charge sheet."

When he didn't put it away, I grabbed it, put it in the pocket of my trench coat, and quickly got out of the car. He didn't look happy, but better that I got arrested for carrying an unlicensed firearm than run the risk of him pointing it at someone.

I leaned back into the car and passed him a piece of paper, making sure my pocket was out of reach.

"This is Graham March's number," I said. "At least it was. It might have changed."

"How did you get this?"

"Believe or not, we worked together on a couple of cases before I realised what he was up to. I'm quite good at remembering numbers. Make yourself useful and fix up a meeting."

"With Graham?"

"Evidently with Graham." What was wrong with the man? He was incredibly edgy. "What time are we flying back?"

"It's booked for eight but it's flexible."

I looked at my watch and did a quick calculation.

"Arrange Graham for three. In a park or somewhere."

"That's such a bad idea."

"You don't have to go to that one either. Just say that seeing him last night made you think of something he might be interested in. Either way, get him out in the open. Then I'll go and have a word. If he knows I'm alive I might as well confront the bastard."

Matt started to shake his head, but I tapped my coat pocket. Of course I wasn't going to shoot him – I never wanted to shoot anyone again – but he was acting weirdly.

"Just do it, okay?" I said. "Trust me."

I closed the car door, and headed to the staircase door. It seemed the logical place to wait.

With military precision, a dark green Vauxhall Omega appeared at exactly 11am. I recognised Joe behind the wheel. He pulled up alongside me, then reached over and opened the passenger door.

"Get in," he said.

I hesitated, then decided to risk it. Once I'd closed the door behind me, he reversed into a space on the far side of the car park, a disturbingly long way from Matt.

"I can't tell you how disappointed I am in you," he said, once he'd turned off the engine. He hadn't changed much. He still looked distinguished behind his glasses, with his grey hair closely cropped either side of his otherwise bald head. He'd been like a father figure to me, and I'd been dreading the thought that one day soon he'd be approaching retirement.

"I know." I wanted to give him a hug and beg for forgiveness, but neither of those were appropriate. Instead, I apologised again.

"Let's discuss that later," he said.

"Agreed. But as for me helping you, do we have a deal?"

"Not yet."

"But you're not arresting me."

"Also not yet."

He undid his seatbelt and turned towards me.

"I fundamentally don't know if I can trust you," he said, his voice hard and scolding.

"I understand that. And there's no reason why you should. But I will do everything in my power to prove you can. And in the meantime, try to think of all the good things I did, rather than the one bad one."

"I think it was more than *one* bad one."

"One bad spree, then." I smiled. In some ways it was just like the old days. Despite feeling hopelessly guilty about the trouble I'd caused, it was good to see him. "How's the case against Graham progressing, by the way?"

"You know I can't discuss that."

"But is he going down?"

"I shouldn't even be having this conversation with you, and I'm certainly not going to have a discussion about internal police disciplinary matters."

I held up my hands in deference.

"I understand that. But like I said on Friday, I have a suspicion

I might come across more information that could be of assistance. If I do, I'll pass it on."

"I think you've done enough already."

We lapsed into a momentary silence while a motorbike approached the top of the up ramp, the throb of its engine echoing off the concrete and drowning out speech, even at low speed.

"Do you want to grab a coffee?" I asked, once it had turned away.

He shook his head.

"Who was that in the Honda Accord?"

I followed his eyeline to the opposite side of the car park. The Accord was partly obscured by a concrete pillar.

"That's Matt Sommer. He's a colleague. He gave me a lift."

"A colleague in?"

"I'm working for an organisation that does a bit of business development, albeit in a fairly altruistic way."

"Is that his real name?"

I shrugged.

"It is as far as I know. Until very recently I was sure he used to be in the SAS, or at the very least the Royal Marines. He's looking after me."

Joe said something else, but I wasn't listening. My attention was on the motorbike, which had pulled in to the space next to the Accord. It struck me as strange when there were so many others to choose from. But then I realised where I'd seen the bike before. And the biker. And the black helmet. At the motel.

Even from this distance I could see that as the rider dismounted, he was holding a gun. And with a sickening sense of horror I realised that because of my petulance, Matt was alone, in the car, unarmed and about to take a bullet.

Chapter 30

JOE had seen it too. In a split second I was trying to get out of the car. I had the Glock. I had to run to Matt's rescue. But Joe held my arm in a vicelike grip and pulled me back.

"He's not there," he hissed, pulling me down below the level of the dashboard. It took me a few milliseconds to process Joe's words.

"He got out just after you."

"Where is he?"

"Crouching behind the yellow Nova."

I'd seen the yellow Vauxhall. It was one of the few other cars on our row, about eight spaces away, the far side of a Ford Mondeo.

"That's who shot Colin Medland," I whispered, in panic, my heart beating in my throat. I peeked up, above the dashboard, just enough to see the biker walk a full circuit round the Accord, testing all the door handles. Though he wasn't very tall, he looked menacing in black leather. The gun was by his side, a noise suppressor adding considerably to the length of the barrel.

Eventually, he gave up and got back on his bike. The engine

roared again. Joe and I both ducked down in our seats as the sound got louder. It was coming towards us, painfully slowly, then seemed to hesitate for a moment when it was at its loudest. I had the Glock ready beneath the dashboard, and with a strong pull, racked the slide to load a round into the chamber. But then the engine note rose and started moving past us. We both looked up as it got further away, just in time to see the bike disappear over the brow of the down ramp.

"What the fuck are you doing with a gun?" snarled Joe, looking down at my hands.

"Believe it or not, ensuring nobody fires it," I said, my face immediately reddening.

"I assume you've got a licence?"

I didn't know if he was taking the piss. So much for not doing anything criminal this morning.

"It's not mine," I said, aware of how pathetic that sounded. "Matt brought it. I took it off him. Don't look at me as though I know what to do with it." Now wasn't the time to mention Rüdiger's extensive training sessions.

"You are seriously pushing me to the bloody limit."

He stopped scolding me long enough to make a call on his phone, reporting the registration plate of the bike. I was impressed that he'd both spotted it and remembered it and gave him a mental pat on the head for getting it right.

Once he'd done that, he opened his car door.

"Matt Sommer. Come here *now!*" he shouted across the car park.

A moment later, Matt appeared from the far side of the Mondeo.

"Get in the back," added Joe, in a tone of voice that didn't leave room for debate.

Matt climbed in.

"Matt, Joe. Joe, Matt," I said by way of completely unnecessary introduction.

"I don't even know where to begin," said Joe.

I passed the Glock back to Matt.

"Yours I believe," I said. "You need to unload it."

Without a word, he removed the magazine then pulled the slide back to clear the chamber. A round popped out. He put it into the magazine and then reinserted the magazine into the handle.

"Give me one bloody good reason why I shouldn't just take the pair of you in now," said Joe.

No reply.

"Should I answer that one?" I asked, turning to Matt.

"You can do what you like. If it'd been left to you, I'd now be dead."

And that is precisely why I'll always be single. I meet men I like, and seriously piss them off. I thought it best to ignore him.

"The point is, Joe, we're not the bad ones here," I said. "But now maybe you believe me when I told you there was a man on a motorbike, going round shooting at people."

"Unless that was all a charade."

"Do you really think I'd do that? And do you really think I'd have got the gun out if I had? Have a word with yourself." In retrospect, that was probably a bit strong.

"Okay. Let's talk about Colin Medland," said Joe, thankfully overlooking my outburst.

I nodded.

"Why were you interested in him?" he continued.

"The organisation we work for was trying to do a property deal in the Docklands," I said. "Colin was the contact. Then at the last minute he pulled out. We thought he might have been getting blackmailed. He wasn't returning our calls, so we went to see him."

"Which is when he got shot?"

"Exactly. We think he was being watched. They really didn't want him talking to us."

"And what made you think he was being blackmailed?"

I thought for a moment. Should I mention the pictures? I didn't really have an option.

"We found some photographs of him with prostitutes," I said. "But we think there was more to it than that. I'm still trying to find out what that was."

"Any ideas so far?"

"In truth, no. Not clues. But possible theories, which was why I asked you about business trips. I want to find out where the pictures were taken. But more than that, I want to find out if they had any other leverage on him. Had he been put on the payroll somewhere? Was he involved in anything sinister?"

"Why?"

"What do you mean why?"

"Why are you so interested? Accept he had a better offer. Move on."

I looked to Matt for support, but he was still silently fuming.

"Because the organisation we work for has a strong moral code. We think he was the victim of some kind of extortion. And now someone has killed him, which doesn't sit easy with me. With any of us. Obviously I'm fairly new at the whole thing, but part of the remit is to do good deals, and another is to fight the bad guys. We've worked with law enforcement and intelligence agencies all across Europe. Not me personally, obviously. Not yet, anyway."

"And does this organisation have a name?"

Again I looked to Matt for support, but none was forthcoming. I didn't know how much of this was top secret. In for a penny.

"It's named after an old East German super-spy," I said. "The Blood Angel."

Joe glared at me.

"Are you taking the piss?" he said.

I shook my head.

"No, why do you think that?"

"The Blood Angel?"

I nodded.

"You're seriously working with them?"

I nodded again.

"You say that as though you've heard of them," I said.

"And what about you?" asked Joe, turning to Matt.

"The same," he said. "Although I've been involved much longer."

"Right."

Joe sat back in his seat and closed his eyes.

"What's up?" I asked, after a moment.

"Nothing's up. I just didn't expect I'd be sitting in a car with two members of the bloody Blood Angel network."

"Is that a bad thing?" This could be the moment where it all unravelled, if he told me a horror story.

"No," he said, his voice noticeably calmer. "Notwithstanding the fact that I still don't know whether I can ever trust you again, that does put a different light on things."

"In what way?"

"In a way that says if you *are* telling the truth, I need to take you seriously."

His eyes still looked kind, despite the horrendous things they must have witnessed during his career.

"I'm telling the truth, Joe," I whispered.

He seemed to come to a conclusion.

"Yes. According to his wife, Colin Medland went to Paris about six months ago," he said at last.

"That would be about right," I said. "Do you know where he stayed?"

"No, not yet. As I told you, I'm not directly involved in the investigation. I don't get involved in that. But the detectives working on it are going through bank statements."

"And do you know about anywhere else? Switzerland? I'm wondering if he had a Swiss bank account."

"Not yet," he said. "But we're looking."

Joe's phone started ringing. He said a few words, but mainly spent the call listening. When it ended, he turned back to me.

"Where were you this morning?" he asked.

"We've been staying at a house in Enfield. I spoke to you, then we got ready and then came straight here. Why?"

He nodded.

"That was the SIO. Colin Medland's wife was out this morning. She got home about half an hour ago and found the place ransacked."

"Shit."

He fastened his seatbelt and turned his key in the ignition.

"I'm going to have to leave you to it for now," he said. "We'll keep in touch."

"Okay," I said. "But do we have a deal?"

He thought for a moment.

"Let's say you're on probation. Keep me informed, and we'll review things. But I'm warning you now, I can't protect you. If you overstep the mark and get caught, all hell will come raining down. But make yourself useful and it'll give me something to think about."

I held out my hand. He looked at it for a moment before accepting the handshake.

"It's been good to see you, Joe," I said. "And thank you."

"And you." He smiled. "I always knew you'd come back. The helicopter crash was obviously bullshit."

I shrugged.

"The whole thing got out of control. I'll make sure it doesn't happen again."

Matt and I got out of the car, then watched Joe pull away and head off down the ramp.

"I'm sorry, Matt," I said, knowing he was still furious with me. "Really, desperately sorry."

"You left me unarmed," he said, his voice cold.

"I had no idea we were going to get ambushed."

"Well, it's a bloody good job I took precautions and left the car then, isn't it?"

"But how did you know?"

"Because unlike you I'm not some wet-behind-the-ears newbie. Christ."

I could have cried again, which was so unlike me.

"That's the point though, isn't it?" I said. "I am still learning. This is a whole new world for me. Isn't that why you're here? To teach me?"

He took a step closer, then held my head between his big, strong hands, and looked straight into my eyes. I looked down, finding it deeply uncomfortable.

"Don't ever, *ever*, do that again," he said. But then his grip softened. "If you get us both killed, I'm going to ask Birgit to stop serving you dessert for a month. Understood?"

I looked up and smiled.

"Understood." My eyes moved over to the Accord. "Presumably we're going to need a different car?"

"Hallelujah," he said, stepping back. "You *are* learning. Just when I was beginning to think there was no hope."

"I'm trying," I said.

"Oh, you're very definitely that." He looked at his watch. "We've got two and a half hours to get to Karl Marx's tomb at Highgate Cemetery."

He noticed my puzzled expression.

"For your meeting with Graham," he added. "Which, given that we're now relying on public transport, means we can't hang around here if you're going to treat me to lunch."

I stepped forward and gave him a hug. I still couldn't quite believe he'd worked in a bank and wasn't some kind of special forces commando. I felt safe in his arms. But I needed to wise up quickly, because I knew there was a limit to how long he'd be there to catch me.

Chapter 31

THE day hadn't gone smoothly, but there was still plenty of time for it to get far worse. I had to make sure that didn't happen.

"What's your plan with Graham?" asked Matt, as we walked up Highgate Hill from Archway tube station.

"I just want to unsettle him," I said. "I left behind a dossier that should have had him convicted. But seven months on, he's still running free."

"These things take time."

"They do. But if he's helping Nicolas Thiel find me, I want to call his bluff. Let him know I'm watching him, and I've still got the capacity to make things extremely uncomfortable." My thoughts turned to Danny. "And I need to make sure he doesn't intend to make life awkward for an old friend of mine."

Matt nodded, looking thoughtful.

"On top of that," I continued, "I'm still working on earning Joe's trust, which is going to be vital if I ever want to operate in London with any degree of security. I've got to prove to him that I can be more use on the outside than in a prison cell. So if I can find out information about Graham, it's all going to help."

"So, in terms of that, you think March is an easy target? The low-hanging fruit?"

"See? Now you're attempting a metaphor but it's not even a good one, because a. It isn't actually a metaphor anyway; and b. It's a cliché."

Matt laughed.

"It's no wonder people want to murder you."

"Only according to you, so you can try to seduce me with your knight-in-shining-armour act."

"Wooah. Who said anything about trying to seduce you?"

I raised an eyebrow and left it there for a moment. The truth was, he was doing a very good job of it, whether he was trying to or not.

———

Matt and I parted when we reached the cemetery. He said he'd keep an eye on me, but stay out of sight. I made the walk to Karl Marx's tomb on my own, paid the entrance fee – which seemed ironic – and saw Graham standing, looking the other way.

He turned round as I approached, his initial shock transforming into a sickening smirk.

"Look who it is," he said. "I heard about the helicopter crash. Terrible business. You're looking well, though. Albeit only in comparison to the average seven-month-old corpse."

"Very funny, Graham," I said, walking right up to him. "Excuse me if I don't shake your hand."

"Believe me, there's not enough antibacterial soap in all of London for me to even consider that. Interesting hair, by the way. Was it a student?"

I lit a cigarette, rather than rise to the jibe.

"Enlighten me," he continued. "What are you doing here?"

"I'm watching you, but trying not to breathe in," I said,

through a mouthful of smoke. "Making sure you behave yourself."

He laughed.

"I'm a changed man. I won't bore you with what I like to call the details. But thanks to you I'm enjoying an extended holiday on full pay. I suppose I should be grateful really." He lowered his voice, trying to sound menacing. "You do know, one click of my fingers and you'd be inside?"

"No," I said, shaking my head. "One click of your fingers and people would think you were delusional. And then a day later they'd discover your body. I think you're aware of my darker side."

"Ooh, tough talk from the little lady. I presume this isn't a coincidence? That you got someone to call me on your behalf. Do you think I wouldn't have turned up if you'd asked me yourself?"

"I thought you'd enjoy the surprise."

"I assure you, nothing about being in your company is enjoyable. So I'm going to go now, unless there's something specific you want from me. Or are you just showing off, and trying to impress me with your questionable fashion sense?"

"I wondered why you were meeting Jacqueline Glover."

That threw him. It looked like he was going to try to deny it, but then reassessed and turned towards me.

"She's an old friend."

"An old client? Or old victim?"

"What can I say? I might have helped her out. It's what friends do."

"You helped hide evidence of her using her club as a front for prostitution."

"In your deluded fantasy. I'm thinking of suing, you know. Both you, personally, and the toilet rag you used to write for. And that idiot boy you hired. What was his name? Daniel something?"

I took one last drag on the cigarette, then dropped it to the ground and crushed it under my toe.

"I'm also here to warn you," I continued. "I know you're a nasty bastard. We both know you can't get me, but if one cell of your warped mind thinks about taking out your inadequacies on Danny, it needs to think again."

"Because?"

"Because if you do, I assure you, they won't actually find your body the next morning. The bits I remove while you're still breathing will be fed through a mincer before your eyes, and the rest will dissolve so you don't even get a funeral. And if you think lemon juice on a paper cut hurts, just wait till you dip the open wounds of severed fingers in a vat of acid."

I'm not a violent person. I'm really not. But something about Graham brings out the worst in me.

"Oooh, you sound so scary." He started to walk away.

"A friend of mine saw you in Cologne recently."

That stopped him.

"Cologne? In France?"

"It's in Germany."

"It wasn't me, then. Not if I don't even know what country it's in."

"What were you doing there?"

"I told you, it wasn't me."

"We both know it was."

"Evidently not, my dear. I think your time away has addled your brain. What little there is of it."

"Who did you meet there?"

He closed the gap between us.

"Are we going to spend all day going round in circles or are you going to buy your Uncle Graham a nice cup of tea so we can have a proper chinwag about the good old days?"

I laughed at the ridiculousness of the man.

"I'll tell you what I'll do," I said. "I'll spare you that pleasure.

But be aware that whatever you're doing, I'll be watching you. I'll always be watching you. And in the meantime, I actually think I could help you."

He feigned surprise.

"You could help me? By disappearing? By turning yourself in?"

"Very funny."

"Why would you help me? You've gone out of your way to make problems for me. Is it because you have a crush and I haven't ever succumbed to the temptation? I'm sorry to disillusion you, love, but despite my genial and charitable nature, I have standards. My services don't extend to mercy fucks for the terminally frigid."

"God, you are delusional."

"In what way is that delusional? I'm a man with a certain reputation for pleasing the ladies, and you're famously shit in bed."

"What *are* you talking about?"

"Just what I hear."

"You know nothing about my private life."

"Oh really? You think that? I'm an elite detective, my dear. You don't think I've spent the last few months mourning your passing, do you? I've been doing my research. I knew you'd reappear. It was merely a question of from which sewer."

Part of me had hoped that Graham would have mellowed, having seen the error of his ways. But nothing had changed.

"Okay. I'll try a different approach," I said. "Thorsten Stötzner."

"What?"

"What were you doing with him?"

"He's a person? I thought you were just spouting random German words."

"You met him in Cologne."

"Oh, not this again."

"Why?" I wanted another cigarette already, but managed to resist.

"Why what, my dear? Why do I keep denying something that plainly didn't happen?"

"Which, again, we both know did. It's not going to help your disciplinary hearing, is it? Canoodling with known criminals."

"To quote you: what *are* you talking about?"

"You know exactly what I'm talking about."

"And to remind you, I'm a detective. I meet the occasional criminal. It's in the job description. My task is to bring them to justice. Which reminds me. I really should be taking you in. You need to come with me."

He tried to grab my arm, but I shook him off.

"Michael Eidinger?" I said, standing firm.

"Who?"

"Nicolas Thiel?"

"You've done it again."

"What do you want from Nicolas Thiel?"

To his credit, he didn't flinch.

"I have no idea who he is," he said. "Is he another one of your made-up Germans? Are you just going to keep randomly suggesting names until I finally recognise one?"

"You're playing a dangerous game, Graham. Mixing with dangerous people."

He took a step back and sized me up.

"I'll give you that. I'm mixing with you, and it transpires you're dangerously insane."

"Are you working with them?" I continued. "Are you their man in London? You do know they'll kill you, once they realise you're a useless prick?"

He smirked again.

"Given that I have no idea who you're talking about, I can't possibly comment. All I'm working on at the moment is clearing my name after the scurrilous lies your underling printed about me. And my charitable good deeds, of course."

I'd made my point. It was time to leave.

"Goodbye, Graham," I said.

"You're not going already? I was enjoying our little catch-up. Are you staying locally?"

"Local enough that I can keep watching you."

"You do know that makes you sound like a stalker, don't you?" he shouted to my retreating back. "But it's not going to work. I hate to be the one to break this, but I'm just not interested. I'm a happily married man. And even if I wasn't, there are three billion women in this world ahead of you. But if it makes you happy, I'll add you to my to-do list once I've exhausted those."

I raised two fingers and kept walking.

"In fact I'd even service young Anna ahead of you. I hope that doesn't sound mean, but you know me, I always tell it like it is. Truth and honesty are my watchwords. It's better that you know. I understand that's painful but what can I do?"

I didn't hear the rest of his nonsense. Just talking to the man made me feel the need for a very hot shower. And we had to somehow get back to Enfield to pick up our bags before catching our plane home.

Matt fell into step as I left the cemetery.

"How was he? Did you learn anything?" he asked.

"No more and no less than I expected to. He denied everything, obviously. But I think I got the message across."

"But he knows you're watching him?"

"For what it's worth. We're not really much further forward. Next stop, Paris."

Matt sighed.

"I told you, I'm not comfortable about you going there on your own. Especially after today."

I tried not to show that I was offended.

"Because of the man on the bike?"

"Because you'll get yourself killed."

"I promise you I won't."

"At least wait until I can come with you."

"We've been through this." I knew better than to ask what he was going to be doing instead.

"But it's a problem, isn't it?" he said. "You're going there to look for the very person who's looking for you."

"I'll do it discreetly."

"For God's sake."

We walked in silence for a bit, neither of us wanting to budge. But eventually Matt caved in.

"Okay," he said. "You go to bloody Paris. But I'll arrange for someone to meet you."

As compromises go, it was one I was happy to accept. Sometimes I'm not actually as brave as I try to sound.

Chapter 32

Sunday, September 12th, 1993

THE journey back to Germany was relatively free of drama. Matt was subdued, as though something was playing on his mind, but he was friendly enough when I prompted him to discuss his favourite books, music and TV shows. That said, with the exception of Propaganda and Kraftwerk, I hadn't heard of any of the German bands he mentioned, and I wasn't familiar with any of the German TV dramas, despite occasionally flicking through the channels in an attempt to improve my language skills. I felt a great sense of relief when we touched down, and an even bigger one when he dropped me off at the Schloss. That's the other reason why I'll always be single. I actually enjoy my own company and the reassurance that the only person I can let down is myself.

I woke up early on Sunday morning, with the urge to go for a run. It would have been an alien concept seven months ago, but for the new me it was an immensely therapeutic way to blow away the stresses of the last four days. After a five-mile circuit, I returned to my room, showered, and went in search of breakfast.

Birgit was in the kitchen and smiled when she saw me. I think the fact that I could now make rudimentary conversation in German helped immeasurably. She didn't ask about what I'd been up to, but instead fussed around me, like a devoted grandparent indulging a small child. Walter popped in at one point, kissed her on the cheek, then nodded at me as he left. I heard the front door close a moment later.

Matt had finally agreed that I should head to Paris first thing on Monday, not that he had any right to argue. We were in this together, but throughout my time in Germany, it'd been stressed that I was an individual and would be free to make my own decisions. Obviously, I was nowhere near the deal-making side of things yet. But I was fairly sure that would come if I proved myself capable of helping to sort out the Colin Medland mess. Matt had arranged for me to meet a colleague called Sylvain Audat, who would act as my local point man, and who would accompany me if needed as I explored the city.

I phoned Rüdiger and asked to meet. He said he'd be at the Schloss by 3pm, which gave me a few hours to myself. I was still restless, so got changed again and then went for an hour in the gym, finishing with twenty lengths of the pool and then ten minutes in the sauna. By the time I'd done all of that, I felt a strange mixture of energised and exhausted, so set my alarm for two and went back to bed for a snooze.

Rüdiger was waiting for me in one of the lounges by the time I came downstairs. I hoped I was looking suitably refreshed and reasonably well-dressed in a mid-length dress, opaque tights and knee-high boots. An open fire made the room both warm and cosy. I was exceptionally pleased to see him. Strangely, it was the first time we'd met in one of the living rooms. I couldn't remember him ever seeing me in normal clothes.

"How was London?" he asked in his heavy German accent, after I'd given him a hug.

"Interesting," I said. "Although it was a bit of a wake-up call too."

"How come?"

I gave him the summary, with details of Colin Medland's murder, my lapses, and the sense that I needed to be more mentally prepared in future.

"But physically?" he asked, which was understandable, given that the physical training was his department.

"Physically I was okay," I said. "Although I didn't like the Glock 20. It took quite a bit of effort to load, which was a surprise. It wasn't a problem standing in the woods, but it was different under pressure."

"Who gave you the Glock?"

"Matt."

He nodded.

"I will give you a 23. This is smaller."

"I didn't really want to have a gun at all," I said, "but it focuses the mind when someone else seems willing to fire one."

There was a knock at the door. Birgit entered and offered us tea or coffee. We both opted for coffee, and a few minutes later she returned with a cafetière, together with a plate of biscuits. She was a darling.

I thought of a question for Rüdiger.

"Do you know a Sylvain Audat who works for us?"

He thought for a moment.

"I don't think so. Is he in Paris?"

"Apparently."

He shook his head. "I don't know many of the French ones. Maybe he goes to the parties, the name is familiar, but I can't recognise him."

"I've never seen you at the parties."

He looked bashful, all of a sudden.

"No."

"Not your thing?"

He took a deep breath.

"No, not really."

Sometimes the things people don't say tell you more than those they do. But my curiosity was piqued.

"Are you married?"

He looked away, then down to the floor. I longed for the day when I was no longer the new girl and could be as secret and evasive with new recruits as the rest of them were with me. I didn't expect him to expand, but then he did.

"You know about East Germany?" he said.

That took me aback.

"In terms of?"

"Athletics."

"Not really," I said. "I remember the blue vests with DDR on the front. And obviously there were always rumours of drug-taking."

He nodded, looking forlorn.

"The records were opened a couple of weeks ago," he said. "The Stasi had control of doping from 1971 until reunification. It was for the national pride. The athletes were heroes. They were the symbol of success of the government and communism."

"But not so much fun if you were one of the athletes?"

"Correct. I was. I was a sprinter. I was supposed to compete at the Olympics in Moscow in 1980 when I was twenty-four, but I hurt my knee two months before. Then again at Los Angeles in 1984 but we had the boycott. By Seoul I was too old. For me there were no more chances."

"Wow. I knew you were fit, but I had no idea you were that good."

"Well, maybe it was for the best," he said.

I poured us both a cup of coffee, to give him time to elaborate, but he seemed content to wait for me.

"The best in what way?" I said, as I passed him his cup.

"Because it was all a lie. They'd pumped me full of anabolic-androgenic steroids. I did not deserve to win. I did not want to win. Possibly I wanted to for me, but not for the country."

"That sounds awful." I took a sip of the coffee while I tried to process the revelation. It certainly explained his physique. "But were there side effects? I don't know much about it, but I've read occasional stories. Funnily enough, one of the features I was working on before I left the newspaper was investigating a company illegally importing drugs into the UK for the bodybuilding and gym market. But I didn't get far."

For the first time, the big strong man in front of me looked vulnerable.

"There were," he said.

"Do you mind talking about it?" I said, my voice softening.

He looked uncertain.

"Depression and infertility, mainly," he said at last. "So to answer your first question, yes, I was married, but it was not possible to have children, and that made the depression worse. I became abusive and had violent mood swings. I am not proud of myself."

I let out a deep breath.

"Rüdiger, that's awful." He looked so incredibly sad. "I do feel for you. None of that is your fault though. You mustn't blame yourself."

"I take strong drugs now to keep things under control," he continued. "But not the kind you get from the doctor. I need stronger. But I have a supply. And that's why I don't have relationships, because I'm worried it would happen again, and why I don't go to the parties. I can't drink alcohol and I think I would be embarrassed to try some of the other things."

Coming on top of the revelations about Anders' family getting killed while defecting, and Matt's wife and their unborn baby, I was beginning to realise that my problems were relatively minor. And unlike the others, I only had myself to blame, which made it all so much more frustrating. But if I hadn't done what I'd done, I'd never have met this flawed but brilliant group of people. I wondered how many of the others in the organisation had similar backstories. All of them, I suspected.

I didn't know quite what to say to Rüdiger, so I went across to him, knelt on the floor, and held his huge hands, resting my arms on his thighs.

"I am so sorry to hear all of that. It is so terribly, desperately sad," I said, looking into his heartbroken face, which was clearly displaying the emotion behind the memories. "I know it's easy for me to say, but you must never blame yourself."

He closed his eyes, and nodded. And we stayed there in silence for a few minutes, just listening to the crackle of the wood in the fireplace and the distant ticking of the clock.

Eventually I gave his hands a squeeze and then returned to my chair. We both finished our coffee. I offered him a biscuit, but he declined.

"You need anything else for Paris?" he asked, bringing the conversion back to the original purpose of the meeting.

"A small camera, I think," I said.

"Camera, Glock 23. Anything else?"

I already had a listening device and lock-picking equipment. If I thought of anything else, I could ask Sylvain for help.

"That's everything," I said.

"You have all the travel arrangements?"

"Matt said he was going to sort all that out, and drop off the details this evening."

"That's good." Rüdiger stood to leave. "I will deliver back to you this evening also, then."

I followed him to the front door.

"Thanks, Rüdiger," I said, as he put on his jacket and took his car keys from his pocket. "For everything. For all the training and all the patience, and for telling me what you told me. You're a good man."

He tried to smile, but it didn't really work. Then he headed out into the late afternoon on his own.

Matt ended his call with Anders. They'd discussed London and Clare's forthcoming trip to Paris. He'd made a note of the suggestions that Anders had given him for hotels, and people to contact in an emergency. He'd type it all up, and leave it in a briefing dossier when he visited the Schloss.

Next on the agenda was finding a hotel with a vacancy for a couple of nights. He struck lucky on the second call. It wasn't far from the Gare du Nord mainline station, which meant it wasn't in the most scenic part of the city, but she wasn't going there to be a tourist.

That left one more call to make. He closed his office door, even though there was nobody else in the house.

"Nicolas Thiel," said a voice when the call connected.

"Nicolas, it's Matt. I have some news for you."

"About time. Progress?"

"The handover is Thursday. Four more days."

"That's good."

Now for the delicate part.

"But I have a favour to ask," he said.

"I don't like the sound of favours."

"Nicolas, you have to trust me. This is in all of our interests."

"And yet you still present it as a favour?"

"Yes." He was aware this could go either way. "I know the most important thing for you is Clare."

"Correct."

"But hopefully Florian has shown you all of the other ways we can work together. Certain products we can supply you with. Yes? I spoke to him yesterday. He tells me he's done a lot of work with you. And all we need to do is shake hands on the deal."

"Also correct."

Matt took a deep breath.

"So my favour request is that I need you to trust me. Clare will be in Paris for the next two days. She might visit your club. I want you to be patient. If you see her, be gentle. I know you could take her there and then, but if you do that, you'll lose all of the other opportunities."

"*Pourquoi?*"

"Why? Because it works best for all of us this way."

"But that makes no sense. The rest of the deal is still beneficial. Just because I get the most important part four days early, does not stop the other arrangements still being mutually beneficial."

Matt cursed under his breath. He'd thought that might happen. He crossed the fingers of his left hand while holding the receiver with his right.

"And that's why it's a favour," he said. "I've spoken to Florian, and we both agree. We have our reputations to consider. On top of that, we still have plans for Clare for this week. There's still something we need her to do. And last of all, she'll be coming with protection. If you try to capture her, it could get messy. So all I'm asking is some restraint, and a little bit of patience. Give me that and on Thursday she's yours."

There was a lengthy pause.

"Why will she be visiting my club?" Nicolas asked at last.

"Because she's impetuous and reckless. She might not, but there's a risk she will. And it's possible you won't recognise her anyway. I didn't need to make this call, but I'm doing it as a courtesy."

"And if I say no?"

"That would be a significant inconvenience. It's only four more days."

There was another pause.

"Okay," Nicolas said at last, although Matt detected significant reservation. It was a huge gamble. "But Thursday has to happen with no excuses and no delays."

"You have my absolute word."

———

Nicolas ended the call and then immediately made another, from the numbers stored on speed dial. Of all of the thugs on the payroll, Serge Benoit was the most capable of extreme, remorseless violence. Although competition for that accolade was tough.

"Clare Woodbrook will be coming tomorrow," he said.

"How do you know?" said Benoit.

"Because the English idiot thought it would be a good idea to tell me. She'll be visiting the club and we need to be ready for her. I'm going to explain to you exactly what I need you to do."

———

True to his word, Matt dropped off an itinerary at some point in the evening. I didn't see him, but there was a folder for me in the hallway when I walked through from the computer room. There was a separate package from Rüdiger too.

I'd spent the evening on CompuServe, finding out as much as I could about Paris, and looking for any reference to Nicolas Thiel. There was very little about him, aside from a picture at a charity fundraising event. There's always something incongruous about bad people using charity as a way of somehow validating themselves.

The printed itinerary showed an hour and a half on a train from Koblenz to Cologne, then a further three and a half hours on an international train to Gare du Nord in Paris. As well as the tickets and hotel details, Matt had thoughtfully left me a choice of three English-language novels to read on the way: John Grisham's

The Pelican Brief, *Meeting Evil* by Thomas Berger and Val McDermid's *Dead Beat*.

I wondered if the choice was deliberate or accidental. I didn't want anything to do with lawyers, so *The Pelican Brief* was out, and I suspected I'd have my fill of meeting evil over the next few days. I chose *Dead Beat*.

According to the blurb, it was about a female private detective from Manchester called Kate Brannigan who agrees to track down a missing songwriter as a favour to her journalist boyfriend.

I thought of Anna, back home. She was from Manchester. She'd agreed to help track down a newspaper writer – me – as a favour to a reporter she'd dearly like to be her boyfriend, even if she's always too scared to admit it. And to make the coincidence even more scary, the restaurant I was supposed to be meeting Danny in, on the day I disappeared, was called Brannigan's.

Had Matt chosen it deliberately? Was it some kind of joke? Or just a coincidence? Was there a secret message hidden in the text? I leafed through the pages, in case a note should fall out, or to see if he'd highlighted a particular passage. But the pages were clean and the paperback spine was perfect, meaning the book was new and had never been read.

I packed it into my overnight bag, along with my Kaarina Mäkinen passport. It was already past midnight. So much for the early night. Monday was going to be a long day.

Chapter 33

Monday, September 13th, 1993

THE train journey was uneventful, but the bustle of Paris was in stark contrast to the calm and beautiful Rhine views of the Schloss. The area immediately around Gare du Nord was especially noisy and chaotic, with preparations well underway for the forthcoming launch of the direct Channel Tunnel train service to London. In retrospect, learning French would have been useful. But at least I could now pretend to be a clueless German person rather than a British one. That might make the locals a little bit more forgiving.

According to the map, it was about a ten-minute walk to the Hotel Trudaine. After the dust and congestion around the station, it was a pleasant surprise to find a beautiful, shaded, tree-lined street, dominated by six-storey classical Parisian terraces on either side. There was a wide choice of shops and restaurants at ground level. Many of the buildings had balconies that overlooked the cobbled street and the raised planted area that ran through the middle of its full length, keeping the two narrow lanes of traffic apart.

Cars were parked on one side of the street: a mixture of classic French Renaults, Peugeots and Citroëns. But in amongst them, about a hundred yards before my hotel, there was a black Porsche with a German "D" sticker on its rear bumper. Immediately I shrank back into a shop doorway. Surely that was too much of a coincidence? But again, there was no sign of the driver. With a deep and tentative breath, I approached the car. What had Matt said? Something about a parking permit from the local hospital on the windscreen? I got close enough to check, but the windscreen was clear. I told myself there must be thousands of black Porsches on the streets of Europe, but nevertheless, something about the way it was just sitting there unnerved me.

The hotel was small but welcoming. Once I'd checked in, I set out into the fading warmth of mid-afternoon, with a glance in the direction of the Porsche. I was relieved to see that it was no longer there. Sylvain had agreed to meet me at 4pm, but that gave me just over an hour to get my bearings.

Montmartre, in northern Paris, is generally considered one of the city's most romantic areas, dominated by the Sacré-Coeur cathedral which sits atop its highest hill. But at the foot lies the altogether less romantic Pigalle district, on the border between the ninth and eighteenth arrondissements. It's an area known for a dark underworld of sleaze, prostitution, drug dens, peep shows and sex shops - alongside the world-famous Moulin Rouge cabaret club that tempts tourists looking for old-school Parisian burlesque. Hustlers and pickpockets prowl the same streets as rival drug gangs. And in amongst it all was *Épice Bleue* - or Blue Spice - the strip club owned by Nicolas Thiel.

Within ten minutes of leaving my hotel, I found the club, nestled on a corner next to a tacky souvenir shop and opposite a video cabin offering the latest XXX films by the minute. It looked exactly like the picture that showed Colin Medland entering a building. I could even see precisely where the car with the yellow headlamp had been parked. It was an excellent start.

I walked the full length of Boulevard de Clichy, the main road running straight through the district. Even in the daylight it was an intimidating place. Several times I felt threatened just by being there, and was frequently hassled into entering clip joints by hollow-eyed people who were unwilling to take no for an answer. I ignored them and walked on, often having to speed up to get away. At the end, I crossed over and made the same journey back on the other side. It was no less depressing. I'd expected Pigalle to be grim, but this was another league. And yet I knew I'd have to return, in the dark, and actually enter Thiel's club if the trip was to prove a success. In retrospect I was hugely relieved that Matt had insisted on giving me a chaperone.

Just before 4pm, I made it to the coffee shop where we'd arranged to meet. I ordered a cappuccino and took a stool by the window, facing the entrance of the Pigalle Metro station. I was looking for a slim man with dark hair, aged thirty-five and 5'10" tall.

But 4pm came and went, and while I saw a few people who possibly fitted that description, only one came anywhere near the coffee shop. And even he arrived with his wife or girlfriend, and when he placed an order it was evident that he was English and hardly spoke a word of French.

I beckoned to a waiter, and asked him to confirm the address, just to make sure I was definitely in the right place. I was. So, I ordered a second drink and continued my vigil, but still nobody showed. At 5pm I thought I'd give it a final fifteen minutes, just in case I'd got my timing wrong, but even with an extra five minutes on top of that, there was still no sign of him.

Reluctantly, I decided to give up, and head back to my hotel. The no-show presented a significant problem, and I needed time and space to come up with an alternative plan.

I was in my room, on the verge of unpacking my overnight bag, when the telephone by the bed started ringing.

"*Bonjour*," I said, hoping they wouldn't immediately launch into French, or I'd be in a world of trouble. Luckily, they didn't.

"Miss Mäkinen, this is reception," said a female voice. "You have a visitor downstairs. A Monsieur Sylvain Audat."

"Ah, brilliant," I said. "I'll pop straight down. *Merci beaucoup*."

Problem solved.

Or so I thought. My real problems were just beginning.

Chapter 34

W HEN the lift doors opened, there was only one person in reception apart from the staff behind the desk. But if it was Sylvain, he wasn't what I was expecting. He was about the right height but looked a good few years older than thirty-five, and his dark hair, at least what was left of it, was showing distinct signs of grey. I'd hardly have described him as slim, either. But he turned as I emerged from the lift, and extended his hand, confirming that was, indeed, his name.

"I apologise for not showing," he said. "I had a problem that delayed me. I think I arrived just after you left."

"Don't worry," I said. "As long as you're okay. Should we go for a drink?" In truth I didn't think I could face any more coffee, but there was always the option of sparkling water.

"Let's go to your room," he said. "Maybe it's better to discuss things in private?"

"Okay," I said, taking a step back towards the lift. It seemed logical I suppose. As the lift doors opened, I saw the receptionist smile. She clearly thought I was up to some sort of bedroom mischief.

On the fifth floor, I led Sylvain along the corridor to my room, then opened the door and showed him inside. It was a small space, with not much room apart from a double bed and a small desk beside the window.

"Can I get you a drink?" I asked, hoping there was a mini bar. Luckily he declined so I didn't have to find out.

Sylvain took the chair by the desk while I sat on the bed, next to my bag.

"How are you finding Paris?" he asked.

"It's okay so far," I said. "I've been for a walk around Pigalle which was horrible, but the hotel seems okay."

"It's Paris. You must come again and I'll show you the good parts."

"I've been a few times over the years, and done lots of the tourist things. But Matt speaks highly of you. I'm sure we'll be okay."

He frowned.

"How do you mean we'll be okay?" he said.

"I mean when we go to Thiel's club."

The frown didn't lift.

"We aren't going to a club," he said.

"We are. That's the whole point."

He shook his head.

"No, I'm taking you to meet someone. You need to come with me. My car is downstairs."

That wasn't in the plan. And it was hauntingly similar to what I'd been told by Henning Bierstadt, back in the hotel in Cologne, in February. Instinctively I began to feel uncomfortable.

"I'm not going anywhere with you apart from the club," I said. "Possibly dinner, but otherwise that is very much that."

I didn't like his expression any more than the fact that he looked nothing like his description. That he hadn't turned up when he should have done, and seemed to have an agenda all of his own. And that he was in my room, when increasingly I was beginning to think that this wasn't Sylvain at all.

"I said, you need to come with me," he said, his voice suddenly hard. And as he started to move towards me, and his jacket fell open, I saw the telltale butt of a pistol in his inside pocket.

I didn't wait long enough to give him the benefit of the doubt. I was up in a blink, and as he reached out to grab me, I ducked and turned, and then punched him hard in the throat, exactly as Rüdiger had shown me. The initial blow took him by surprise but didn't stop him. The second and third did. And as he fell to the floor, I added a fourth for good measure.

While he was out cold, I went through his pockets. There was no ID, but there was a gun, a roll of gaffer tape, and a phial of clear liquid that was possibly intended to drug me. Moving quickly, I wrapped his wrists together behind his back with tape. More tape secured his knees and ankles, and I attached those to the leg of the bed.

Looking at the pistol, I was tempted to finish the job properly, but a dead body in a hotel room could only ever draw attention to myself, and if there was one thing I was trying to avoid in Paris, aside from being murdered, it was that.

Instead, I decided to wait till he came round so I could question him. Then I could decide where to take this from there.

Gradually, he opened one eye, squinted and tried to open another. If he was surprised to find himself on the floor, taped up, he must have been even more surprised to see me sitting over him, pointing his own gun at his head.

And then he closed his eyes again. But not before a smile crept over his battered face.

It took me a second to realise why. The bastard.

He should have had the job done by now. The fact that he hadn't would have alerted his backup. They'd be on their way.

They could be with me at any moment. They could be about to charge down my door now.

With one last elbow to the face and then an uppercut under the chin that seemed to knock him back out cold, I quickly grabbed my bag and room key. I edged open the door and scanned the corridor. It was clear.

I elected for the stairs, rather than the lift. That was a serious misjudgement. Before I'd reached the second step, I saw a black-clad man approaching me, two flights below, gaining fast, his weapon looking primed and ready.

I raced back upstairs and along the corridor. Thankfully I had a two-flight head start. With a bit of luck, the lift would still be on my floor. A distant ping as the doors opened gave me a surge of hope. But as I turned the corner it fell away.

Another man was standing there already, blocking my way, his arm outstretched and the barrel of his gun pointing at my heart.

Chapter 35

"YOU must come with us," said the man by the lift, in English with a heavy French accent. He was dressed in black, with Mediterranean-looking skin, dark hair and cold eyes.

Behind me, his colleague was approaching. I turned. He had slowed to a walk, but his gun was also pointing at me.

"Really?" I said, in a calm voice, then shrugged and started to walk towards him. "Okay."

I think that surprised him. I like the element of surprise. There was another one coming.

In one fast and fluid movement, I reached for the Glock 23 that was loaded and hidden in the back of my waistband, and before he'd even had a chance to process what he was seeing, a bullet exploded into his arm, causing him to drop his weapon. But the shot alerted his colleague, who opened fire just as I dived to the ground.

Suddenly the gunshot to the arm was the least of the first man's worries. The second and third from his friend blasted his chest wide open, saving me a task. I returned fire, using the corpse as a shield, but the stair man had seen enough. He turned and fled, just as I could hear shouting and screams coming from all directions.

I collected my bag from where I'd dropped it, pocketed the Glock, then pressed the button for the lift, taking a moment to catch my breath while I waited for the doors to open.

Sometimes looking like an innocent female tourist has its advantages. By the time the lift reached the ground floor, police were streaming into the building. The gunman emerged from the stairs, and shouted something in my direction, but two heavily armed officers wrestled him to the floor.

"Excuse me, what's happening?" I asked the nearest policeman in my most polite voice.

"Clear the lobby please," he said by way of reply.

I nodded and walked past him, and headed out into the evening. And past the black Porsche that had reappeared on my street.

I had no contact and now no hotel room, but I still had my phone. When I was a couple of blocks away, I called Matt.

"How's Paris?" he asked.

"So far so good," I lied. The last thing I needed was any kind of *told you so*. "Sylvain didn't show, though. Do you have his home address?"

"I'll call you back in a moment."

While I waited for him, I practised the lessons I'd learned in my counter-surveillance training: cutting through buildings, doubling back, abrupt changes of direction, and all sorts else. I didn't think anyone was following me, but the events at the hotel had been a warning. I had no idea what the police would think when they found a body in the corridor and an unconscious man taped up in my bedroom, but once they started looking for me too, my problems would grow exponentially.

Logic suggested this was all far too dangerous. That I should get the first train back to Germany. But if I did, then I went back a failure, and the bad guys won. I would just have to be more careful.

One thing bothered me above all others.

How?

How did they know where I was? How did they know who I was supposed to be meeting?

It was surely impossible that somebody had been following us from London. I suppose we could have been tailed to the airfield, and then someone else could have picked us up in Germany. But really? Because then they'd have to have followed me on the train all the way to Paris, and even if they'd done that, even if they'd followed me to my hotel in a black Porsche, how could they possibly have known about Sylvain?

I'd left my bag in my room, with the printed itinerary. But that only had the details of my trains and hotel reservation. There was no mention of the meeting. So even if someone had broken in while I was walking round Pigalle, there was nothing that would have given them any indication.

So no, there was absolutely no way Thiel could have known I was heading to Paris. And no way he'd have known who I was meeting with, unless there'd been a leak somewhere.

That led me to a conclusion that was both logical and horrifying. Somebody must have either bugged our phones or the Schloss itself.

It would be impossible to bug the phones. They were mobiles. Short of hacking into the mobile phone signal across multiple countries, I couldn't see how that could be done. Yes, they could theoretically access a mailbox, but we hadn't left voice messages. In fact we hadn't even discussed the itinerary over the phone. So that left the building. But when? How? It was time to think the unthinkable.

Had anyone visited while we were in London? No, whoever

this was had information from before that. I wracked my brain for any recent unexpected guests, but I couldn't think of any. The last time there were lots of visitors was the last party, just over three weeks ago. Any of the guests could have had ample opportunity to set bugs while we were all otherwise distracted, but that was a horrible thought. It meant there was a traitor in our midst. And it meant everything that had been said in the Schloss for the last three weeks could have fallen into enemy hands.

But even that didn't make sense. Thiel was after me. As far as I was aware, he didn't have any other gripe with our organisation. Yes, I could prove a link between Colin Medland and his club, but that could easily be explained. Thiel's partner, Saskia, was Florian Straub's cousin. Straub was the villain here, wasn't he? Even if Matt didn't think so. Straub wanted to blackmail Colin, and took him to Paris to a club he knew through his family connections. It didn't mean Thiel was involved any more than that.

And yet if Matt was right and this wasn't Florian Straub's style, who was behind it? Graham bloody March? Had he had a sudden transformation from corrupt idiot to ruthless criminal mastermind? I really couldn't see it.

So that brought me back to Nicolas Thiel. I needed to see inside his office. I needed to look at his computer, if he had one. And yet even before I'd stepped into the place, they'd been onto me and tried to kill me.

I took a deep breath, and lit a cigarette for the first time since arriving in Paris.

My phone started ringing.

"Hi Matt," I said.

"Hi, I've got you Sylvain's address," he said. "Have you got a pen?"

"One moment."

I had a pen in my trench coat pocket. My bigger issue was paper. I folded back the lid of my cigarette packet and told him to fire away. He gave me an address that meant nothing to me. It could have been next door. It could have been a dozen miles away.

"Thanks," I said. "I'll pop round and see if he's there."

"Is everything else all right? You sound on edge."

"I don't know Paris as well as I'd like to, that's all. I'll get a taxi."

"Okay. Good plan."

"There is just one thing, actually, while you're on."

"Go on."

"Just a security issue. How often do we sweep the Schloss for bugs?"

"What makes you ask that?"

"Nothing really. It was just something I thought about on the train coming over."

"Okay. Walter does it weekly. Sometimes more often. But as far as I'm aware he's never found anything."

"That's good." I thought for a moment. "And that's not just because he's using faulty equipment?"

Matt laughed.

"No, I assure you, it's working properly. But you're obviously asking for a reason."

"No, just curious, that's all. We have parties. People come from all over. I just want to make sure that nobody could leave anything behind."

"Well, you don't need to worry about that," he said. "Apart from anything else, you have to be one of the most trusted to even get an invitation. But no, if anybody ever did, it would be found immediately and there'd be a major investigation."

"Okay, that's good to know."

I ended the call. Was it good to know? In one sense it was. But in another it raised an even bigger question, which took me back to the beginning. How?

———

By the time the taxi dropped me outside Sylvain Audat's house, it was dark and the streets were filled with yellow headlamps. It was such a typically French scene, but already there was the odd set of white ones amongst them. The end of an era was imminent.

Conversely, Sylvain's house was dark. It was a small, detached property, deep into the outskirts of the city. There was a Renault 21 in the drive, but it didn't look like anyone was home.

Nevertheless, I knocked at the door. And when it wasn't answered, I walked round to the side, where a smaller door opened into the kitchen. I tried it, but it was locked. A few minutes later I'd fixed that.

I flicked on the kitchen light. It looked a reasonably well-appointed room, with modern high-gloss units and integrated appliances. A doorway led to the hallway and from there to a choice of either a staircase or a living room on the ground floor. There was a strange, cloying aroma.

I tried the living room first. I didn't need to go any further than that. The description of Sylvain had been quite accurate, but there was a recent addition: the bullet hole between his eyes that had removed the back of his head. The body had been left taped to a chair in the middle of the room. At least that explained why he hadn't come to meet me.

I didn't have time to feel nauseous. Because a noise from the kitchen had me reaching for my gun.

Chapter 36

I SWITCHED off the living room light, then peered into the darkness of the hallway, my finger on the trigger of the Glock. The noise came from the kitchen again. I edged forward and found the source.

A black and white cat was standing on the kitchen counter. It must have followed me in when I opened the side door. It mewed as it saw me, then jumped down and rubbed itself against my legs. I thought the poor thing must be hungry. I needed to get out of there, but it was heartbreaking enough to think of a cat losing its owner without also thinking of it going hungry.

Wrapping my hands in my sleeves, I opened a couple of cupboards until I found a box of dried cat food, then shook out a generous helping into a bowl. I refilled the water bowl too, wished my new furry friend the very best of luck, and then headed back outside.

Things were going from exceptionally bad to substantially even worse. I now had no idea where I even was. A colleague had died. And the people who were after me were clearly as ruthless as they looked. It was decision time.

I went back into the house and did a search for a set of

Renault car keys. It didn't take long. The engine fired up at the first attempt, and I pulled onto the road and looked for signs to central Paris. When the buildings started to get larger and closer together, I began to keep my eyes peeled for a Metro station. It didn't matter which.

Eventually I spotted one. Porte de Charenton. I parked the car, making sure to wipe my fingerprints from the steering wheel and gearstick, for what it was worth, then locked the door and started walking towards the station entrance.

And then I stopped. The police would only be looking for the car once they discovered Sylvain had been murdered. Until then, it was mine to use. Traffic in central Paris was horrendous, but it gave me a degree of flexibility and the possibility of making a getaway that would be denied if I went back to relying on public transport. The key thing now was not to panic. To keep an element of control.

I called Matt again.

"So soon?" he said. "What's up now?"

"I don't like to bother you, because I know you're busy, but there is something I thought I should tell you," I said.

"You're missing me?"

"Obviously that, but something serious."

Cars were streaming past, Parisians heading to who knows where. Maybe for a safe night at home, watching TV with their loved ones. I'd rarely felt so alien.

"That doesn't sound good."

"It isn't. I found Sylvain. He'd been murdered."

"*What?*"

I paused for a moment to let it sink in.

"What do you mean murdered? How?"

"Taped to a chair, bullet to the forehead. Single shot as far as I could tell. I didn't hang around long enough to look for others."

"Fucking hell."

I don't think I'd ever heard him use the F-word before. It was time to explain about the hotel. I told him about the fake Sylvain, who, to the best of my knowledge, was still out cold on my bedroom floor. The two gunmen, one arrested, and the other dead.

"You need to come back," he said.

"No. I'm here to do a job."

"It's too dangerous. We need to regroup. Rethink. Give you suitable backup at least."

"And again, what was that about everyone being equal? No chain of command?"

"I'm not giving you orders. I'm giving you advice."

"Okay. Well, thank you for the advice. But I didn't come here to fail. I've just spent more than half a year getting into shape for this."

He used the F-word again.

"And we don't want to run the risk that all that effort is wasted by a bullet on your first trip out," he continued.

"I won't get shot. And if I do, you can tell me you told me so at my funeral."

"It's not funny."

"I'm not attempting to amuse you. I pride myself on doing a job properly. And in seeing the dark side of everyone I meet."

"Me included?"

"You don't even want to begin to think about my perception of your dark side. But the point is, I'm astute. I'll be alert."

"And yet you nearly got captured at the hotel."

"Oh come on, that was seven months ago."

"No, I mean this afternoon."

My laugh was suitably derisive.

"You think I nearly got captured? At no point was I ever in any danger. Trust me. Trust Rüdiger's training. You'll notice that this time I didn't need you to come to save me, much as I welcome your attempts at seduction. I'm learning."

He sounded exasperated.

"You don't know how many people are after you."

"No, but I do know it's at least two fewer than this afternoon. So the way I look at it, my odds just improved substantially. And even at the old odds, I've already fended off three of them."

"You're going to go through with this, aren't you?"

"I've told you, I'm not coming back to Germany a failure."

By the third F-word, the novelty was wearing off.

"Do we have any contacts here other than Sylvain?" I asked.

"We do, but no one that knows anything about Thiel or his club."

I thought for a moment.

"But I could meet them?"

"For backup?"

"For cover. I think I'd draw less attention to myself if I was part of a loved-up couple, having a romantic night out, exploring the seedier side of Paris."

"Jesus. Wait there. I'll call you back."

Matt hammered Nicolas Thiel's number into his phone.

"What the fuck is happening?" he snarled when the Frenchman answered.

"Is that Matt Sommer?" asked Thiel.

"Yes, it's bloody Matt Sommer. And I specifically told you not to lay a finger on Clare. Not to let anyone else lay a finger on Clare. That I was going to deliver Clare to you on Thursday. And so back to the original question: what the fuck is happening?"

Thiel hesitated for a moment.

"I genuinely don't know," he said. "You tell me."

"I'll bloody tell you. The man she was meeting was murdered. Three people turned up at her hotel, trying to capture her. One of them's dead. One has been arrested. And God knows what happened to the third."

"Let me stop you there," said Nicolas. "I promise you, none of that is anything to do with me."

"You expect me to believe that?"

"Yes, I do actually. Because despite the overwhelming temptation, and despite what you think of me, I'm very much a man of my word. For your information, we're looking out for Clare but so far we haven't seen any sign."

Matt paused for a moment to gather his breath.

"Well, somebody did," he said.

"And again I assure you it isn't me. When you rang me and told me she was coming, I called one of my men, said we need to be ready, and here's what I want you to do. And do you know what that was? Against every instinct, I told him that we needed to protect her, and that he was responsible for making sure that none of my staff did anything to cause her any harm in an attempt to impress me. And do you know why I did that? As a gesture of goodwill to you. So do not ring me up and start throwing around accusations or I'll tell you what will happen. I'll cancel the deal. And I *will* take her tonight. And then all bets are off."

"Even if that's true, there's somebody out there," said Matt. "And they've killed one of our people in Paris."

"And to reiterate, I don't even know who your people in Paris are."

That was actually a valid point. Matt sighed.

"In that case, I can only apologise," he said. "And thank you for your understanding."

"Is she still coming in?"

"You know what? I really don't know."

"If she does, I guarantee you that nobody here will cause her any harm today. But I cannot say the same for Thursday."

"I understand."

Matt ended the call, then redialled the number for Clare.

"Have you still got that pen?" asked Matt.

"I have."

"Then make a note of this."

He gave me a number, then read it back to make sure I'd got it right.

"Who's that?" I asked.

"Philippe Huguet. And before you ask, I don't know much about him. He's young, but he's in Paris and he should be available. Try not to get him killed."

"I'm going to try not to get anyone killed."

"You especially."

"Your concern is touching, Matt. It's almost as though you like me."

He didn't laugh so much as make a strange gurgling noise.

"Just make sure you get home safely," he said. "What are you going to do now?"

"I'm going to call Philippe, then find a new hotel, and then hopefully have an exciting time exploring nightclubs."

"Let me know where you're staying."

"Does it matter?"

"Of course it does. I might need to contact you."

"You've got this phone."

I ended the call, then rang Philippe and arranged to meet him outside Pigalle station at 10pm. That gave me less than two hours to find a hotel and grab food from somewhere. Or maybe forgo food and resign myself to spending the night in the car.

This time, nobody knew about the meeting apart from the two of us, but I would still have to be on my guard. If somebody tried to kill us, I'd only have myself to blame.

Chapter 37

THE new hotel was reasonably awful, with a room even smaller than the last one, but at least it had vacancies. That said, judging by the state of the place, it was no real surprise. It was close to the Poissonière Metro station, which even my limited knowledge of French told me was something to do with fish, but sounded a lot more deadly, and I hoped that wasn't an omen.

It didn't seem worth unpacking my bag, but there was time for a very quick shower to freshen up. Once I was dry, I tied back my hair, applied very quick make-up, then changed into a black dress that was slightly shorter than my trench coat, and in retrospect made me look like some kind of female flasher. God, I wasn't having a good day. I added a scarf for warmth and a hat to hide the hair disaster, then tried on the reading glasses. They still made my eyes go funny, but it was the best I was going to manage in terms of disguise.

Sadly, Poissonière was on a completely different line to Pigalle, and taking the Metro would have involved two changes. But I didn't really fancy going down on the Metro on my own late at night, in any case. To walk, it was less than three-quarters of a mile, but that didn't hold much appeal either. So I took the car. It took four times as long to find a parking space as it did to drive, but nevertheless, I made it to the meeting point with a couple of minutes to spare.

I was exhausted, hungry, and still suffering from a degree of shock, but I tried to put on a brave face. That said, something about Philippe immediately annoyed me. I don't know whether it was his choice of shoes, which were overly showy light brown slip-ons, or his slight air of arrogance, but I found it a struggle to hide my irritation. He was about six foot tall, with slicked-back hair, and an equally annoying cheap pale grey suit with a sheen that reminded me of the dull side of a roll of Bacofoil.

All that said, he was one of us. He was there to help me. And I therefore had to give him the benefit of the doubt. We shook hands, I thanked him for coming, then we linked arms and started to weave our way through the late-night throng.

"This is it," I said, when we reached *Épice Bleue*.

"And you're sure about this?"

"Not really, but I need to see inside the place. We don't have to stay long."

With a deep breath, perhaps my last-ever out in the open, I took a step forward.

I don't think the door staff were used to men taking a female partner, but nonetheless, they took our money and held open a dark blue velvet curtain to let us inside.

It was every bit as dingy and dismal as I'd expected, despite the abundance of black leather and red velvet. Even as someone who has the occasional cigarette, I almost coughed at the thick smoke in the air. There was a stage at one end, with a shiny pole and a mirrorball, and a further three smaller podiums dotted around among a dozen or so neon-lit alcoves. The stage was empty, but bland eurodisco was pumping out of the speakers.

Once my eyes had adjusted, I calculated that about half of the alcoves were occupied. A couple of tired-looking, bikini-clad strippers were sitting either side of a man who looked old enough to be their grandfather, while another was gyrating in a corner in front of a pair of legs that were presumably attached to someone else.

Philippe led me to an empty alcove in the far left corner, behind a low, sticky-looking table. It gave us a great view of most of the club, although it was at an oblique angle to the stage. That was no great loss to the world of entertainment.

Almost immediately, a waitress descended, with a drinks menu and ashtray. Philippe ordered a Kronenberg, which would almost certainly be a watered-down version of something else, while I opted for a Coca-Cola Light. I lit a cigarette while we waited, loathing everything about the place. While I regretted almost every aspect of my criminal aberration, I felt no guilt at all about defrauding the man who profited from this. I offered Philippe my packet of Silk Cut, but he lit something foul-smelling and French instead.

As soon as the drinks arrived, a gaunt-looking stripper approached, and asked if we would like to buy her one too. I'd seen the extortionate dancer drink prices on the menu, so politely declined. She didn't seem happy, and rubbed her hand on Philippe's thigh and whispered something into his ear. He shook his head and she departed, but it had attracted the attention of a couple of bouncers, who were now staring in our direction.

I crossed my legs, grateful to feel the reassuring heft of the Glock in my pocket.

"What did she want?" I asked, leaning in to Philippe, and resting my head on his shoulder. At least there was no chance of being overheard over the synthetic pulse of the music.

"She thought I might be more willing to buy her one than you were," he said. "I suspect she'll be back."

I kissed his cheek, for no reason other than I hoped it made us look like a couple, then snuggled in as he put his arm around me. It felt strange to be intimate with a total stranger, but it was all part of the role.

Eventually, a dancer appeared on the main stage, giving a half-hearted striptease that lasted the duration of one 2 Unlimited track, and earned a muted round of applause.

There was no sign of Nicolas, but there was a doorway at the back that was guarded by the most brutal-looking bouncer of all. Occasionally we saw a stripper lead a customer through a curtained-off area at the far side.

Another woman approached and asked if she could join us. We declined, but she sat down anyway, on Philippe's left. Immediately the waitress appeared, and told us we needed to buy her a drink. After much protest, which nearly turned angry, they both departed. But I knew our time was running out.

It was definitely the right place. I recognised it from the pictures. But I didn't think we were going to gain any more by staying, apart from possibly a thorough kicking from the bouncers.

"Let's go," I whispered. I'm not sure he heard me, but got the message when I started to stand up. Feeling the glare of the eyes of all of the staff, we made our way through the dark blue curtain and then back out into the night. I couldn't stop an involuntary shudder.

"Well, that was awful," I said, as we linked arms. "I'm not a prude, and I can admire the female form, but God, that was depressing."

Philippe didn't say much, but I hoped he at least agreed with me, rather than finding it in any way a turn-on.

This, however, was where my afternoon excursion began to pay dividends. I led Philippe to a bar across the street that had a small lean-to annexe on the pavement at the front. Most of the customers were inside the main building, where it was warmer, but we took a table by the window, which afforded us a view of *Épice Bleue*.

"Did you learn much?" he asked.

"As much as I needed to," I said, relieved to be able to remove the glasses. Obviously I still wanted to get into Nicolas Thiel's office, but I didn't feel the need to discuss that. "Have you heard of the place before?"

He shook his head.

"I know the area, of course. But this is mainly for tourists and drug addicts."

A waiter appeared. We ordered the same drinks again, and then a bowl of French fries. It was hardly Parisian fine dining, but hunger was getting the better of me. I offered to share with Philippe when they arrived, but thankfully he declined, and I wasn't in the mood to insist.

As we watched the club, I asked him about his life, what he did, and how he got involved with the Blood Angel network. I have no idea if anything he told me was true, but in any case, there was the traditional lack of detail.

"Have you ever been to any of the parties?" I asked.

"In Koblenz?" His eyes lit up. "It's my dream to be invited to one of the parties."

"Really?"

"Of course. Have you?"

I hesitated, not wanting to give the wrong impression of either myself or my standing within the network.

"I've heard they're quite lively," I said instead.

"They're meant to be incredible."

In fairness, despite my original reservations and his dreadful fashion sense, I was warming to him. His French accent was kind of sexy, as French accents always are. He was far from my type, but it wasn't a hardship to spend time in his company, and I began to look forward to perhaps meeting him again, if I ever needed to return to Paris.

Throughout it all, we kept watch on the club, keeping track of people going in. Single men. Groups of men. Occasionally somebody would be escorted out by one of the door staff, who then walked with him to the nearest cash machine. Occasionally one would leave with a woman he didn't go in with. Eventually the women returned alone. It was clearly a front for prostitution.

I sensed our bar staff hovering, and when I looked round, realised why. All of the customers had left, and they were getting ready to close up.

"Is that everything for tonight?" asked Philippe with a shiver as we returned to the street.

"Nearly," I said. "I want to look round the side of the building and see if there's access from the back."

He let me lead the way. We crossed the street, but further down, away from the club itself. I didn't want to run the risk of encountering the door staff.

The side street that ran alongside the club was dark, which was both a good and a bad thing. It gave us cover, but equally only added to the intimidating feel of the area. I half expected to be jumped upon by a crazed junkie mugger. At the back, a deserted alley ran along the rear of the block. That looked scarier still. I could just make out a rear entrance and fire door at the back of the club, although from a distance it appeared to be blocked by a bottle skip.

From the alley we heard the sound of a car engine bursting into life, and just had time to shrink back into the shadows before being picked out by its headlights. A moment later, a sleek black Mercedes pulled past us. I shrank back further still, recognising the figure of Nicolas Thiel in the front passenger seat. He didn't see me, but it was due to luck rather than judgement.

Once it was safe to move, we walked back to the Pigalle

Metro. I offered Philippe a lift to wherever he was headed, but he insisted that he could take a taxi.

It had been a curiously depressing end to a dark and terrifying day. But as I watched Philippe disappear back into the night, I knew it was far from over for me.

Chapter 38

I DROVE back to my hotel to give myself a chance to think. It was time to come up with a plan.

Above all else, I needed to see inside Nicolas Thiel's office. I could hardly attempt to approach him and gain his trust. He'd know who I was, and kill me.

But breaking into the club carried huge danger. Even once the door staff left for the night, there would be strong physical security, as well as an alarm. So, even if I could break through the locks, I wouldn't have long before trouble arrived.

There had to be a better way.

The more I thought about it, the less likely it was that Nicolas would keep any evidence in his office. I needed to know where he lived. But then, if he had any sense, he was unlikely to keep anything at his house either. And the security there would be even more intense. I wasn't sure of the law in France, but if he caught me breaking in to his home, there was a fair chance he could kill me and claim it was self-defence.

The only option, then, was the club. It closed at 2am. That was still an hour away, and I should probably leave it for an hour after that, to make sure the coast was clear. But even then, the alarm issue wasn't going to go away. I lay on my bed and closed my eyes to think, but not before setting my alarm, just in case the overwhelming tiredness claimed me.

Nicolas Thiel answered a call on his mobile phone, as his driver carved a path through the late-night Paris traffic.

"Who is this?"

"Sorry to call you so late," said the voice. "It's Philippe Huguet."

"Philippe. Calling to make arrangements to clear your debt? You do understand I'm not a patient man?"

"I do. And possibly." The voice sounded nervous. "I've got some information for you that I think could be worth something."

"That depends on the type of information."

"I've just spent a couple of hours in the company of Clare Woodbrook."

Nicolas ran his hand through his hair, then turned to his driver and smiled.

"Really? Where is she now?"

"She was going back to her hotel."

"Which is?"

"I don't know."

"And precisely what use is that to me?"

Philippe sounded almost pleading.

"At least you know she's in Paris. And hopefully I'll be seeing her again."

"And you're absolutely sure it's her?"

"One hundred percent."

"If you're lying to me, I could make things even more difficult for you."

"I promise you I'm telling you the truth. I'll bring her to you."

Nicolas did a quick calculation. He'd promised Matt Sommer that he wouldn't do anything to harm Clare on Monday night. But if she was hanging round Paris for a couple of days, he hadn't made any promise about Tuesday ...

"Speak to me again when you know the hotel," he said, then ended the call. He had to make one of his own.

I parked in the alley, turned off the headlamps and waited. The car's digital clock showed 1.58am. Two minutes later, I got out of the car, lifted a small backpack over my shoulder, and crept along towards the club. My hand was on the Glock, which was loaded and ready. At the back of the club, I crouched down behind the bottle skip. My black sweatshirt was much less stylish than the trench coat, but it did a far better job at camouflage.

A couple of taxis pulled into the alley, and the rear door to the club opened. The dancers emerged, and then were whisked away. More taxis appeared. This time it was the bar staff. Three of the bouncers left next, but the lights inside were still on.

Finally, at about 2.30am, the final person emerged. I heard the beep of an alarm being set as he locked the door behind him, and then started to add a heavy-duty padlock for good measure.

He was twice the size of me. But I had the element of surprise. I had Rüdiger's training. And I had an empty wine bottle from the skip that I brought crashing down on his skull.

The first blow bounced off, but was enough to grab his attention. He turned and yelled, then made a lunge for me. I was agile enough to leap aside, then followed with the butt of the Glock against his temple. This time he looked dazed, and off balance. My knee to his groin took his breath away, but the final blow was delivered by a wooden pallet that, with every ounce of my strength, I smashed over his head.

When I was convinced he was out cold and likely to stay that way, I helped myself to his keys and alarm fob, unlocked the door, disabled the alarm, and headed inside.

Chapter 39

WITH a mental note of gratitude to Rüdiger for all of his strength and conditioning work, I dragged the security man inside, then looked for something to tie him up with. I found several lengths of electrical cable and decided they would do. I wrapped them tightly round his wrists and ankles, then added some gaffer tape from the backpack for good measure, before patting down his pockets, looking for a phone or weapons. I found both. My first instinct was to take them, but equally I had no idea what crimes the gun might be linked to, and I had to hope he'd be too ashamed to report his failings. Still, I put them in my bag for the time being.

Once he was secure, I headed through the kitchen into the club itself. It was even less welcoming in darkness. A faint glow of neon from the bar area cast an eerie glow over the main room. I stashed the gun and phone behind the bar, but that wasn't my main focus of interest. In the dim light, the smell of the place seemed even stronger. It was a nauseating mixture of stale cigarette smoke, disinfectant and bodily fluids.

I took a torch from my backpack, then quickly checked the curtained-off area. A short corridor led to a door. I opened it. A mattress lay on the floor in the centre of the room. Beside it, a wastepaper basket was overflowing with tissue paper, wet wipes and used condoms. Nice. That confirmed prostitution, beyond any reasonable doubt. I took a couple of pictures for evidence, the flash momentarily blinding me on each occasion.

Aware of the time, and the pounding of my heart, I returned to the main room, then tried the door that had been guarded by the biggest bouncer. It opened to reveal a staircase. At the top, there was a locked door.

I tried all of the keys on the keyring. None of them worked.

I reached for the Glock and weighed up my options. I could shoot out the lock, but then they'd know I'd been there.

On balance, that was not my problem. I wasn't going to get this chance again. I took aim, and fired.

The office was huge. It was dominated by a large desk that faced a leather sofa across a Persian rug. All along one wall were a collection of filing cabinets.

I started searching through them. Some were unlocked, but they only seemed to contain information relating to the club itself. Receipts, purchase orders, staff records.

Others I had to force. I wasn't bothered about leaving evidence of a disturbance. I was more intent on finding what I came for.

Again, a lot of it was business-related. There were bank statements, copies of accounts. Handbooks for pieces of equipment.

I thought I heard a noise. I stopped dead, my hand gripping the Glock.

Slowly I edged back to the door and looked out to the landing, and down to the stairs. But it was still dark and there was no sign of movement. I put it down to my nerves which were on edge, a sense of panic creeping up and threatening to overpower me.

I ran back to the filing cabinets and rifled through them, but there was still nothing to incriminate Thiel.

I took a deep breath, trying to steady my hand, aware that my heart rate was getting dangerously high. Knowing that my time was running out. And still I'd found nothing.

But that left the desk.

A set of drawers filled the space under one side. They, too, were locked. I didn't have time for niceties.

I rammed a letter-opener into the gap and wrenched them open. And finally I hit the jackpot.

There were more pictures of Colin Medland, and this time I knew exactly where they'd been taken. I recognised the mattress and the overflowing bin.

Then there were more of him in one of the alcoves of the main room. But the real gold was who was sitting alongside him. Michael Eidinger, Florian Straub's right hand man, plus Thorsten Stötzner, Thiel's man in Cologne. That proved links between Straub and Colin Medland. The only thing lacking for the full set was Graham March. I still didn't know what the link meant, but at least I had proof that there was one. I quickly bundled up the pictures and put them in my backpack.

I was so consumed by the pictures, I'd taken my eye off the door. That was a massive error. Because there was a man standing in the darkness, and as I shone my torch in his direction, all it did was illuminate his gun. And it was pointing directly at me.

Chapter 40

IT took me a moment to realise it was Philippe.

"God, you scared me," I called out, relief flooding my veins, but my heart still pounding. "You didn't need to come back. I'm getting on fine. You can put the gun down."

But he didn't put the gun down, and the relief was quickly replaced with an even more heightened sense of panic, as he flicked on the overhead lamp and took a step towards me.

"Stop what you're doing and put your hands in the air," he said, his finger dangerously close to the trigger.

"What the fuck are you on about?"

"I said hands in the air."

There was no other option. I let go of my backpack and raised my hands.

"We're on the same side here," I said, struggling to process what I was seeing.

"No." He shook his head. "We were but we're not now."

"What do you mean?"

"I mean I need to take you to Nicolas Thiel."

Nothing made sense.

"What *are* you on about?" I asked again. I could see him

thinking, presumably trying to work out exactly how he was going to get me out of there. But my brain had kicked in too.

Thiel wanted to kill me himself. Having my remains spread about his office was presumably not part of the plan. That way, he'd never be fully rid of me, always discovering specks of my blood, staining the walls, the floor, the furniture. Never quite managing to banish the aroma of death. And if Philippe wanted to shoot me, he could have already done it. So presumably, he would at some point need to escort me from the building. Unless the plan was to keep me there until Thiel arrived, and that was not an attractive option.

"I don't understand," I said. "What's happened? Why are you working for Thiel now?"

He didn't answer. But then it came to me. It was the only thing that made sense.

"Do you owe him money?" I said. "Is that it?"

"Shut up," he said, taking another step forward me, narrowing the angle of shot.

"What is it? Run up too big a bar bill? Gambling debts?"

"I said shut up." His voice was rising, sounding increasingly volatile. I was playing a dangerous game. But then, I quite liked dangerous games, and I'd never been known to lose one. Yet.

"Because whatever it is," I continued, "you should have told me. He's no friend of mine. I'd have helped you."

"Shut u –"

He didn't get to finish the sentence. The security guard that I'd left downstairs leapt on to his back from behind, bringing them both crashing to the floor. Philippe's gun went skittering across the floor towards me. But I didn't stop to pick it up. I had to take my chance before the guard reassessed the situation and realised just how catastrophically he'd misread it.

I grabbed the bag and made a dash, jumping over them. An arm reached out to grab me, catching my ankle, causing me to stumble and then slam into the doorframe. The impact took my breath away, but I didn't have time to breathe. Both men were getting up, fighting each other to be first to catch me. I took the first three steps and then one giant leap to the bottom of the staircase, landing heavily. Pain went shooting up my leg from my ankle, but there wasn't time to feel pain, either.

And then I ran, through the club, through the kitchen, throwing myself at the fire door and hoping it would open. It did, but only a fraction before smashing into the bottle skip. But it was just enough to squeeze through. There were footsteps and voices close behind me, gaining fast.

I ran across the yard as the rear entrance burst open. I glanced back as I ran. It was the guard. He moved quickly for such a big man. But I was quicker still, and the Renault was right ahead of me. I wrenched open the door and got the key in the ignition just as he caught up with me. As he grabbed the door handle, I managed to slam it into reverse, floor the accelerator and drop the clutch. The car shot backwards. He tried to hold on. So I slammed on the brakes, causing him to lose his grip and go skidding across the tarmac, before I hit first gear and floored the accelerator again.

He was just getting back to his feet as I reached the end of the alley, then turned left to get the hell out of there.

I didn't want to hang around till morning. But I was buggered if I was leaving my lovely trench coat behind. I drove back to the hotel, sprinted up to my room, collected my bag and coat, then nodded at the night receptionist as I ran back to my car, and set off to drive to Germany.

It took a moment to catch my breath as I navigated the narrow streets close to my hotel. The last thing I needed was to attract police attention, so despite the empty roads, I managed to resist the urge to pile on the speed. I had no idea in which direction I was travelling. It didn't matter. All I needed to do was put as much distance as possible between me and where I'd been.

As the roads opened out, and the area became more industrial, I spotted the welcome glow of an all-night petrol station. With a glance in my mirrors to check I wasn't being followed, I pulled over onto the forecourt.

Of course I wasn't being followed. That was just paranoia. Or was it? I hadn't expected my Parisian ally to turn on me either, nor for my life to be inadvertently saved by one of Nicolas Thiel's security guards. God help him when he had to explain that one.

With a full tank of petrol, I studied my newly-acquired Michelin road map, trying to assess the scale of the task. It looked like about 350 miles. Perhaps six hours through northern France and then Luxembourg before finally reaching Germany.

Two hours later, as I was approaching Reims, still in France, and still with a very long way to go, fatigue had replaced any last drops of adrenaline. Following signs to a national park, I found a rest area that was both deserted and out of sight of the main highway, and then closed my eyes, just for a moment. Or at least that was the plan.

Chapter 41

Tuesday, September 14th, 1993

BY the time I opened my eyes, it was daylight. The car's digital clock said just after 7am. I was stiff, uncomfortable, in need of a stretch, but glad to be alive. The car park was still deserted, but I could hear a lot more traffic noise as I got out of the car and took in deep lungfuls of crisp morning air. Everything started coming back to me, but the main thing was that I had the pictures. I needed to call Matt and I needed to speak to Joe, but it was still too early for either. I got back into the car and decided to at least try to make it to Luxembourg before stopping again.

The morning traffic was horrendous. Nearly four hours later, shortly after entering Luxembourg, I was hugely relieved to see a service station, in more ways than one. I took my bag into the toilets to freshen up as best I could, decided it was going to take extensive plastic surgery rather mere mascara to look presentable, and then went in search of coffee.

Once I was back in the car, I called Matt and briefly explained what had happened. My phone battery wasn't looking good.

"In all the time I've been involved in this, that's the first time I've ever heard of anything like that," he said. "I am so sorry."

"Don't worry about it," I said. "The main thing is I've got the pictures."

"But I do worry. I take it personally. That's a major security breach."

"Is it not a risk of the job? We take outcasts and misfits with criminal records. I'm sure he's not the only one who's run into trouble."

"But that's not the point. You've got to be able to trust the people you work with. Put your life in their hands if need be. Where are you now?"

I looked around for any hint of a road sign, but this could have been any service station, on any road, anywhere.

"Somewhere in Luxembourg. I'm driving back. I'm going to have to go, though. I'm running out of battery."

"Driving?"

"I acquired a car."

"I won't ask. Take care and I'll come and see you at the Schloss tomorrow afternoon."

"You're not around today?"

"I've got a few loose ends to tie up today. But I'll be there tomorrow, some time after lunch. Try to stay out of trouble."

"I will."

I ended the call and then dialled the number for Joe.

"Where are you?" he asked.

"Luxembourg," I said. "Don't ask. Actually you can ask, but it's not really very exciting, and kind of a long story, so I was just saying that to save you a job, rather than to make it sound all mysterious, or because I'm up to anything, because I'm not. I'm in Luxembourg, but I could be anywhere, and frankly it doesn't look much different to anywhere else, because I'm basically standing in a service station next to a motorway."

"Are you okay? You're babbling."

"Am I?"

"Yes."

"Sorry. I don't mean to babble. I've just had a long day."

"It's ten o'clock in the morning."

"Ah yes. I forgot about the time difference." I was aware I was probably making things worse. "Anyway, this is a quick call because I'm nearly out of phone battery."

"At ten o'clock in the morning?"

"I didn't get a chance to plug it in overnight. But the point is, I've been to Paris."

"Today?"

I had to work that one out.

"Technically yes, although I prefer to think it was yesterday. But listen, I'm very tired, so don't try to confuse me."

"Okay. And did you find out anything?"

"I did, yes. I found more pictures of Colin Medland, linking him irrefutably to Florian Straub."

"Who's Florian Straub?"

"Ah. I was about to come onto that in the car park when you were called away. He's a German gangster, based in Frankfurt. But the main point is that back at home I've got more pictures from Cologne, showing meetings between a representative of Nicolas Thiel ..."

"Who's he?"

I was aware I needed to slow down, but the phone had started beeping, warning that the battery was critically low.

"He's the bloke who runs the strip club in Paris where the pictures of Colin were taken. Anyway, it was his representative, and Florian Straub's right hand man, and guess who was meeting both of them?"

"That makes sense. Colin Medland?"

"What? No, that was in Paris, later. I'm talking about Cologne, earlier this year. Graham March. Which sticks him right in the middle of it, and establishes a link with London."

"Our Graham March?"

"The very same."

The phone beeped again.

"Listen, the phone's about to die. I'll speak to you properly when I get back."

"Okay," said Joe. "Just one thing before you go. I've been looking into your friend Matt Sommer. You need to be very, very careful. He's not who you think he is. He's been ..."

And then the phone finally gave out. I wanted to slam it on the steering wheel in frustration, but it was an expensive bit of kit, so decided against it, and screamed instead.

What did Joe mean, he'd been looking into Matt? That was understandable, I suppose. But why did I need to be *"very, very careful"*? Had he found out about his fraudulent past? If so, big deal. I knew about that. But surely Joe would realise that, and it hardly presented a risk to me. *"He's not who you think he is."* Did he mean Matt Sommer wasn't his real name? That was hardly a surprise either. But then, *"He's been ..."* He's been what? In prison? Not to my knowledge. Something else? What on earth was he referring to?

I frowned, trying to wrack my brain. I hate not knowing things like that. And the way he'd said it ... I didn't like the sound of that at all. It bothered me more than it probably should have done. I was sure there was an innocent explanation. But it gave me one more thing to think about when my head was already spinning from the events of the last twenty-four hours.

I thought about more coffee, but opted for a cigarette instead, so got out of the car, and leaned against it while I tried to make sense of what Joe had said. Why should I be scared of Matt? He was the one person in all of this who had my back. Who'd gone out of his way to teach me, and protect me, and be there whenever I needed someone to speak to.

The Silk Cut didn't help, and only made my head spin even more. I went back into the service station, bought breakfast and a cappuccino, then popped back to the bathroom for one last time before restarting my journey. All I really wanted was to be home.

Home.

Germany.

What was going on in my life?

———

It was late afternoon by the time I finally arrived at the Schloss, having parked the Renault and collected my own car from Koblenz train station.

I nearly stumbled over several crates of wine and Champagne when I opened the door. It was a welcome sight, and I resolved to start working my way through them immediately, but then remembered it was party night again on Saturday, and that they'd be there for that, rather than me. Pity.

From the kitchen, Birgit called out hello to me, so I popped my head round the door before heading upstairs. Immediately she looked concerned, and told me I looked tired. At least, I hoped that's what she said. The German word for tired is *müde*. She may have just been accusing me of being moody.

Nevertheless, she insisted on pouring me a glass of wine, which was very welcome, and offered to provide dinner for 7pm. That would give me time to unpack, have a shower and get changed. I gave her a hug. Exhausted as I was, her unrelenting kindness made me all the more emotional.

I headed upstairs, after nearly bumping into Walter, who was carrying the wine boxes through to the storeroom next to the kitchen. I offered to help him, but he smiled and shook his head.

I plugged in my phone and tried to call Joe, but it went straight to his answering service. I thought it best, again, not to leave a message.

After dinner, I hit the pool, but my heart wasn't really in it. I managed twelve lengths before feeling like I could fall asleep at any moment, and it's never wise to do that when you're submerged in water.

There was still no luck with Joe, so I took my Val McDermid book to bed and started to read. But I don't think I'd even managed a page before my eyes started closing. And a moment later I was falling fast asleep, still wondering what on earth Joe had been referring to.

Chapter 42

Wednesday, September 15th, 1993

I WOKE up late but feeling better than I expected, hit the gym for an hour, then spent the rest of the morning trying to evaluate the evidence. After lunch it was time to get changed to meet Matt. I chose a reasonably short dress and perhaps put a little extra effort into my hair and make-up. Maybe that was for his benefit. Or possibly I was continuing to delude myself that I wasn't interested in ways other than strictly professional. Three further attempts to contact Joe ended in unanswered failure, although on the final one I did leave an anonymous and innocent-sounding message saying I hoped he was okay.

I saw Matt's car coming up the track from my bedroom window, so grabbed the folder of pictures and went down to the main entrance to meet him.

"Good trip?" he asked with a wry smile when I opened the door. He was carrying a bouquet. I blushed, going all gooey inside, and reached out to take it.

"Aw, Matt, you shouldn't have," I said, but was secretly delighted he had.

His expression changed to a quizzical frown before the smile returned. This time it reached his eyes.

"I haven't," he said. "These are for Birgit and Walter. It's their wedding anniversary."

"Is it? Shit. Why did nobody tell me?"

"I just did. Hold on, you didn't think these were for you, did you?" He started to smirk.

"For me?" I laughed. "No, of course not."

"You did, though, didn't you?"

I was saved further embarrassment by the appearance of Birgit, who gushed with gratitude and gave him a hug. Part of me was worried he'd squash her, and part wished I was more fluent in German so I could fully understand their conversation. I added my congratulations, not knowing if it was polite to enquire about the precise number of years, and then Birgit hugged me too. Walter appeared and shook us both by the hand.

Birgit took the flowers, and I led Matt through to the drawing room. He joined me on the sofa, but kept a considerable distance between us. I turned and folded my legs so I was sitting sideways, hoping that he'd notice them, but suspecting he probably wouldn't.

"What have you been up to?" I asked.

He shrugged.

"Odds and ends of things I needed to attend to," he said. "More importantly, are you okay?"

I had to think about that for a moment.

"I'm fine. It wasn't quite as smooth as I'd hoped, but equally, more successful than it could have been."

"I'm so sorry. None of that was supposed to happen," he said.

That struck me as odd.

"What do you mean it wasn't supposed to happen?"

"That's not what I meant."

He reached out to the folder that was on my lap, but I moved it away.

"Patience," I said. "What was with the books?"

"Which books?"

"All of the books. You left me three books."

"Oh, they were just three English books I managed to pick up. I thought you might appreciate something to read."

"I did. It was very kind. They didn't have any special meaning?"

"No. Should they have done?"

I decided to leave it for now and give him the benefit of the doubt.

Birgit arrived with a tray of coffee and muffins, which she placed on the table in front of us. We both smiled and said thank you. She clearly had a soft spot for Matt. She closed the door behind her as she left.

I relented and passed Matt the folder. He removed the pictures and started looking through them.

"I can't believe you actually managed to get these," he said. "Tell me in detail what happened."

And so I recapped everything, from my initial walk round Pigalle, to the fake Sylvain, the escape from the hotel, the black Porsche, finding the real Sylvain's corpse, borrowing his car, my evening with Philippe, and his ultimate treachery once I'd broken in to the club. Matt seemed genuinely impressed.

"You've done very well," he said.

"Thank you. I must admit, I was quite pleased. But anyway, the pictures prove links between Florian Straub, Nicolas Thiel and Colin Medland in London. So that puts Florian at the centre of things. It points to him trying to gazump us. It suggests he was trying to blackmail Colin to make sure that happened. So now we need to find out why, because if we can do that, we can get the deal back on, get justice for Colin, and hopefully put Straub out of the picture."

Matt nodded, but didn't appear to share my enthusiasm.

"And there's one big obvious other connection with London," I continued.

"Graham March."

"Exactly. So I know you've said it's not Straub's style, but the evidence is stacking up."

"And Graham March is what? His chief negotiator?"

I sat back.

"No. I'm still working on that. I might be doing him a disservice, if that's even possible to do, but he's a small-time bent copper. He's not a criminal mastermind. He might be useful on the ground, helping to bury things, but you wouldn't put him in charge of anything important."

"And it wasn't him on the motorbike," said Matt.

"No."

I sighed, aware I was finding holes in my own theory. Some of it added up, but that could be mere coincidence. And worse than that, it was as though somebody was always one step ahead of us, always aware of what we were up to. I needed to clear my mind and rethink everything, take a fresh, lateral look at all of the evidence.

"What do you think?" I asked, before pouring the coffee to give Matt time to compose his reply. I couldn't resist one of the raspberry muffins. It was deliciously light and fresh. Crumbs fell onto the front of my dress, but I brushed them off onto a small side plate.

"I take on board what you say about Florian Straub, but I've met him. It's out of character," said Matt, lost in a world of his own. "If we go back to basics, we're looking for somebody who wanted to sabotage our deal with Medland. Maybe they wanted to do a deal of their own, but it's possible it was purely out of spite."

That was a new angle.

"What do you mean by spite?" I asked.

"I mean, we piss people off. We've got enemies."

"Such as?"

"How long have you got? Organisations we've disrupted in the past, or beaten on a deal, or associates of any of the above. It's a complex world of unusual alliances out there."

"I can imagine."

"But if that's the case," he continued, "we could be looking at anyone. We've got the pictures. We know where they were taken, but we don't know who was behind the camera."

"Presumably somebody who works for Thiel," I said. "Stötzner? Otherwise how did he end up with the pictures? And I know he hates me, but he wouldn't have any idea I was working with you, would he? Well, he might now, depending on what Philippe's told him. But not before."

Matt was quiet, looking thoughtful. My mind was going off in tangents, too.

"There's one big thing that's bothering me," I said, after a pause. "It's like somebody is following us. I told you about the Porsche but it's more than that. We went to meet Colin Medland. He gets shot. How did that happen? I went to Paris, but someone killed Sylvain and there was a welcoming party in my hotel. They're one step ahead of us. It's like ..."

I stopped. Desperately fighting against the thoughts that were beginning to form at the outer reaches of my brain.

It all pointed back to me. To the bounty on my head. It all pointed to a leak.

Somebody knew everything we were planning. Somebody knew we were going to London to meet Colin. They managed to intercept him at his motel as we were taking him away. They managed to find our hire car and trace us to the London car park. All of that could be explained if we agreed that they were watching Colin, and followed us from there, but if they'd done that, why not strike at the safe house? How did they manage to find our car?

More worrying than that, they knew I was going to Paris. They knew which hotel I was staying at, and who I was supposed to be meeting. That wasn't Philippe. He only got involved later. So it had to be someone else within our organisation. And while I didn't understand why, as Matt had said, it was a complex world of unlikely alliances. Somebody was betraying us. More specifically, somebody was betraying me. Somebody I trusted. Somebody who knew my plans. Perhaps somebody who arranged my agenda.

I tried to shake the thought as soon as it came. It was ridiculous.

But why did Matt ask me which hotel I was moving to? *I might need to contact you.* He had the phone. Why would knowing the hotel make a difference?

What did he mean, *"none of that was supposed to happen"*?

And then Philippe. What was that about? He was supposed to be working for us. He was there to protect me. But then he turned. Coincidence? Or had that been planned all along?

"Just one thing before you go. I've been looking into your friend Matt Sommer. You need to be very, very careful. He's not who you think he is. He's been ..."

Joe's words were bouncing around inside my head, adding to the cacophony of impossible thoughts. Matt didn't ever want me to meet Joe. Why? Did they have history? Or was it something more?

Then I remembered something else Joe said yesterday. Something tiny. I hadn't even noticed it at the time, but in retrospect I should have done. I'd mentioned Nicolas Thiel. He asked who that was. I'd said, *"He's the bloke who runs the strip club in Paris."*

He'd said *"that makes sense"*.

Why did it make sense? What was he referring to?

Why would Matt stop me from being captured if he was

subsequently going to betray me? Unless he wanted the reward for himself.

"I've been looking into your friend Matt Sommer. You need to be very, very careful. He's not who you think he is."

"You're looking thoughtful," said Matt, pulling me out of my trance.

"I ..." A sudden sense of foreboding made me hesitate. "Nothing. I need to think it through." From nowhere, I was overcome by a sudden rush of survival instinct. Perhaps it was paranoia, but a switch had flicked inside my head. I had to get out of there.

"I need to go now, lock myself in a room and clear my head," I said, standing up, and hardly daring to meet his eyes. Because when I finally looked in his direction, it was as though I was seeing him for the first time. And I might have been completely mistaken, but his eyes had a cold, calculating depth that I'd never noticed before.

Chapter 43

WITH a growing sense of panic, I got changed into dark jeans and a black shirt before throwing on my trench coat and hastily packing an overnight bag. I didn't know how long I'd be away. It might be a while. I opted for my new black Dr Martens boots instead of heels. I'd bought them as a tribute to Danny's friend Anna, but resolved never to let her see me wear them, in case she thought I was copying. She didn't like me as it was. There was a knock at my door. I ignored it.

But something was missing. Where was the Glock?

The panic intensified. I wasn't thinking straight. What had I done with the Glock? I'd had it in Paris. Had I seen it since? It wasn't here. It wasn't anywhere. How could I lose a gun?

I didn't have time to search, so I made a quick decision.

Rüdiger answered almost immediately.

"Where are you?" I said, aware my voice sounded breathless.

"In the garages, talking to Walter. Why?"

"The garages at the Schloss?"

"Yes."

The sense of relief was measurable.

"I need a gun," I said.

"Another gun."

"Yes, another gun. Have you got anything?"

"There is a SIG-Sauer P228."

"That'll do. Perfect. Can you meet me at my car in five minutes?"

"*Natürlich*. Are you going somewhere?"

"Yes. Just for a day or two. But it's a bit of a rush. Thanks, Rüdiger."

I ended the call. Tried to think. Was there anything I was missing?

I took one last look around, aware I was seeing these four walls for perhaps the last time. It had been fun. It had been life-affirming. But if ultimately it ended in my murder, then really, what was the point?

Matt was at the foot of the stairs as I descended.

"There you are," he said. "I wondered where you'd gone."

"Sorry. Something came up." I could hardly bear to look at him.

"Where are you going?"

"Just out for a bit."

"With a bag? And you've got changed."

I tried to push past him, but he moved to block my way.

"Listen, Matt, I haven't got time to explain now," I said, feeling my irritation rising along with a desperate urgency to be away from him. "I'll be in touch, okay?"

"But I came up here to see you."

"I know. But you've got the pictures. Keep working on them. I'll be in touch soon."

"You're acting weird."

I didn't respond to that. I'd seen a gap, swerved round him, and was running for the door.

"Clare!" he shouted, but I ignored him. There was no going back. I was desperately sad I hadn't had a chance to say goodbye to Birgit, after everything she'd done for me. I'd send her a card. I knew where she lived.

Rüdiger was waiting by my car. I threw the bag onto the passenger seat, then took the gun from him.

"You look like you're in a rush," he said.

"Kind of. But don't worry. I'll see you soon. And thanks again, that's really useful. In fact, thanks for everything."

I didn't hear his reply as I was already behind the steering wheel, firing up the engine. I floored the accelerator, narrowly avoiding Matt who'd run out of the Schloss to stop me. He stood, watching, as I powered down the track, heading for freedom. But before I could achieve that, there was one big, important thing I needed to do.

Chapter 44

WAS I being ridiculous? Or was this the first sensible thing I'd done all year?

My phone rang as I was about to join the autobahn. I ignored it. It rang again. I couldn't put it off forever.

"You left in a rush," said Matt when I connected the call. There was a hard edge to his voice.

"Yeah."

"Where are you going?"

"I don't know yet. For a drive. Bit of shopping, maybe."

"I asked you where you were going."

"And I just told you."

"With an overnight bag and a gun?"

He'd clearly spoken to Rüdiger. Shit.

"You never know when you might run out of petrol and need to fight off a bear, Matt," I said.

"This isn't wise, Clare."

"I make a habit of doing things that aren't wise."

"I'm being serious. We need to talk."

"Talk to me then."

I pulled into the outside lane and flexed the full power of the five-litre engine. I'd driven this road before, but never with such a sense of urgency.

"Face to face," he said. "We're supposed to be reviewing the evidence. Coming up with a plan. Trying to put the pieces together. I'm only here this afternoon."

"Can I get back to you on that?"

"Where are you going?"

I gave an exasperated sigh.

"You don't tell me where you go and what you get up to. You're going to have to trust me on this. I'm doing it for the right reasons."

"Fine." I could tell he was getting angry. I didn't feel guilty. It was his own fault for plotting to kill me.

"Do you know Joe?" I asked, as I slammed on the brakes to avoid hitting the back of a Volkswagen that had pulled out in the lane in front of me, the driver having misjudged my approach speed.

"Which Joe? Your Joe?"

"Yes, my Joe. Have you come across him before?"

"No. Should I have done?"

"I just wondered."

His reply was lost in static as the signal faded.

"I'm losing you, Matt," I shouted. "The signal's going. I'll call you when I need you."

He said something else but the syllables were syncopated. I took the opportunity to end the call.

The overhead gantry said it was 110km to Frankfurt. Florian Straub seemed to be key to all of this. It was time to meet him, or at least his henchman Michael Eidinger. Finding either in a city with a population of nearly 700,000 wasn't going to be easy, even assuming that was really where they lived, and they weren't away on business somewhere. But I had an idea where to start.

The Volkswagen pulled back into the middle lane. The road

ahead was clear. And my Mercedes 500 SL showed exactly what it could do at the limit.

———————

Frankfurt's red light district lay between the city's *Hauptbahnhof*, or main train station, and the skyscrapers of the financial district. Logic dictated that Straub, or at least his influence, wouldn't be far away.

The streets themselves looked as grubby as I'd expected. Even though it was still just about daylight, there was an abundance of neon, all competing to pull punters in the direction of casinos, sex shops and Eros Centres. It was my second depressing trip into the gutter within three days, but I could only blame myself for the company I kept.

There was an immediate conundrum. It didn't look like a suitable place to park an expensive car, but equally, I didn't really want to be walking around. But then, as I cruised up and down the intersecting roads, I had a realisation. Unlike Paris, there was an immediate honesty and openness to Frankfurt. Less of a tourist trap, more of an acknowledgement of its own shortcomings, and those of the people who frequented its seedy delights. In the end, I parked a couple of streets away and set off on foot. I didn't feel safe, as such, but I'd had experiences that were much, much more scary.

The only option was to start asking questions. I thought I'd try the sex shops first.

Aware of the eyes turning in my direction, I approached the counter of the first.

"Do you know where I might find Florian Straub?" I asked.

The assistant shook his head and denied having heard of him, but suggested I could look amongst the racks of explicit VHS cassettes. It wasn't quite what I had in mind.

The next couple yielded a similar response. I wasn't getting very far, but at least my initial nerves were wearing off.

As darkness descended, I decided to try an Eros Centre. A central staircase ran through the middle of the building. On each floor, there were rooms for individual working girls. Most of the doors were closed, but occasionally I found one open, with a prostitute sitting, waiting for a customer. I'm not sure they were expecting an English woman, but there again, I thought it was probably far from the weirdest thing they'd encountered.

Again, however, I got nowhere. I spoke to some of the girls, but they denied any knowledge. Whether they were being truthful or were just too scared to speak to a suspicious-looking stranger, it didn't really matter. Either way it was proving fruitless.

I tried a different approach in the second, asking for Michael Eidinger first, before mentioning the name of Florian Straub. Even though I was quite fit, the relentless slog of endless staircases was causing my legs to ache, and all for no reward.

After the third fruitless brothel, and with time cracking on, I decided to try a casino. It wasn't the glamorous kind as seen in countless James Bond films. Instead, it was like a dimly-lit penny arcade, with walls of one-armed bandits and other gaming machines interspersed around the occasional roulette wheel or blackjack table.

I approached a seedy-looking man who was counting chips behind a Perspex screen. He was far from alone in looking seedy in the place, but his lank, greasy hair, poor complexion and faded black Motörhead t-shirt all added to his allure.

He looked up as I approached and sneered. I think it was a sneer. It might have been an unsuccessful attempt at a seductive smile.

I decided to start with Michael Eidinger.

He'd never heard of him.

I played the wild card: Thorsten Stötzner.

No again.

The joker: Florian Straub?

He stopped what he was doing and looked me up and down.

"Yes I know him. Who's looking for him," he asked in English.

"I am."

"I mean what's your name, pretty lady?"

Where to even begin with that?

"Charlotte Sadler," I lied.

"Charlotte," he repeated, pronouncing the final e as a separate syllable, in the traditional German manner. "Pretty name for a pretty lady."

"Can we quit with the pretty lady shit?" I said, losing my patience, then immediately regretting it. This was the closest I had to a lead. He might be obnoxious, but he was still better than nothing.

"I only tell the truth," he said with another attempt at a smile that only made him look even sleazier. "What do you want with Florian?"

"I just want to talk to him."

"You looking for a job, Charlotte?" Again the e was pronounced.

"No, I just need to speak to him."

"And what if he doesn't want to speak to you?"

"Let's give him the chance to decide for himself, shall we?"

He opened the door at the back of his booth, and came out to join me. He was slightly taller than me, even allowing for the soles of my DMs, so about 5'9" or 5'10". His jeans badly needed a wash, and I dreaded to think about what would happen if he removed his filthy, once-white trainers.

"You're not from round here," he said.

"Good spot."

"And what is in it for me?"

I sighed.

"How much?"

"A blow job."

"Dream on."

He looked disappointed, as though I'd even have considered it.

"Okay," he said. "A hundred."

"Pfennig?"

"Deutschmarks."

"Are you trying to be funny?"

He shrugged.

"I can't help you, pretty lady, if you're going to take that kind of attitude."

"Fifty and I don't break your ankles?"

That made him laugh.

"I like you, Charlotte," he said. "Okay. I will take you for fifty."

"You don't need to take me. I just need the address."

"It's just round the corner but hard to find. All part of the service."

I doubted that, but while not wanting to overstate my own credentials, I suspected the thought of leaving the building with a reasonably glamorous woman in tow was a novelty he'd quite enjoy.

"Okay," I said.

"Money first."

"Half now and half when we get there."

He laughed again.

"You don't know how this works, Charlotte. Full amount now or we're not going anywhere."

I had no option other than to give him the money. He asked another member of staff to cover his booth and led me towards the door, and then back onto the street.

We turned left at a crossroads, then took a shortcut through the ground floor of an Eros Centre into a courtyard at the back. It was dark. There wasn't much moonlight with six-storey buildings on all sides.

"Follow me," he said.

We reached a door. He pressed a buzzer. A moment later it clicked open, and he stepped inside and indicated for me to follow. There was a rank aroma of sweat, smoke, and assorted other unpleasantness.

"This way," he said.

We reached another door. This time he had a key. He unlocked the door and stood aside for me to walk through. Feeling wary, I did as directed. But there was no sign of Florian Straub. It was, at best, a storage room, but one that looked like it might have a significant problem with rodents.

My tour guide slammed the door behind him and flicked on the overhead light. His sleazy smile intensified.

"Now Charlotte," he said. "About that blow job."

"Really?" I said, more out of disappointment than fear.

He took a step towards me, then reached out to grab my arm. It was the last step he took. A second later he was on the floor, gasping for air, his eyes watering with the shock and severity of my response. I really didn't want to make any further contact, for health reasons alone, but couldn't resist smashing my boot into his groin, and wishing the soles weren't made of rubber.

I retrieved my money from his pocket, realising I'd now need to wash it, then aimed the SIG at his head.

"I take it this was a complete load of bollocks, then?" I said, standing over him. He couldn't reply with more than a whimper. "Honestly, you should be utterly ashamed of yourself."

I moved my finger to the trigger.

"Say *auf wiedersehen*," I said.

The panic in his eyes was accompanied by the involuntary release of his bladder. I stepped back to avoid getting the foul-smelling liquid on my boots, then turned, opened the door and slammed it behind me, leaving him to fester.

Breathing raggedly, I headed away from the brothel, trying to seem calm. I weaved between the figures on the pavement, head down, dodging left to avoid a bulky man approaching me. He dodged the same way. We collided. As I tried to extricate myself, I looked up at his smirking face and felt a sick sense of recognition.

It was Graham March.

Chapter 45

"WELL there's a surprise. Discovering you in the middle of a red light district," I said.

"Bit late for your lunch break, isn't it?" he said. "I can't imagine you've had many clients, although I doubt you charge much. Are you going to show me your room?"

I took a step back, and then reached into my pocket for cigarettes. If I was going to have to put up with this shit, I might as well enjoy myself.

"What are you doing in Frankfurt, Graham?" I asked, lighting a Silk Cut.

"You kept mentioning Germany. I thought I'd come and see it, see what all of the fuss was about. It's not really my kind of place, looking at the surroundings, although I can see how you'd fit in."

"And the real reason?"

"Well, I must admit. There is, what I like to call, an ulterior motive."

I folded my arms after blowing smoke in his direction.

"Amaze me. Actually, let me guess. You'd heard they had world-leading sexual health doctors and you wanted someone

258

who'd take care of your rash before the long-suffering Mrs March found it?"

"Very good. Slightly insulting on several levels, but I understand the psychology of envy." He leaned back against a shiny black BMW 7 Series that was parked incongruously beside us. "No, something much more rooted in reality, although I must admit, my enthusiasm for the task is diminishing rapidly."

"Go on then, enlighten me."

"I'm here to get you out of trouble."

"Right."

"No, seriously. I told you, I do a lot of good work for charity these days, and here I am, in person, to offer a helping hand to the weakest and most vulnerable members of society. Viz, you. I appreciate you might wish to thank me with some display of carnal gratitude, but really, there's no need. In fact, I'd prefer it if you didn't. No offence."

It was one of the most ridiculous things I'd ever heard.

"Okay, and how are you going to get me out of trouble?" I asked.

"The word on the street is that you've been walking into every bar, casino and whorehouse, asking if anyone knows Florian Straub. Probably not your most sophisticated of undercover missions, but I make allowances for you being long past your prime."

"And in which parallel universe would I ever need you to save me?"

He was clearly enjoying himself.

"Word also has it that you made a run from your friends who've been providing you with free accommodation," he continued. "Did I ever tell you about my work with the homeless? I have contacts if you decide a lovely clean hostel is preferable to a rat-infested gutter. Although I understand why you'd feel more at home in the latter. So you're here, on your own, making yourself a nuisance. And much as I'd quite enjoy seeing someone rip you to shreds, your old Uncle Graham has been asked to look after you as a favour to a friend."

"Which friend would that be? Presumably an imaginary one."

"Florian Straub."

That made me laugh.

"Florian Straub asked *you* to look after *me*?"

"I know. It's terribly unsporting. But those are the facts, alas."

I took a step back and rested my back against the wall, then drew on the cigarette to give myself time to contemplate the bizarreness of the situation. A dazed-looking man staggered between us, nearly bumping into me, his knees looking shot. He was either on his way to see a prostitute, coming back from a particularly heavy session, or most likely just feeling the effects of all the staircases.

"Just to clarify. Is this the same Florian Straub you claim not to know?" I asked, once the man had passed.

"When did I ever claim that?"

"Four days ago in London."

"No, no, no. You mentioned Thorsten somebody, Michael somebody-else and even a Nicolas. You never asked about Florian Straub. I'd have remembered. Typical lack of attention to detail."

I let it pass. I couldn't prove otherwise, but even if I had, he'd have denied it.

"So you're saying you do know Florian Straub?"

"I can neither confirm nor deny. Not that it matters. You'd make something up, either way. It's what you do."

"And what form does this looking after me take?"

"Ah, now that's where it gets delicate," he said.

I dropped the cigarette to the floor and ground it out with the toe of my boot, fantasising for a moment that it was actually Graham's head.

"Delicate?"

"Obviously I rejected his first proposal."

"Which was?"

"You don't want to know, but I declined on taste grounds. So in the end I agreed that when you came off shift and staggered into the street, presumably looking for a fix, I'd find you and take you to him. Before anyone tried to kill you. Perhaps he wants that pleasure himself. Did you sell him any paintings, by the way?"

"Not to my knowledge."

"Let's hope not, eh? Apparently there are some bad people in the world who aren't too happy about you ripping them off. Or so I've heard."

Was that an admission that he knew Nicolas after all? Not that it had ever really been in doubt. But his relaxed confidence was slightly concerning.

"And what if I don't want to be taken to him?" I asked.

"That would be ridiculous, given that you've been shouting your mouth off asking if anyone knows where he is." He reached back and opened the rear door of the BMW. "Get in."

I didn't like this. I didn't like the thought that I wasn't in control. And I specifically didn't like the thought that Graham March held my destiny in his filthy, nail-bitten hands.

And yet what option did I have? I needed to find Florian. This was my best chance, even if it meant I was completely forgoing the element of surprise. I stepped forward, with my hands in the pockets of my trench coat, one of them fingering the grip and trigger of the SIG. It wasn't as reassuring as I'd hoped. Then lowered myself into the car.

I recognised Michael Eidinger in the driving seat. Graham got into the front and then, without a further word, we pulled away.

Chapter 46

THE drive took less than three minutes. I'm not really sure why we bothered. Michael parked up, got out of the car, then opened my door. He grabbed me roughly by the upper arm as I emerged, his fingers digging sharply into the flesh through my clothes. I tried to shake free, but the grip intensified. I could sense the bruises already forming.

He led me into a building under a flashing red Eros Centre sign, down a garishly-lit corridor to a staircase. Graham followed a couple of paces behind, clearly enjoying my discomfort. Thankfully we only had to climb two flights of stairs to reach the first floor, whereupon Michael unlocked a door and led me down a further corridor into an office.

My two companions followed me through. And there, behind the desk, was Florian Straub. At least my hunch had positioned me within the correct postcode. He was well-built, balding, and smartly-dressed, albeit in a strange, old-fashioned way, in a tweed suit and bow tie.

"So, Clare Woodbrook," he said, in accented English. "You have quite a reputation."

"As do you," I said, moving across to the chair that he indicated. Michael and Graham remained by the door.

Straub laughed.

"Have you been talking to Matt Sommer? What am I asking? Of course you have. Tell me, how is life working for Angelica? Have you met the mythical lady?"

"I can't confirm or deny," I said. There was at least sixty stone of male fat and muscle in the room. If I had to fight my way back out, it could prove a challenge.

"Why were you looking for me?" he asked.

"Because I want to know what you're up to."

He laughed again, more heartily this time.

"And you expect me to tell you? Here you are, working for a rival organisation, and you come in here and expect me to tell you all of my plans? I thought you were supposed to be the new prodigy, but that is either very naive or very stupid."

The P228 was still safely in my pocket. They hadn't searched me. That was something.

"You probably think you're in danger," he said.

"It crossed my mind."

"You're not at risk from me."

"Did Colin Medland think the same?"

"Colin Medland?"

"Don't try to tell me you don't know Colin Medland."

He stretched out his arms, opening his hands.

"You're going to need to enlighten me."

"I'm sure Graham can fill you in."

For the first time, he appeared to acknowledge the presence of the others. He stood up, told them to wait where they were, then headed towards the office door, beckoning for me to follow. We set off along the corridor.

"How long have you known Graham?" I asked, falling into step behind him. The opportunity to get answers was more important than the chance to run for freedom.

"A little while," he said.

"And what's his involvement?"

We started to descend the stairs, heading back towards the street.

"He's helping me on a project."

"You do know he's suspended. Don't you?"

"Yes, he told me. Some made-up allegations by a British tabloid newspaper, wasn't it?" He smiled and clicked his fingers. "That's where I recognise your name. You were the journalist."

"They weren't made up," I said. I didn't mention that technically Danny had written the piece from my research.

"He insists they were."

At the bottom of the stairs we turned left, away from the street, and then out through a doorway into a courtyard that was similar to the one I'd been taken to by my potential casino rapist. Florian stopped walking and leaned against the wall. It was even darker now. The moon had disappeared behind thick clouds. The only real light came from closed windows on the floors above.

"The one thing you need to know about Graham is that he never tells the truth," I said, joining him against the wall.

"That's a shame. He told me I could trust you."

"He ... What?"

Straub laughed.

"I'm playing with you. He told me you were - let me quote the exact words - an evil, lying bitch who would steal from her own mother. The worst kind of scum, with more diseases than the average hospital."

"It's a viewpoint."

"Which you contest?" He took a cigarette from a packet, then offered me one, which I accepted.

"Of course," I said as he lit them, the flame momentarily illuminating his face. "I don't know what shit you've been told but I'll tell you the truth. I did one bad thing. I admit that. I didn't think it through. But once the dust settled and I could look back with clarity, I realised just how stupid I'd been."

"He also mentioned you were stupid."

I laughed, suddenly feeling relaxed. But maybe that was part of his plan. Mindful not to let my guard down, I started taking in my surroundings, trying to notice the details, the colours, the pattern of the brickwork. Checking for potential escape routes. But it was too dark to see anything.

"I told you, he talks rubbish," I said. "It was a one-off. I did the perfect crime that I could never be caught for. But I have been caught, by my own conscience. And I'm in prison because I can't go back to my old life, and see the people I care about."

"And so you ended up with Matt and Anders."

"I did."

"And you believed everything they told you."

"I make up my own mind."

"But you made up your own mind to believe them."

He had a point. But that was then. I needed to change the subject.

"Let's go back to Colin Medland," I said. "You claim you don't know him. But I've seen pictures from a strip club in Paris, in which he's sitting alongside your right hand man."

"Michael?"

"Yes. But Colin is now dead. He was killed last week in London, by someone who knew him, who by all accounts was a business rival of ours. You can see why I'm interested."

"Mmmm." Florian nodded, looking thoughtful. "I remember that now. Michael mentioned he'd been to Paris. He was invited by a guy called Thorsten Stötzner who wanted him to meet his boss, who happens to be married to my cousin. But nothing came of it. He said they met some weird English guy who looked nervous but then got carried away with the girls - especially as everything was on the house."

The cold was starting to seep through my trench coat. My

fingers were stiffening where I was holding the cigarette. I took one last drag then dropped it to the floor, barely two-thirds smoked.

"Have you met this Thorsten?" I asked.

"Once or twice."

"Which is it? Once or twice?"

"Three times."

"God. I thought Germans were supposed to be efficient with things like numbers." There was just enough light to show his smile. "What do you make of him?"

"He's brutal," said Straub. "Word has it, he recruited a guy in Cologne to take you down. And when he failed, he killed him."

"Yes, I heard about something like that. Tell me about him."

"There's nothing to tell. He thinks he's hard. He knows better than to mess with us, though."

"But why does Nicolas need a man in Germany?"

"You've heard of Schengen?"

"Yeah, of course."

"Well, it's all to do with that. You know about trafficking?"

"Not first hand."

I got the impression he was about to tell me. He didn't disappoint. I hadn't expected him to be so talkative.

"You've got source countries, destination countries and transit countries in between," he said. "In Europe, the big transit countries are Poland and the Czech Republic. Everything to the east of that is a source country. Everything to the west is a destination. In Germany we have a near 500km border with Poland and about 800km with the Czechs. So if that's what you're into, then Germany suddenly becomes very important."

"But Cologne?"

"What about it?"

"Why was he in Cologne? Because that's in the north-west, which is the wrong side completely. Why not somewhere east, like Dresden or Nuremberg, or even Berlin?"

"It's not to say he wouldn't have contacts or visit all those places. Even Leipzig ... " He paused and glanced at me, as if waiting for a reaction. Was he trying to establish a link with Angelica? "But Cologne is right next door to the Netherlands and Belgium."

"So he's not only interested in supplying girls to Nicolas?"

"It's more that Nicolas is looking to expand."

That made sense. There was a limit to how much he could make from one seedy club in Paris, even if I suspected the bulk of his income came from illegal add-ons.

"And are you into this as well?" I asked. "Don't get me wrong, but you seem to be in a similar trade."

He paused.

"I need to talk to you about that."

"Meaning?"

"Meaning not now."

"At least give me the one word summary: yes or no."

"It's not as easy as that."

"I think it is. Either you are or you aren't."

He discarded his cigarette, then turned to face me. He was probably at least twice my weight, but if necessary I'd be prepared to fight him. And yet there was no obvious sign of threat. Instead, he was sounding quite reasonable, almost friendly. He shook his head.

"It's only an easy question if you're looking at it in the simplest of terms," he said. "We think in the long term. We get approached, of course. And sometimes we have to give the impression that we want to do things in order to improve our position when it comes to what really matters. But no, everything we do is legal."

I laughed.

"I very much doubt that."

"Okay, not strictly legal. But not importing girls illegally. Everyone who works for me chooses to be here."

I still didn't understand why we were standing in a courtyard. Maybe he just wanted to talk out of the earshot of Michael and Graham. It was time to delve deeper.

"So going back to London," I said. "You claim you weren't involved with the Docklands deal. And had nothing to do with the murder of Colin Medland. But you know about it? Both the deal and the murder?"

"I heard Matt was doing something over there," he said. "It's not my area of interest, so I didn't make further enquiries. I did hear that Nicolas Thiel was looking for you, though. And I heard that Thorsten Stötzner was furious when you escaped in Cologne. He blamed Matt and the last I heard, he was going to do everything he could to fuck up something in revenge."

"So, you're saying he sabotaged the London deal? Out of spite?"

"It's what I've heard."

"On Nicolas Thiel's instruction?"

"That I don't know. But Thorsten is - how should I put this? A maverick. He takes his own decisions at times."

It was all beginning to make sense. But if that was Stötzner on the motorbike, why didn't he kill me when he had the chance? Unless I was more valuable if he captured me and handed me to Thiel to do the job himself. That made sense as well. But one thing still didn't. It was time to add some flattery into the mix.

"Thank you," I said. "That's definitely something to think about. But I still don't understand why somebody successful and reputable like yourself would want to get involved with Graham March of all people. What is this project?"

"Ah," he said. "That's why I told you you were in no danger."

"Because?"

"Because we need your help. Yes, he has his limitations, but he could be useful for us. We need your help to clear his name."

I couldn't help but laugh.

"But it was me that got him suspended!"

"Precisely."

"So why would I help reinstate him? I'm not sure if you noticed, but we don't get on."

"Because we will pay you."

"I don't need money."

"And we will protect you."

"I don't need protection."

"Really?"

"Really."

"Because you've got Matt and Anders. Who you've run away from?"

"I just needed time to think."

"But you think Matt is double-crossing you?"

How did he know all of this? Unless it was so blindingly obvious, and as ever I was the last to know.

"I think that's between me and Matt and not something I want to discuss with anyone else," I said.

He started walking to the far side of the courtyard. I followed.

"But let's say he is," he said. "And if he is, then you can come to work for me."

We stopped as we reached the end. It was my turn for a head shake.

"No disrespect but this isn't me," I said. "I appreciate the offer, but I don't want to get involved in prostitution. Or drugs, or guns, or whatever else you're into."

He didn't deny any of them.

"Okay, not work for me, but I'll still protect you. I'll do something that saves your life. And in return you look after Graham. And even though you don't need the money, I'll still pay you as a token of my gratitude."

I didn't know how to respond to that. It sounded ridiculous.

"I can see you're not convinced," he said. "I'm not looking for an answer now. Let's discuss this when you realise you owe me. I believe you're probably honourable, despite what Graham tells me."

"I am, but I'll still try to make sure that doesn't happen. No disrespect."

"We'll see," he said.

He turned towards the wall and reached towards it. Straining my eyes, I could just about make out a door that was hidden in the corner, in almost complete darkness. I reached into my pocket for the reassuring touch of the SIG.

"Come with me," he said. "I want to introduce you to someone."

"Who?"

"A friend of yours."

I followed him inside the building. He flicked on the overhead light and then my mouth fell open in shock.

Chapter 47

PHILIPPE was sitting taped to a chair in the middle of the concrete floor. He was gagged, his face beaten, his head lolling to the side. He looked barely conscious.

"This is what happens to traitors," said Florian.

He took a handgun from his pocket, attached a noise suppressor, and fired a single bullet into Philippe's brain. The chair toppled over and the Frenchman fell to the storeroom floor. A pool of blood started to form beneath him. I watched on in horror, as though time was standing still. Suddenly the affability had gone, replaced by the brutality I'd expected in the first place.

"We don't mess about," said Florian.

"Was that really necessary?" I asked, my voice cracking.

"The most important quality in this business is loyalty. He was prepared to sell you out to pay off his own debts. That was a big mistake."

"And this is what you call saving my life? And now I'm supposed to be indebted to you?"

"No. This was for me. I cannot stand dishonesty. That will come later."

He seemed so sure he was going to save my life, it was actually more terrifying than if he'd threatened to kill me.

"So what now?" I asked.

"You go home. You don't need to worry about Matt. I promise you he's not going to betray you. And if he did ... Well, you've seen what happens. Go to sleep. Wake up tomorrow and focus on Thorsten Stötzner."

Against all the odds, it sounded plausible. Maybe I had rushed into running away. Perhaps there was an innocent explanation for Matt's behaviour, and for the things that Joe had started to tell me. The more I thought about it, there had to be. If Matt wanted to kill me, he'd had ample opportunity.

"Okay," I said, heading back towards the door. Florian pocketed the gun and we headed back out to the street.

"It was nice to meet you," I said, when we got there. I almost meant it, but I couldn't shake the image of Philippe falling to the floor.

Was it appropriate to give him a handshake when he still probably had gun residue on his palm? I didn't want to appear rude, so when he reached out, I didn't really have an option.

"We'll meet again," he said.

"Will we?"

"You'll be looking after Graham for me."

"Don't count on it."

"And again, we'll see."

He smiled again as I turned to leave. It had been another extremely strange day.

Once I'd got my bearings, I set off back to my car, four blocks away, feeling an uneasy mix of emotions. On one hand, it had been a successful trip. I'd tracked down Florian Straub, which was an achievement in itself. And I was pleased to have met him.

He was a monster, but if anything, he'd been respectful towards me, and I hadn't expected that. Obviously he hadn't been completely honest with me, but I did believe what he said about the London project.

So, based on the evidence linking Colin Medland to Nicolas Thiel, I was prepared to believe his theory that Thorsten Stötzner was behind it. But had Stötzner done it purely as an act of sabotage, to punish Matt for protecting me, or was he planning a rival bid of his own?

In truth, I suspected the former, but Matt and Anders had been elusive on the exact scope of the deal, beyond the acquisition of a property, so it was hard to know for sure.

Something else bothered me more. If it was the former, that meant it was done specifically to get back at me. But why then kill Colin? Because Stötzner thought he was still working with us? Or maybe to frame us, knowing that any involvement with the police in London could have serious long-term consequences for my liberty? Was I responsible for Colin's death? That thought made me feel nauseous.

Except Stötzner didn't know that I knew DSI Joe Leyland. And while Joe's willingness to agree to a deal was still up in the air, at least it was something. If I could help him solve a gangland murder, it would prove I had some worth to him as a source of intelligence. And I now knew for sure that Graham March was working for a German gangster.

But that then presented another problem. Straub's little show of the effects of disloyalty hadn't gone unnoticed. He'd pretended it was to reassure me about Matt, but it didn't take a genius to understand the real message. If I caused more problems for Graham, it would be me in the chair next time, and the treatment would be just as merciless.

I continued in the direction of the financial district. It was getting late, and the further I walked into the darkness, away from the bright neon lights of the brothels, the more apprehensive I felt. Frankfurt was supposed to be one of the safer big cities, but I remembered one of the first things Matt ever said to me. I had a target on my back now. And I'd made myself vulnerable, alone, in the open.

I crossed the road, glancing behind me. A sixth sense was warning me of danger. And the sensation was getting ever stronger. I speeded up, half jogging, as I turned into the street where I'd left the Mercedes. It was almost pitch black, but I could see my car, about a hundred yards away. I speeded up again. My car was getting closer. I started to run, closing the gap, my senses on red alert, warnings screaming through my brain.

But they weren't enough to save me. As I reached the car, I sensed movement from behind, but before I had a chance to react, somebody grabbed me roughly. There was nobody else on the street to hear my scream.

Chapter 48

FLORIAN Straub made a call on his mobile before returning to his office.

"Thorsten," he said. "Florian Straub."

"Florian. Good to speak to you. Do we have an update?"

"We do. She just left."

"And?"

"She knows about you. She knows about London."

Stötzner paused, as if processing the development.

"And is she going to do anything with that information?" he asked at last.

"Not tonight. But tomorrow, I think she'll try."

"We need to stop that."

"We do," said Straub. "It's time to take her to Nicolas. Everything is in place. Matt is on his way there. I'm taking the helicopter in the morning. I look forward to seeing you there."

———

I winced as I was pushed roughly back against the wall, crushed by the weight of a body, and an arm across my throat, making it difficult to breathe.

"I don't like you," said Graham March, the foul stench of his breath so close to my face adding an altogether less pleasant aspect to proceedings. His arm was restricting my air supply.

"Florian thinks you're going to need my protection," I croaked, trying to wriggle free, but the pressure intensified.

"Florian thinks a lot of things," he said. "But so you know, I won't forget what you did to me." Finally the pressure lessened, and I gasped for air. "One day you'll regret it."

"Big threats, Graham." I said, still with a waver.

"I could kill you now," he said. "I could shoot you with your own gun. Make it look like suicide. And don't say you're not carrying one because I can feel it." He dropped his arm to the front of my coat, and pressed the pocket. Then he let his hand wander, and I added sexual assault to his list of crimes. I pushed his arm away, flinching at his touch.

"So why don't you?" I said, trying to stay calm and not immediately castrate the bastard with the SIG.

"Because that would be too good for you. Just so we're not in any doubt, here, I loathe you. I loathe everything about you. I currently loathe the piece of ground you're standing on. I couldn't loathe you any more if ..."

"You've made your point. It's eminently mutual. Jesus."

"But what I don't understand," he continued, spitting venom with every syllable, "is why you investigated me. Why you decided you should compile a dossier on *me*."

"Because you're corrupt, Graham."

"And yet all the while you're doing things ten times worse! I've never murdered anyone."

"It was self-defence."

"Was it shit. You're worse than I ever was. And that makes you the worst kind of hypocrite. So when I'm cleared and back on the Force, I want you to know that I'm coming after you. I'm going to take you down, with force if necessary. And I'm going to make your life a misery. It's going to be my entire focus, every day, and I want it to be the only thing you think about too. Because every day I'm going to be out there, creeping up behind you, until one day I lock you up. And I'll spread rumours about kiddie-fiddling while I'm at it, so that every minute you're inside, for twenty-five years, you're watching your back for someone who wants to attack your face with a razor."

"Have you finished?"

"I haven't even started."

I tried to suppress the contempt before it turned into a giggle, but could feel I was struggling.

"So before you continue, let me tell *you* something," I said. "A lot of bad people are looking for me. Most of them don't have your level of halitosis, admittedly, but you don't scare me. Because I want you to know that if you do somehow manage to clear your name, despite everything you've done, I'm going to be out there every day, creeping up behind you, until one day you finally get what's coming to you. And yes I do have a gun. And tempting though it is to shoot you now, I'd much rather you suffered the trauma of knowing I'm coming for you too. What are you doing with Florian?"

"That's none of your business."

"He seems to think it might be. He's offered me money to keep you out of trouble. So that tells me two things. First, he knows you're going to fuck up, because it's what you do. And second, he knows that I'm the only one who can save you. Though why he should want me to do that, God only knows. And you know what? I'm tempted to take the money just so that at some later date I can have the joy of taking you down myself."

With one last almighty shove against the wall, he finally loosened his grip. I took a step towards the Mercedes, keen to get away from the man.

"Nice car," he said, as I unlocked the doors. "Shame it's wasted on you. Let's hope you don't have an accident."

It was nearly midnight by the time I made it back onto the road. It was too late to call Joe, but it could wait until morning. A decision was made. I'd return to the Schloss, sleep with the SIG, if necessary, and reassess everything in daylight.

What had I really learned? Florian was brutal, but that was hardly news. Philippe was a traitor, but likewise. Graham March was up to something but I didn't know what. Either it was an elaborate bluff or Straub genuinely had no interest in the deal in London. Which according to Matt would have been out of character anyway. So everything pointed to Thorsten Stötzner. I'd speak to Matt. Apologise for being hasty and hopefully he'd not hold a grudge.

Searching for music to keep me company on the journey home, I put Duran Duran's *Wedding Album* into the car's CD player. It was a while since I'd listened to Duran Duran but I'd bought their latest CD in a moment of curiosity, to see what they were up to. I'd loved them when they started, when I was in my teens.

The first song was rockier than I was used to. But when track two, *Ordinary World*, came on, and I started to listen to the lyrics, I nearly crumbled. It was as though they'd written it for me. My life had changed but I couldn't afford to shed tears for yesterday. It was a steep learning curve, but I was determined to survive.

When it ended, I played it again, then turned the music off, and drove the rest of the way in silence. There was no point having regrets. No point trying to recapture my old life. I had to make the best of what I had. Make amends with myself, first and foremost. Learn to forgive myself before I could truly expect forgiveness from others.

Getting justice for Colin was a small step in the right direction. But if Florian was right, and it was all done out of spite for me, then I was as guilty of his death as the person who'd pulled the trigger.

With a heavy heart, I pulled up at the Schloss, hoping everything would be better in the morning. The big, glorious, imposing building looked peaceful in the starlight. The only sound was my feet crunching on the gravel as I got out of the car. I'd have a night in my own bed, trying to put the vision of Philippe out of my mind, and start again. Another day older, another day wiser.

I didn't notice the person creeping up behind me as I locked the car, and didn't react to them putting a chloroform-soaked rag over my face, until I was falling to the ground, powerless to do anything other than succumb.

Chapter 49

Thursday, September 16th, 1993

WHEN I regained consciousness, I was in the back of a van, being jolted around with every bump in the road. It was dark, hot and airless. I was gagged. My arms and legs were tied. I had no idea where I was, where I was going, or who had taken me.

More importantly, I had very little way of finding out. There was a tiny amount of light creeping in through a gap in the doors. It wasn't enough to illuminate the inside, but at least it told me it was daylight. But morning? Afternoon? How long had I been knocked out for?

The road noise hinted that we were moving quickly, but how far had we gone? I had no idea. With a growing sense of dread, I realised I could be anywhere.

Florian Straub's helicopter touched down in the grounds of a country estate to the east of Paris. While the pilot attended to the controls, Straub collected his briefcase, climbed down, and walked across the lawn, where he shook hands with Matt Sommer, Anders Hagström and Nicolas Thiel.

"Glad you could make it," said Thiel. "You're just in time for Champagne."

"Good journey?" asked Matt, as the Frenchman led them towards the house.

Straub nodded. Why was Anders there?

"It beats the autobahn. And Anders, it's a pleasure to meet you again."

"I thought I would come along to witness the final exchange," he said, as if sensing the question.

"Any word from Stötzner?" asked Florian.

"The pick-up went okay, apparently, but other than that, nothing yet," said Matt. "Not long now, though."

"If I'd thought, I could have given them a lift." He winked, and Matt raised his eyebrows, before smiling in response.

"Come in, gentlemen," said Thiel, as he reached the door to the huge conservatory that ran along the back of the building. He waited for the others to pass then followed them inside, closing the door.

"I hope you don't mind, but one can never be too careful," he continued, as a bodyguard stepped forward and frisked the new arrival. Florian handed over the briefcase and held out his arms. He'd expected nothing less. The bodyguard kept hold of the briefcase once the search was completed.

The conservatory was cool, with blinds obscuring most of the polycarbonate roof panels. There was an abundance of plants in giant pots on the cream tiled floor. Wicker furniture surrounded a pair of low coffee tables. One of the tables held an ice bucket, a bottle of Champagne and six glasses.

"Expecting company?" asked Straub.

"I very much hope so," said Thiel.

He offered his three visitors a chair, and then opened the bottle and poured each of them a glass.

"It is a truly wonderful day," he continued, handing out the drinks. He nodded in the direction of the briefcase. "A sample of the merchandise?"

"Indeed. Call it a token of our esteem," said Florian. "I think you'll do very well with it."

The bodyguard placed the briefcase on the table. Florian opened it, then turned it to face Nicolas. The plastic-wrapped bundles met with his approval. Some were white. Others brown. The street value would be significant.

"To a happy partnership," said Anders, raising his glass. The others followed suit.

"And I'd like to thank you for your patience," added Matt. "I appreciate it can't have been easy, but I'm sure the wait will be worth it."

After a few minutes of small talk, Florian cast a glance in Matt's direction.

"Where are they, by the way?" he asked.

Matt checked his watch.

"They're on their way. They're due any minute. In fact, in precisely five."

Five minutes later, Florian noticed Matt checking his watch again. He looked nervous. Any second now.

But nobody turned up. Another five minutes passed. Still nothing. Another ten, and Florian started to get the sense that perhaps something had gone terribly wrong.

Chapter 50

THE road noise changed to the crunch of gravel, then after a few moments, the motion finally stopped. The engine was turned off, and a few seconds later the van doors opened, momentarily blinding me with the bright daylight.

I recognised Thorsten Stötzner as soon as I was able to focus. He looked as wiry and creepy in real life as he had done in the pictures. He cut the binding around my ankles, but there was no point in kicking out. My hands were still tied behind my back, and I was sure his gun was loaded. If I tried to run, I wouldn't get far.

He dragged me from the back of the van. Pins and needles made it almost impossible to stand, but he wasn't in the mood to make allowances. I felt filthy, aching and desperately thirsty. He removed the gag, but not my wrist ties.

"Where are we?" I asked, trying to sound a lot more confident than I felt.

At first it didn't appear that he was going to answer, but then he warmed to his moment.

"In France," he said. "We've come to see somebody you ripped off, and who isn't very happy with you."

He pushed me in the direction of an expensively-renovated country house, showing impressive strength for a little man. I staggered at first, but then gradually regained my composure. I could feel the gun barrel poking into the centre of my back.

The door opened as we approached, and he pushed me inside.

"Turn left," he said.

I followed his direction into a well-appointed living room. There was a huge fireplace, and two large leather sofas. Paintings adorned three of the walls, while a display cabinet held a collection of small sculptures.

Thorsten pushed me down into a chair in the middle of the room. Ominously, there was a big polythene sheet beneath. He attached my legs to those of the chair, and then finally undid the bindings on my wrists.

So this is Thiel's house, I thought. Not quite as I pictured it.

But it wasn't Thiel who walked through the door at the far end of the room. It was a woman, perhaps in her mid-sixties, chicly dressed with expensively cut hair.

"Clare Woodbrook," she said. "At last."

I think she could sense my confusion.

"Not who you expected?" she continued, in a German accent, which was weird as we were apparently in France. "Let me introduce myself. Suzanne Köppen. You were responsible for selling me some artwork, but it turned out to be a rather expensive mistake. For you, rather than me."

The name rang a bell.

"It wasn't me who ..." I stopped. What was the point? A change of approach was required. "I do apologise."

"You apologise?"

"I'm sorry you got caught up. It wasn't your fault."

"And you think that's going to help? You saying sorry?"

She looked pleased rather than angry, which worried me more.

"Tell me how I can make it up to you," I said, looking down at the plastic sheet, and expecting it was pointless.

"I want my money," she said.

"I don't even know how much it was."

"Eight million francs. Plus interest. Let's call it twenty."

I did the calculation. That was about two million pounds.

"That's ridiculous. I don't have that kind of money."

I did, but not that I could get access to, not in a hurry.

"It's going up every minute. It's already twenty-two," she said.

"Oh, come on. Give me time and I can try to get the original money back, but as I think you might have noticed, I'm not carrying a case of cash around."

"And how long will it take?"

"I don't know. A few weeks?"

She snorted.

"I don't think you have any intention," she said. "In any case, nobody rips me off and lives. Your death will be some compensation."

I raised my eyes to focus on hers.

"You don't think I can escape?" I asked.

"I know you can't escape. I left your hands free so you could put them together in a final prayer. To atone for your sins."

I let my right hand fall to my side, discreetly checking that the SIG was still in my pocket. It was. I didn't want to use it, but if needs must ... But where was Thorsten? Still behind me? I needed to get him out in front so I could see what he was up to. The moment he dropped his aim, I could end this.

It wouldn't be my proudest moment. But I'd killed in self-defence before. Even if I was the only person to believe that.

"Do you have any final comments?" she asked.

I thought for a moment. There was something I needed to know.

"I have a question," I said. "How did you find me?"

She started to laugh.

"It wasn't hard. It was more a case of choosing the right moment to bring you in."

Thorsten passed through my peripheral vision. My eyes flicked sideways. His gun was at his side. The moment was coming.

"Meaning?"

"Nicolas Thiel wanted the pleasure, but I think he would have let you off too lightly. I'm a bit more old-school, as I think you English call it. I know where you've been living. I have a man on the inside who's been keeping me informed of your progress."

"Matt." I knew it. The bastard. I'd heard enough. I felt the fury rising. How could he have done that. I felt huge gratitude to Joe. At least he'd tried to warn me. And once I was out of here, Matt would be made to suffer. He could spend a night in Florian's chair of doom, and I'd be the one pulling the trigger. But that was for another day. I had to end this now. It was time. Thorsten first, then Suzanne if necessary. Then get the hell out of here.

In a flash, my hand delved into my pocket. The SIG was loaded. I pulled it out and took aim in one fluid movement. I couldn't possibly miss. This wasn't the time to think about consequences, only freedom. I pulled the trigger.

And nothing happened. I pulled it again. Still nothing. I racked the slide and tried again. Still nothing. Oh fuck.

Suzanne laughed again.

"Matt Sommer?" she said. "You think I'd work with Matt Sommer?"

And then, to compound my sense of dread, Rüdiger walked in. Without a word, he came over, took the SIG from my hand, then took a step back and placed it on a table. He could hardly bear to look at me.

"You didn't think he'd give you a gun that worked, did you?"

Suddenly, it made sense. So that's where the Glock went. He knew about today and that's why he'd swapped it. Of course he was the leak. He knew everything. I didn't know why it hadn't occurred to me before.

So this was it. It was just a question of who would pull the trigger. As if reading my mind, Thorsten passed his weapon to Suzanne. He and Rüdiger went to stand behind her.

"Say your goodbyes," she said, her finger closing on the trigger.

I thought of Matt and Anders, Danny and Anna. Birgit. Walter. Joe. But there wasn't time to say goodbye to any of them. The barrel was about six inches from my face. Suzanne's finger started moving back, as though in slow motion. And then there was an almighty bang.

Chapter 51

MY first thought was that it hadn't really hurt as much as I thought it would. The next was that there was a terrible ringing in my ears, followed swiftly by *how on earth am I hearing that if I'm dead?* I opened my eyes just in time to see Suzanne falling backwards, half of her face missing.

A second shot followed a split second later. Thorsten flew backwards as the bullet connected. Rüdiger opened his mouth to shout something, but was silenced by a third that entered just above his right eye.

I felt someone coming up behind me. I turned.

"Walter!" I gasped.

He knelt down beside me, groaning with the effort, as befitting a man in his seventies.

And then I remembered how Matt had introduced him, that first night at the Schloss. *"He was an elite sniper in the German army."* He'd clearly never lost the knack.

"Come on," he said, cutting through the ties round my legs.

It was the first time I'd heard him speak. He had a beautiful voice, with the softest of accents.

"I thought you were deaf?" I said.

He shook his head.

"It's useful that people think that, but I hear everything. Let's get you out of here."

———

Matt noticed Florian Straub casting an anxious glance in his direction.

Where was Thorsten Stötzner with Clare? They were already half an hour late.

He returned the look, but he didn't know either. Anxiety was taking root in his brain.

"Is there a problem, gentlemen?" asked Nicolas Thiel, after making a show of checking his watch. He stood up and walked to the window. "I thought they were supposed to be here by now?"

"They'll be here," said Matt, trying to sound confident. "I expect it's traffic."

"Really? In the countryside? We are not known for it."

"On the way to the countryside," said Matt, struggling to keep irritation from creeping into his voice.

Ominously, the bodyguard returned, alongside two similarly armed colleagues. They stood either side of the doorway that led through to the rest of the house.

"I'm beginning to think you have let me down," said Nicolas. "They're not coming."

"I assure you, they're on the way," said Matt. "You spoke to Thorsten yourself."

"Ah yes. I did."

Thiel turned back to his guests. Suddenly, his voice dropped half an octave.

"All three of you, up against the wall, now," he said.

"What?" said Anders.

"I said now."

As if to stress the point, the three gunmen took a step forward, raising their weapons in unison.

"Hold on," said Florian. "For the sake of Saskia, what are you doing? It's like Matt said. You can't blame us if there's traffic."

"Now!" growled the Frenchman.

Matt, Anders and Florian reluctantly went to the back of the room, one of the guards following close behind.

"Now sit on the floor, back to back," shouted Thiel.

"What the fuck?" said Matt, and got a rifle butt in the face for his trouble. Immediately, he could feel blood running down, past his nose, and dripping onto the front of his white shirt.

"Silence!"

The gunman returned to stand next to his colleagues. All three aimed their weapons at the three men on the floor.

"What the fuck is going on?" shouted Florian, but stopped when the guard lunged forward again. "All right," he said instead, raising his hands.

"I told you, they are not coming," said Nicolas, running his hand through his slicked-back hair. "I wasn't lying. There has been a change of plan."

"What do you mean, a change of plan?" asked Matt, suddenly feeling extremely nervous. If the plan had changed, Clare could be in serious danger.

"I mean I spoke to Thorsten and told him not to bother. Instead to take them to a friend of mine, not too far away. Suzanne Köppen. Do you know her?"

"Should I?" asked Matt.

"She was another of Clare's victims. We've swapped notes. She's as keen to see the bitch as I am. But you know what I've never understood?"

"What?" asked Matt, panic mounting, with an overwhelming sense of powerlessness close behind.

"You stress loyalty. Integrity. And yet you expect me to believe you'd sell out one of your own."

"She was disposable. We look at the bigger picture." But Matt knew that sounded pathetic.

Thiel was warming to his subject.

"All along, that wasn't your real agenda, was it?" he asked.

"How do you mean?"

He laughed, almost hysterically.

"Do you take me for an idiot? The stupid French man? Gullible enough to be ripped off over artwork, so an easy target again. You think I wouldn't take precautions? I asked myself, why are these people so keen to work with me? What is it? They could deal with so many people in this new, united Europe, but it's me they come to. So I've done my homework."

"I'm sure our record stands up," said Anders.

"Shut up!" screamed Thiel, standing up. He took a couple of steps to compose himself and then continued in a calmer voice. "Oh, it certainly does. But then I thought: why would they give me Clare Woodbrook? And if they were happy to do that, why not back in February. Why wait till now?"

He raised his hand to stop anyone else speaking.

"Why spend so much time training her? Teaching her self-defence. Working on her fitness. Getting her battle ready – if all you're going to do is hand her to me?"

"It was something to keep her there. To keep her interested," said Matt.

"I told you to shut up. I will tell you when you can speak, unless you want me to kill you now?"

Matt shook his head, desperately trying to think of a way out of this, but every thought was as hopeless as the last.

"What perhaps you do not know is that Rüdiger Heutmann was working for me. And for Suzanne," Thiel continued. "The two of them have known each other a long time. Suzanne was his counsellor. He needed specialist drugs to control his anger and depression. Doctors said they were illegal, but Suzanne managed to find them. He is dependent on her. So I know all about the

Schloss. I could have come to collect Clare at any time. But I was curious to learn what you were really up to. And then, between us, we worked it out. So I'm going to tell you. Nod if I got this right."

He made a gesture to the three gunmen, who took up position facing the captives, their guns pointing directly at them.

"For whatever reason, you decide you want to work with Clare Woodbrook. Maybe you see something in her that the rest of us missed? Maybe you all want to fuck her? Who knows? But you've got a problem. You know that I'll always be coming for her. And one day I'll strike."

He leaned back against the wicker sofa.

"So you offer me Clare to get close to me, promising all kinds of deals. But your real motivation is to put me out of action permanently. You bring me drugs. You link me with evidence of sex trafficking. You bring me Clare. But then, any second now, you send a signal and the police turn up and arrest me, because suddenly I am in possession of illegal narcotics, and linked to the trade in human misery. You make your escape; I am locked away. I am no longer a problem to you. You go back to Koblenz, to Frankfurt. And God knows what arrangement you made with each other, but you'd sort that out in due course. Feel free to nod."

None of them moved a muscle.

"But you forget I am not a stupid man," continued Thiel. "And this is the only reason why I did not take Clare on Monday when she made a mess of my club. Because I wanted to see the three of you together, and watch you suffer. I spoke to my friends at the police. I said to them, do you know of anything like this? And do you know what they said? They told me yes, you *had* been in contact with them. That you would be taping our conversations. I wonder if that is true."

He reached down and ripped open Matt's shirt. Finding nothing, he moved on to Florian. When he made it to Anders,

Matt knew that the game was up. Thiel grabbed the wire and yanked it away from his body.

"You forget that this is Paris," Thiel continued again, his voice rising. "This is my city. These are my people. They look after me. And so they told me all of the details and promised to turn their eyes away if I wanted to kill you. Because believe me, we have had historical problems with the Germans and the English and there is some poetic justice, is there not? Suzanne will deal with Clare. I deal with you. And when the message gets back, I understand that I will be a target. But your organisation will also know that we are not to be messed with."

He took a step back, out of the firing line.

"And on that note," he yelled, "who is going to volunteer to die first?"

Chapter 52

WALTER floored the throttle of his black Porsche, sending plumes of gravel back in the direction of the house.

"I don't know what to say, but thank you," I said, still half breathless in shock. I desperately wanted to give him a hug, but he was in an almighty rush to get out of there, and the inside of the car was cramped.

"You can thank me when everyone is home safely," he said.

In retrospect, it was a strange thing to say, but my mind was consumed by the car.

"Was it you?" I said, my brain overloaded with mismatched thoughts.

"Was what me?"

"In this car? Following me?"

A smile crept through the deep lines of his face.

"You haven't needed protection. Not until today. But yes, when you've been out on your own, one of us has never been far away. Often it was me. It's been fun to get back in service."

I genuinely didn't know what to say.

"You've been in danger," he elaborated. "Matt and Anders came up with a plan to fix that, but there were bigger risks in the short term. So they asked me to arrange to have people in the shadows, just in case anything went wrong. One of them nearly bumped into you in Frankfurt when you were talking to Graham March."

I thought of the man staggering along the street, apparently on his way to see a prostitute. I had so many questions, but still the words wouldn't come. What plan? What risks?

"And now we need to extract them. And Florian Straub."

"What do you mean, extract them?" I said, my gratitude for something else to focus on outweighed by new concerns that I didn't understand.

And so he told me their plan. How they were at Nicolas Thiel's house, awaiting my arrival. Not to betray me, but to set me free.

And how their lives might be in danger now Rüdiger had betrayed us.

"But why is Florian Straub involved?" I asked. He'd said he was going to save my life. I saw that now, but it still didn't make sense. Why would he risk himself for me? Was Graham really so important?

"For Florian, it's personal," said Walter.

"You mean because Thiel is married to his cousin?" Even that didn't make sense. It'd be one almighty family feud. But Walter was shaking his head.

"No. You met Michael Eidinger?"

"His henchman?"

Walter nodded.

"Michael's brother, Karsten, was in Paris in December. He got drunk on a night out, and ended up at *Épice Bleue*. Thiel's club. You've been there, I believe?"

"I have. It's awful."

"And you saw the prices of the drinks?"

"They're bad enough if you're buying for yourself. Don't tell me he paid the dancer prices?"

"He did."

"But they were extortionate."

Walter nodded again.

"By the end of the night, he was given a bill for over twenty thousand francs."

I did the calculation again. About two thousand pounds.

"He didn't have the money," said Walter, changing down a gear and blasting past a slow-moving car in front. "So two of the staff took him to a back room and gave him a beating. They left him on the street, with the rubbish. But he was so badly injured, and the night was so cold, he died."

"Jesus."

I didn't think it was possible for me to loathe Nicolas Thiel any more than I already did, but he'd just eclipsed even Graham March.

"And that was the start of it," said Walter. "Traditionally the Blood Angel group does not get on with Florian Straub. But there is a grapevine. Anders heard about what had happened, and he got in touch."

"Really? I get that it's horrific, but why would Anders want to help Straub if he's normally an enemy?"

"Because Anders is very concerned about Schengen. He's working on a project to do with stopping smuggling but needed someone like Straub to get involved. This gave him an opportunity to have a conversation. Anders offered to help bring down Thiel if Straub would repay the favour on the smuggling plan."

"Hence the uneasy alliance?"

He nodded.

"They met and that's when they started to think of ways they could get back at Thiel. Anders asked Matt to investigate, and that's when they first came across you."

"Because Thiel was after me?"

"Yes."

Walter pulled off a main road onto a narrow country lane, but the speed was maintained. It was terrifying.

"Matt started looking into you and identified you as someone who would be perfect for the organisation, so they struck a deal. Take Thiel down together. Florian gets revenge for Michael's brother. Matt gets you for the organisation and Straub helps with the Schengen project. I overheard Anders on the phone to you, telling you Matt has unusual methods. He does. But he was also right to say that you can absolutely trust him."

"So what was the plan?"

"Matt would talk to Thiel. Tell him he'd hand you over if he agreed to various things that would incriminate himself. Taking a supply of drugs to sell in his club, and in time girls smuggled through Germany. But it was all a bluff. Of course, the handover was never going to happen. The police would swoop first. You'd be safe and never have to worry about Thiel again. But it was going to take something as dramatic as that to get you free of him permanently. And in the short term, it bought time and stopped him looking for you. At least that was the plan."

"But it went wrong?"

"It looks like it. It was always very high risk. It put both Matt and Anders in very big danger. And Straub, towards the end. But those are the risks they were prepared to take. They clearly think a lot of you. And that's why they asked me to arrange to have you followed, as a safety net. They thought they could control Thiel but his man in Germany was less predictable."

"Thorsten Stötzner?"

He nodded again.

"Stötzner was always a risk. He'd been made to look a fool when Matt rescued you in Cologne, and he'd been trying to get revenge on us ever since. I heard Matt tell Anders about what happened in London, about how Stötzner turned up in the car park and would have killed him. Possibly both of you."

"But why didn't they tell me? I could have helped."

"Because they realised you'd try to talk them out of it."

He had a point. I would have done. The thought of someone potentially putting their life on the line, merely to save me from being hunted, was both humbling and terrifying. I didn't deserve it.

"And what about Graham March?"

Walter steered round a bend, and approached a slow-moving farm van at speed. I braced myself for emergency braking, but instead he put two wheels on the verge and powered past it, jolting us both towards the low roof in the process.

"That was also part of the deal," he continued, as though death-defying driving was a daily occurrence. Perhaps it was. "That's what Anders is most concerned about with Schengen: the rise in sex trafficking. That's his next big project. He knew that Straub wasn't involved in that, but he could help stop at least one Polish group that was targeting Germany and England. But they needed someone in London."

"March?"

"Exactly March. It had to be somebody the bad people would believe was corrupt, but who was seeking a project to try to clear his name."

"Wow." Even that made some kind of sense.

"But they'll need you to keep an eye on him," said Walter.

"Oh, that'll be fun."

"It's for the future. I told you. I hear everything."

My mind was racing. Walter slowed for a T-junction and had to wait for a Peugeot van to trundle past. A second later he was behind it, then powering past on the approach to another scarily blind corner. I hardly dared to look.

"So it was definitely Thorsten Stötzner who killed Colin Medland?" I said.

Walter nodded, without taking his eye off the road. A small hill was approaching. I had visions of us taking off.

"He did," he said. "And Sylvain Audat."

"But how? Why?"

"Stötzner had gone off grid. He was working for himself as much as for Thiel and Köppen. He wanted you as some kind of trophy. So he killed Sylvain, and hired three local contractors to come to your hotel. That was the closest I'd come to stepping in, before today. I was in the lobby. I don't think you saw me. I was very proud of how you dealt with them on your own."

"Wow. You're right. I didn't. But why kill Sylvain though?"

"Hatred, pure and simple. For you. For us. I heard Rüdiger on the phone, telling someone where you were going, and who you were meeting. He saw the details of the hotel in the itinerary that Matt left for you at the Schloss. I blame myself for not realising the risk to Sylvain and putting a stop to it."

"Hey, I'm the only one allowed to blame themselves round here. You couldn't have known what Rüdiger was up to. None of us did. So the three at the hotel were working for Stötzner rather than Thiel?"

"Kind of. The one who was arrested has confessed, apparently. They were just supposed to rough you up, and take you to Stötzner. But then you drew a gun and he panicked and accidentally shot his friend. They weren't killers. They were just lowlife he could pay to do a job. Like the one in Cologne."

"Wow. He wasn't great at recruitment then."

I let out a deep breath. Then another thought occurred.

"Hold on, do Matt and Anders know you're not deaf?"

"No," he said. "Only you. But I like you. I like how hard you've worked and how you try to speak to Birgit in German. It's the small things that make a difference."

He started to chuckle.

"What is it?" I asked, beginning to smile.

"You don't know this, but she speaks fluent English."

"Birgit?" I was shocked.

"That is our secret too."

A large house came into view as we turned a corner. At last Walter slowed the car, then pulled in. The house was still a reasonable distance away, but it looked huge and imposing. There was a helicopter parked on the lawn.

He passed me a Glock 23. Possibly the one that Rüdiger had stolen from my room.

"You know how this works?" he said, handing me two further fifteen-round magazines.

"I do."

"It's loaded, and won't let you down. But hopefully you won't need it."

"All I have to do is go in and get them out?"

Walter nodded but his expression had turned serious.

"Hopefully it'll be that easy. I'll be following behind, but I'm not as fast as you."

Chapter 53

SO this was it. Matt and Anders had decided to save me. Now it was my turn to repay the compliment, but I could hardly claim credit when it was my fault they were in danger in the first place.

And to think I'd doubted them. Matt especially. God. What an idiot.

There was no time for self-recrimination. Leaving my trench coat in the car, I ran towards the house as fast as I could, trying to keep under cover of the trees that were dotted around the gardens, while looking out for anyone keeping watch. I made it all the way to the front of the house without attracting any obvious attention, but that was the least of my problems.

It was an old, sprawling building, but had been substantially extended. The ground floor was dominated by a large front door with big windows either side, but lots of smaller windows at different levels above indicated a potentially unusual floor plan. Either way, the doors and windows were firmly closed, and there was no obvious way in.

I continued round the side of the house, then stopped, my heart thudding, when I heard shouting from inside.

It was brief. One word. *"Now!"* It was coming from the back.

I edged further round, past an opulent dining room. Then, when I reached the corner, I saw them.

And what I saw was terrifying.

There was a conservatory about fifteen paces away, with floor-to-ceiling windows. Matt, Anders and Florian were being ushered to the far end of the room, pursued by a man with a gun. Two other gunmen were standing in the middle of the room, next to somebody I decided must be Nicolas Thiel, even though he had his back to me. There was a chance I could run up to the window and open fire, but it'd be suicide with three of them against me. Shit.

Worse still, it looked like they were making arrangements for a firing squad. The captives sat on the floor, then one of the gunmen whacked Matt in the face with the butt of his rifle while Thiel shouted again.

Time was running out, and logistics were not on my side. There was only one thing to do.

I ran back round the side of the house, looking for the lowest protruding window that might give me a point of entry. Better still if one of them was open. None was.

I sprinted back to the front and round the other side, catching a glimpse of Walter making his way slowly towards the house. I wanted to call out to him, but it was too dangerous. Two of us would improve the odds slightly, but we'd still be outnumbered.

None of the windows on the other side was open either. But there was a low-hanging slanted roof over something that looked like a downstairs bathroom.

Levering myself up, with the assistance of a cast iron drainpipe, I managed to perch on the slates, but the slant was precarious. My boots did their best to provide grip, but it was a losing battle.

Just above, though, was a dormer window. I took a deep

breath and made a run for it, over the slates, aware that if I didn't make it, I wouldn't get a second chance.

My boots slipped again. With the window agonisingly close, I felt them sliding away altogether. I made one desperate final lunge and reached out, trying to grasp anything I could. My legs gave way, but my fingers somehow managed to latch onto the concrete sill that ran across the bottom of the window.

It was agonising. My whole bodyweight was supported by the tips of my fingers. I was beyond giving thanks to Rüdiger, the duplicitous bastard. This was all now down to me.

I didn't dare look down. Again, I could feel my grip failing, but with the extra support from my hands, my boots found traction on the slope of the roof. I managed to edge my way round to the side of the dormer, and then work my way up to take hold of the guttering. From there I was able to pull myself up on top of the dormer, and from there, make a run to the apex of the main roof itself. Again, there'd be no second chances if I got it wrong.

I didn't get it wrong.

Keeping one foot either side of the ridge, I made my way forward until I could see Walter, who had now nearly reached the house. I dared to whistle. He looked up and saw me.

Thankful that we'd spent the previous seven months communicating by hand gestures, I made signals that I hoped he'd understand. *Three gunmen. Round the back. Be careful.*

He nodded. But I suddenly had a terrible rush of guilt. Elite sniper or not, he was taking a huge risk against men far better armed, far younger and far fitter.

I'd just have to fix things before he got there.

Chapter 54

THERE was a matching dormer on the far side, but it was quite a drop, and the roof looked even steeper at the back. Reaching it, however, was my only chance. I'd have to slide down the roof, hope my aim was good, and trust that I'd manage some form of braking with my boots before I sliced myself in two on the ridge.

The braking was nearly successful, but not as good as it could have been. I collided with the ridge of the dormer at a frightening speed, picking up bruises that I wouldn't want to show anyone. Winded and wincing, I nearly lost my balance. That would have been a disaster. Because the only thing below me, to break my fall, was the roof of the conservatory itself.

Taking a second to regain my breath, I raised my Glock and checked that it was loaded and ready to fire. I held onto the guttering, using the dormer as a shield, poking my head around. But my view of the action below was largely obscured by blinds over the conservatory roof.

Most, but not all. There wasn't a blind over the end panel, but it was frosted, blurring most of what was below. Unless they'd moved, that was where Matt, Anders and Florian were sitting on the floor. I thought I could detect a shape. It could be furniture, but then there was a slight shift as something, or someone, moved back under cover of the blinds.

And I heard a yell, from somewhere close to the middle of the room. A French accent. *"Who is going to volunteer to die first?"*

"Nicolas, don't be stupid," said Florian, in a desperate voice. "We can discuss this. Blame me if you want. This is my fault. I started it. But I'm family. Think of Saskia."

Matt admired the bravery, but thought it was unlikely to save them. He wasn't a religious man, but momentarily considered praying, as another, more pressing thought ran through his mind. *So this is how it ends.*

And then, from nowhere, three gunshots perforated the roof panels in the middle of the room, ripping the blinds and sending shards of polycarbonate falling to the floor. One of the gunmen took a hit to the shoulder and fell to the ground. Thiel dived for cover while the other two turned and returned fire. In an instant, a hail of bullets was flying in both directions. Everyone was shooting blind.

But as more bullets hit, the roof panel in the middle of the room collapsed. Suddenly Matt could see the sky, and a familiar arm, extending from behind a dormer window, taking aim, now with a clear view, but risking death by coming out of cover.

And then two more shots shattered the glass of the windows. They were coming from outside. Walter. Both hit their targets. The two gunmen fell to the floor, each taking a single hit from Walter's rifle. Further shots smashed into them from above.

Then the firing stopped, and Matt looked across to where Nicolas Thiel was cowering by the window, shaking in shock and fear, his arrogant self-assurance having deserted him.

As the roof collapsed, I had a clear view of the room below. One gunman on the floor, blood oozing from his shoulder. Two others pointing automatic weapons in my direction, firing with increased intensity now they knew where I was. I moved behind the dormer to reload my magazine, then looked back just in time to see them fall as the windows shattered. Both taking a direct hit from Walter. Rounds from my Glock arrived a moment later, finishing the job once and for all.

So, Walter had made it. I'd have to be quicker next time.

With all three gunmen down, the shooting ceased, but the sound was still reverberating in my head. The room below was chaos, where my random shots had connected with furniture and porcelain planters.

"Everything clear?" I yelled.

"All clear," shouted Matt in return. Thiel was crouching on the floor, looking every bit the coward. Walter was standing by the window, his rifle by his side, as though on parade. I wondered what was going through his head.

"Anyone injured?" I called.

"Three men down, but we're all safe."

I trained my gun on Nicolas Thiel. I couldn't be sure he wasn't armed. But if he tried anything, I'd stop him in an instant.

Through the haze of gun smoke and debris, I saw movement at the far end of the room. A moment later, Matt appeared, brushing dust from the front of his ripped shirt. He grabbed Thiel by the arm and dragged him to his feet.

I continued to survey the chaos. I couldn't believe my luck. I must have hit one of the gunmen when shooting blind. The one on the floor when the roof collapsed, with blood oozing from his shoulder.

But then, with a sense of dread, I realised I hadn't been lucky enough. He wasn't dead. He was only injured. And in the split second between me seeing him move and training my Glock in his direction, he had a chance to raise his gun. In the milliseconds it took for the bullet to leave my barrel and finish him for good, he fired twice in the direction of Matt and Nicolas Thiel.

And I watched in horror as both of them collapsed to the floor.

Chapter 55

ISCREAMED, then jumped down from the dormer window, landing with a thud on the part of the conservatory roof that was still intact. From there, I dropped down into the room itself, my boots crunching on the debris. Thiel was dead, no question about that. The bullet had hit him in the throat. Matt was still alive, but in a very bad state. Anders and Florian were already by his side, but I pushed them away to get through to cradle his head in my hands. There was a gaping hole in the front of his chest, and blood was oozing out on to the floor.

He looked at me, with half-closed eyes, and tried to smile.

"Don't you dare die on me," I whispered, my voice breaking. "Everything's going to be okay. Just keep your eyes open."

Anders was applying pressure to Matt's chest, trying to stop the blood. But the more he pressed, the more his hands were covered in a seemingly endless river of red.

"I knew you'd come to the rescue," croaked Matt, his voice slow and fading.

"It looks like I did a bloody shit job of it."

He tried to smile again, but his eyes were closing.

"I said to keep your eyes open. Matt. Come on, talk to me."

He tried to open them. Tried to acknowledge me. Tried to speak. I lowered my head to get closer, desperate to hear his words, putting my arm around his shoulder to cradle his whole body.

"I want to say thank you," I said. "For everything. And apologise if I ever doubted you. Stötzner was behind London. Everything's okay now. Just stay with me. An ambulance will be on the way."

But despite my pleading, life was slipping away. He tried to say something again, but then stopped. And suddenly he became heavier as finally, his consciousness slipped away, and he died as my hero in my arms.

Chapter 56

Friday, September 17th, 1993

ANDERS said he would stay in France for a couple of days, to supervise a clean-up at both properties. He wasn't talking about the broken furniture. Florian flew back to Germany in the helicopter, with Matt's body alongside him. And I accepted a lift from Walter.

I don't remember much about the journey. Apparently it took about six hours, but all I can recall is looking out of the window, my mind numb, and thinking that ABC were onto something with *Tears Are Not Enough*. I'd never felt so alone. We reached the Schloss after nightfall. It felt different. Nothing would ever be the same.

After a shower, which washed away the dirt but not the horror of the day, I tried to fall asleep. But sleep wouldn't come. My mind was far too active, replaying the events of the day, and everything that had happened in the last seven months. And blaming myself for all of it.

At some point, in the middle of the night, I got up, wrapped myself in a bathrobe, and went down to the front door. The night was quiet. The air cool. In the distance, I could see the lights of a cruise boat moving slowly along the Rhine. I lit a cigarette and watched the orange tip glow in the darkness, aware of the irony of smoking while I was consumed by thoughts of the fragility of life.

I returned to my room and lay in the darkness, but I couldn't switch off. I tried to read, but the mere act of picking up the book reminded me of Matt's selfless acts of thoughtfulness, and that set me off again.

Birgit was sitting in silence at the kitchen table when I went downstairs in the morning. She'd been crying too. She stood as I entered, and then, without a word, came over and gave me a much-needed hug. Neither of us wanted to let go.

Eventually, though, she released her grip and took a step back, holding my hands in hers. I knew she was looking at me, but I could only focus on the floor.

"I'll make a cup of tea," she said at last. Walter was right. She could speak English. Part of me wanted to smile, but it didn't reach my eyes.

She made a pot and then joined me at the table.

"I heard about everything," she said.

I nodded.

"I don't know what to say, really," I said, my voice barely audible. "I feel so guilty. Matt did everything for me. I doubted him and yet he ended up giving his life."

"But it's not your fault," she said.

"Isn't it? If he'd never met me, he'd still be alive. Everything I do turns to sh ..." I stopped myself, not wanting to swear in front of her.

She reached out and held my hands again.

"But you're not the bad person," she said. "You risked your life, trying to save him. And Anders and Florian."

"But they wouldn't have been there if it wasn't for me."

"Of course they would." She let go for long enough to stir the pot of tea and then pour me a cup. "Don't forget, they identified Nicolas Thiel as a target long before they found out about you."

It was a good point, but it didn't make me feel any better. The only thing that mattered was that Matt hadn't come home with us.

I tried the tea, but it was still too hot.

"We've cancelled the party for tomorrow," Birgit said, after a moment.

That took me a second to process. I'd forgotten all about the party.

"Of course," I said. "Nobody would be in the mood."

I still didn't know what she made of the parties, but it definitely wasn't the time to ask.

"Do you know what you're going to do now?" she asked.

"About?"

"About everything. Life. Work. Living here. Working for us?"

I took a deep breath and sighed.

"I don't know where I stand, really. I know what you just said, but I wouldn't blame everyone for hating me."

"Oh shhh." She squeezed my hands. "Shall I tell you what I see?"

I did smile that time, albeit in a fairly half-hearted way.

"I expect you see everything."

"I do." She let go of my hands and sat back. "I see somebody who came here with problems, but who's worked exceptionally hard. Somebody who's learned a lot, but acknowledges there's more to do. Somebody bright, and most importantly with the right values. And, on top of that, somebody who is brave. I heard about what you did at Nicolas Thiel's club. Going to Frankfurt. Finding Florian. Climbing on top of a building and risking your life to save other people."

I shrugged.

"I just want to do the right thing. I've always wanted that, really. Apart from once. And ever since I came here, it's been about trying to make amends. Although there's still a lot more to do on that score."

"But you've made a good start."

"Have I?"

She nodded.

"You know, when I was growing up in Leipzig, it was a very different world. I did bad things too. And sometimes they weren't for very good reasons. But I learned, and I realised what was important. At times I hated myself, but now, I like to think I make a difference. And make things better where I can."

"You grew up in Leipzig?" I said. Why did that seem so important?

"And I see part of myself in you," she said.

"You grew up in *Leipzig*?" I said again.

She smiled as she saw the realisation dawning in my eyes.

"You're Angelica," I said.

She nodded.

"You're the Blood Angel?"

She put a finger to her lips.

"Not so loud. But yes."

"Wow! I ..." My mouth dropped open while thoughts of that first night with Anders and Matt went through my mind, as though on a VCR set to fast-forward. From Stasi spy and femme fatale to the person who'd been so kind looking after me. It didn't make sense. But of course it made sense. It was her greatest-ever undercover role. Hiding in plain sight. Seeing and shaping everything.

I wasn't sure if I should be in awe or be petrified.

"Welcome to my organisation," she said, taking my hands again. "The world is yours."

"I don't know what to say. It's a mixture of a sense of privilege to meet you and even be in the same room as you, enormous respect, awe at everything I've heard, and absolute humility that you confided in me."

"You've earned it."

"And I'm utterly terrified of you."

She laughed.

"But I've got so many questions," I continued. "Does Anders know?"

She chuckled.

"One thing at a time," she said. "One thing at a time."

Chapter 57

Thursday, September 30th, 1993

Matt's funeral was another emotional day. He was buried alongside his wife and unborn child in a cemetery in Frankfurt. I vowed to visit the grave from time to time, never forgetting what he did for me.

In the meantime, I finally managed to speak to Joe, and told him what had happened, and explained everything about Colin Medland. Well, not everything, but the edited highlights that were least likely to make him put the phone down on me.

"What did you mean when you said you'd been looking into Matt?" I asked. "You said I needed to be very, very careful and he wasn't who I thought he was?"

"You told me he was a Royal Marine, and was there to look after you," he said. "But he wasn't. He worked in a bank."

"Oh."

"I was concerned you thought he was some kind of personal bodyguard. But if you were in danger, he might not have been quite as qualified as you hoped."

"Ah, that makes sense."

"What did you think I meant?"

"I don't know. Sometimes my imagination is my worst enemy."

I decided against giving him any more information about Graham March. That needed more thought, and probably would be better in person.

"When are you next in London?" he asked.

"I'm not sure yet, but soon, hopefully."

"Let me know when you get here and we can have a chat. Leave the gun at home, though."

"I told you, it wasn't mine." I laughed. He didn't. "Does that mean we've got a deal?"

"Let's just say I'm applying some thought to the framework of one, but I'm not going to make any promises."

Florian came to the Schloss a week later, to talk me through exactly what he wanted me to do in terms of looking after Graham. Birgit brought us coffee while I sat in the armchair, and he took the sofa that I'd occupied on my first ever visit. It seemed fitting, somehow.

"Technically I saved *your* life," I said, once the pleasantries were concluded.

"You did, and I am grateful."

"Also technically, I think that means I don't need to look after Graham for you."

"Technically."

"And in any case, we hate each other."

He laughed.

"We all hate each other," he said. "Do you think I'm a natural ally of your organisation, or you of mine?"

He had a point.

"No, but Graham and I have a special level of extreme mutual loathing that actually transcends normal hatred."

"I know. But think about it as a temporary truce in pursuit of the greater good."

"I can't think of any 'good' that would be great enough to qualify for that."

"I'll stress the temporary, then."

I sighed.

It was all a game. I'd already made up my mind to say yes. I owed it to Straub. Even though I'd saved him at the end, and even though he'd had his own reasons for targeting Nicolas Thiel, he'd been instrumental in Matt's plan that had ultimately delivered my freedom. At least in terms of being pursued by crooked French art collectors.

"But I really, really don't want to," I persisted, with a pout.

"And I did say I'd pay you."

"How much?"

"Twenty thousand Deutschmarks."

"For being nice to Graham? Surely we're talking at least fifty."

"I'll go to thirty, final offer."

I pretended to consider it.

"Okay," I said. "We'll agree forty, but only on the condition that you pay me in cash so that I can donate it to a charity of my choosing."

He leaned forward and extended his hand. I took it, and we shook.

"You won't regret it," he said.

I stopped myself short of saying there's a first time for everything.

The end.

SPECIAL THANKS...

The Blood Of Angels was a lot of fun to write and research, with memorable trips to Cologne, Frankfurt and Paris, and a drive along the Rhine past Koblenz.

Huge thanks are due to the following:

Chris Pohl from the brilliant German band Blutengel for making the music that has encouraged me to learn German, an inspirational work ethic, two fantastic nights in Cologne, and for not telling me to go away when I mentioned Angelica's nickname. The language skills are coming on, *langsam*, and I look forward to more trips to Germany once this virus thing goes away.

Anders Hagström from the wonderful Swedish band Ashbury Heights for supplying much of the soundtrack the book was written to and for saying hello after a fantastic show during the research trip to Frankfurt. It was a pleasure to meet you. For the avoidance of doubt, the real Anders is a hugely talented songwriter and bears no relation to Clare's one.

Marc Massive from the fabulous British band Massive Ego, who were on the same bill as Blutengel in Cologne and Ashbury Heights in Frankfurt. Lots of the book was written to Beautiful Suicide and it was lovely to meet you too. See if you can spot the secret mention buried in chapter 27...

As ever, special thanks to my editor Carrie O'Grady for insight, inspiration, and lots of polish. I am forever in debt to Carol Lewis for exceptional proof-reading duties. Hopefully this one cost me a bit less in wine. And many thanks too to Mary Cafferkey for never putting the phone down when I drone on endlessly about writing, and to Caroline Vincent for kind words and spotting things I'd have otherwise missed.

And, of course, thank you to you for reading this far. I really hope you enjoyed it. There will be more... :-)

After *Cold Press*, the story continues in *Out Of the Red* and *Fade To Silence* - two more gripping mystery thrillers with breathtaking twists, and dashes of dark humour.

All three are now available in a great value box set for less than the price of two!

The full Anna Burgin series:
1 Cold Press
2 Out Of The Red
3 Fade To Silence
4 Court Me Kill Me
5 Illusions Of Warsaw

If you enjoyed *The Blood of Angels*, you'll find more about Clare in the Anna Burgin series of mystery thrillers. *Cold Press* is the story of her disappearance. **And the ebook is available FREE at Amazon, Kobo, Apple, Google and Nook!**

London. 1993. Investigative journalist Clare Woodbrook goes missing on the brink of unveiling her biggest-ever story. Is it kidnap? Murder?

Worse still, the police investigation into her disappearance is being headed up by a corrupt DCI - himself the subject of one of Clare's current investigations.

Clare's researcher Danny Churchill sets out to find her, and enlists the help of his flatmate - feisty fashion photographer Anna Burgin. But they soon realise that nobody can be trusted. And as the search becomes ever more desperate, suddenly their own lives are very much on the line.

Packed with intrigue, twists, conspiracies, and dark humour, Cold Press is a hugely entertaining British thriller, with a sting in the tail.

If you enjoyed *The Blood Of Angels*, watch out for the sequel!

Secrets Never Die is book 2 in the Clare Woodbrook series. It's a gripping thriller of conspiracy, corruption, and surprising confessions.

Would you confess to a murder you didn't commit?

Secrets Never Die is coming in December 2020.

FEEL FREE TO SAY HELLO... :-)

If you enjoyed the book, have any queries, or just want to say hello, I'd love to hear from you via www.davidbradwell.com. While you're there, you can also download a **FREE copy of the Anna Burgin series prequel** - In The Frame:

Photography student Anna Burgin didn't expect to be arrested, but she's the only suspect for a series of crimes, and the Police have found damning evidence in her room. But Anna has no recollection of doing anything wrong. Was it a moment of madness? Or is somebody setting out to destroy her? And is the stranger in the bar really trying to help, or just part of an evil conspiracy?

You can also follow me on Twitter: @dbshq - or see what Anna is up to: @AnnaBurginNW1